ALVERNE BALL

Blue Religion

First edition

ISBN: 978-1-944536-02-2

Editing by Sacha Hamilton
Editing by Michael Peterson
Cover art by Terrence Davis

This book was professionally typeset on Reedsy.
Find out more at reedsy.com

Acknowledgement

To Tarvares "Boodie" Richardson: my dear beloved friend, I miss you everyday

To my Uncle Skeet: thank you for instilling in me so many virtues and for teaching me how to be a man

To Mayra: thank you for pushing me towards my destiny, who knew that life could be stranger than fiction

Chapter 1

I was born in death.

At least that's how my father put it whenever I'd ask him about my mother. In truth, I guess he's right, because she died during childbirth. Some people say it was her last selfless act, but I've been told that a mother's love is unconditional, and no matter how one tries to spin it, the fact is, she died so that I could live.

I don't know the full details. Just what my father told me—that she was rushed to the hospital while hemorrhaging, and before anyone knew what was happening I was born, and she was dead.

These are the thoughts that keep me up at night, tossing and turning, unable to shake the feeling that death and I are in some ways kindred souls—lone soldiers cut from the same dark cloth. Sometimes I wonder if my sole purpose for becoming a homicide detective, after doing a four-year stint with the Navy chaplain corps, is so I can be near death—to know what it looks like day in and day out, and to know that deep down when I see it, I feel at home, like a child in his mother's arms.

I roll over and steal a peek at the digital clock on the nightstand. 1:00 a.m. glows in blood-red. Sleep and I are at war again. I place a pillow over my head. If it's not the thought of my mother's death haunting me, it's the dying cries of families from so many years ago in Fallujah that keep me awake.

My phone chirps from the nightstand. I roll back over and pull it off the charger, then flip it open. The message on the screen reads 666*911. The 666 is my captain's code. Before I can close the phone, it rings. "Yeeeeah?" I answer with a drawn-out yawn.

"You up?" the voice on the other end asks. It's my new partner, Fred Lions.

"Yeah, I'm up," I say, throwing back the sheet and sitting up on the side of the bed.

"You get the captain's text?"

"Yeah, I got it."

"Good, I'll be pulling up in ten. Be out front." The line goes dead.

I take a second before rising, allowing the coldness from the hardwood floor to soak into my copper-colored feet and up into the rest of my body. Lions is one of the few cops in the department who's actually willing to be my partner, knowing full well that my father is incarcerated for killing my last partner.

I trek seven feet across the room to the bedroom door, where my dark blue suit hangs. When you work homicide, you learn to expect that at any given time you'll be called into action, especially when your number's up.

I dress quickly, without giving much thought to my appearance. All I can think about is the 911 behind the captain's code. To any normal person those three numbers spell out emergency, but for me they spell out trouble, with a capital T.

* * *

Ten minutes later, Lions pulls up in front of my Greystone two flat in his classic Cadillac Brougham. The car is burgundy, with white walled tires and a burgundy suede interior. Lions reaches across the front seat and pops open the door. His face is grim, with the hue of a milk chocolate candy bar.

"We gotta hustle," he says as I close the door.

I run a hand over my clean-shaven face. "What's wrong?"

"We got an officer down."

He pulls away from the curb and heads down the partially lit street.

I turn and look at him. Lions hasn't changed in all the five years that I've known him. He's rocking a salt-and-pepper, box-styled haircut as though it's still in fashion, and his gut is as bulbous as ever. His eyes are circular and wide, as if he saw a ghost at a young age and has never been able to erase the image.

"Anyone we know?" I ask as the car bounces along the potholed street.

"Don't know. Just told officer down and since we're on call—"

"It means this one goes to the top of the pile."

"Yep, and it's going to be sprinkled with all the brass fixins', too."

I sit back and say nothing for a while. Just the fact that an officer is down turns every cop's demeanor into sour mash, as one realizes that at any given moment, it could be you.

When we pull up to the crime scene it's already taped off. There's a helicopter hovering overhead, shining a large spotlight down over a residential section of Franklin Street, in the 3300 block, where a technician is working to install multiple generators.

I count at least twenty patrol and unmarked vice cars, with their red and blue lights dancing against the backdrop of three-story Brownstones and two-story wooden frame homes. Mixed

3

amongst the hodgepodge of departmental vehicles are the medical examiner's white van and two dark windowless vans belonging to forensics. Farther beyond the taped-off perimeter, I make out the silhouette of the Garfield Park Conservatory, looming behind the bright lights of news cameras popping on all around us. When an officer goes down, the lights of the media circus come on.

We exit the car with an urgency that says we mean business. The September morning is brisk, and the downward wind from the copter's blades isn't making it any more comfortable.

Lions nods his head in the direction of Captain Haggerty, who's standing next to a Hispanic woman and a blond-haired white man in an ash-gray suit, with a crimson necktie that cuts down in between his open jacket. The woman is Adriana Estrada, the department's spokesperson. The man is Dennis Perlenski, the new Assistant State's Attorney.

The captain is decked out in a long black overcoat with two silver bars adorning the lapels. His white and black officer's hat is pulled low over his brown eyes, hiding his sandy colored hair. In his right hand he holds an unlit cigar. He catches a glimpse of us out of the corner of his eye and holds up a hand for us to stay put.

Lions rolls his eyes and kicks a piece of broken asphalt. "Great," he says. "Now we're going to be part of the dog and pony show."

"It all comes with the job," I say, trying to stay as upbeat as I can. But he's right. The media's going to start snapping pictures like mad dogs, and sooner or later they'll have to be thrown a bone.

Officers move all around us, acting as crowd control or assisting evidence technicians with setting up spotlights, so they can properly examine the scene.

"I got twenty bucks says the captain tells us we've gotta do the Jerry Lewis bit for the cameras," Lions contends.

"You don't know that, Fred," I say. "Just because the A.S.A. is on the scene doesn't mean we'll have to take part in the show."

"All I'm saying is that I got twenty, Frank."

Before I can answer, Captain Haggerty makes his way over to us. He sighs and looks over his shoulder to make sure that the A.S.A. isn't within earshot. "This is fucked," he says. Lions and I say nothing as we allow the captain's words to settle in. "Follow me." We cut in between two squad cars heading for the taped-off crime scene. "We have an off-duty along with a civi," he says over the rising voices of the reporters, who are beginning to gather at the perimeter.

"Wait, there was a civilian casualty too?" I ask, wanting to make sure I heard him right.

"Yeah, and right now it's not looking good."

We duck under the yellow tape where two four-by-four spotlights illuminate the actual crime scene. There's a black SUV with its driver's side door ajar, parked in between a silver sedan and a blue hatchback.

A few feet away from the open door of the SUV, a white sheet is draped over a body. Forensics has already marked off the spent shell-casings with yellow triangular cones designated with black Roman numerals. I count eight so far.

"I want you two to assess the scene before forensics finishes doing their thing," Captain Haggerty says.

We all bend down in front of the first body and Captain Haggerty lifts the sheet. The victim's head is turned towards us. She's a strawberry blonde with flushed pink cheeks, a small pointy nose, and even smaller lips. The back of her head is matted with blood, and I can see clear into her skull.

"This is the civi," Captain Haggerty says. "Her name's Katherine McNabb. She's a social worker for United Children's Homes, or at least that's what her work ID says. No formal ID has been found as of yet."

Lions pulls a pen out of the pocket of his suit coat and begins slowly picking through the victim's blood and membrane-splattered hair.

"Do we know the make of the weapon?" he asks.

"You can get all that from forensics," the captain says, dropping the sheet on our dead social worker.

We move around the trunk of the hatchback to the passenger side of the SUV, where we find a forensic photographer taking crime scene photos. The flashes from his high-tech camera cast an almost black cutout of the body on the concrete.

"This is Officer Richardson," Captain Haggerty says, pointing to the wretched corpse lying face down in a puddle of blood. The man is wearing black sweatpants and a blue shirt stained dark with blood.

I move in closer. I want to get a good look at the officer whose face will come to represent the mantle of justice across the five areas of the Chicago police department. I turn on the Maglite attached to my keychain, and squat down in front of the fallen officer. The hue from the bulb highlights his butterscotch complexion. His right eye is closed, and the other is dotted out, with a deep black burn mark left by a bullet, but the contour of his sharp nose and small angular chin tells me instantly that I know him.

"Is his first name Tavares?" I ask, still crouched over and staring down at the body.

"Yeah, Officer Tavares Richardson," Captain Haggerty says.

"He's a rookie."

"You knew him, didn't you, Frank?" Lions asks.

"Yeah," I say over my shoulder while outlining the body with my eyes. "This here is Paul Jeffries' brother."

"Who?" Captain Haggerty asks while Lions whistles in disbelief.

I look up from the body and into Captain Haggerty's eyes. "Paul Jeffries is better known on the streets as Prince Paul."

Chapter 2

" I 'll be fucked," Captain Haggerty says as he searches his
coat for a lighter. Lions and I both know he doesn't have
one because he gave up smoking two years ago. "You
sure?" he asks, planting the unlit cigar in between his lips.

"Yeah," I say, standing up from the body. "I'm sure." I don't
want to tell the captain, or even Lions, that the reason I'm so
sure is because I helped Richardson get into the academy, and
that I did so as a means of paying back a favor to Prince Paul.

"I've got to let the Deputy Superintendent know about this,"
Captain Haggerty says as he turns and scans the small pool of
officers gathering just beyond the perimeter of the crime scene.

"I'll take the civi and you work Richardson," Lions suggests.
"Then we'll switch and compare notes."

"Yeah, yeah, you two do that," Captain Haggerty says still
scanning for the Deputy Superintendent. "Fucking Prince Paul,"
he whispers to himself, shaking his head as he sets out towards
the crowd.

Lions follows the captain, making his way back around to
McNabb's body.

I stand in the spotlights for a full minute, wondering how
such a good kid could have come to such an ugly demise. I'm
not shocked by the sight of death, having seen my fair share in

Iraq, but looking down at Richardson's body paralyzes me with a blood-boiling anger. I feel as if my head is going to burst open and overflow with rage.

I take a deep breath, then pull out a pair of latex gloves from my pants pocket and slide them on. After taking three long steps back from the body, I stand there and look at the layout of the scene. If there's one thing I can say I've learned from Lions, it's that every detective has a different method of approaching a crime. Lions has to get up close and personal to examine the scene, whereas I am the total opposite. I always need to pull back and see things with "God's eyes," as Lions so eloquently puts it.

Officer Richardson's body is laying halfway between the sidewalk and a section of weed-infested grass. A small patch of bright yellow dandelions is forever stained with his blood. In his right hand, he holds his badge, a silver five-point star. His lips are covered with dried blood and next to them is an open cell phone. I pick up the cell and look at the display. The blue numbers that glow up at me are 911. I return the phone to its exact position and notice for the first time that a pool of blood has poured out from the left side of Officer Richardson's abdomen.

Even though there isn't an exit wound in his back, I'm certain that once I roll him over, I'm going to find a bullet wound somewhere near the lower half of his body. The kill shot had to be the round that entered behind his right earlobe and exited through his left eye. Half a foot away, a yellow cone marks the single shell casing.

I feel as though I'm about to blow as I stare up, scanning the windows of the four-story apartment buildings and two-story brick flats that line the street. If anyone cared to look out their window, they would have seen the shooter as clear as day, but deep down I know that no one did. I wonder then, even though I tell myself not to, what Officer Richardson must have felt as his murderer stood over him, knowing that his possible salvation was just a few feet away—if only someone had been brave enough to take a peek.

"You ready to switch?" Lions asks.

"Sure," I say, thinking the switch might ease my ever-growing temper.

On the driver's side of the SUV, the crime scene is open for just about anyone to see. It feels more chaotic than usual because of the large spotlight beams drowning out the constant red and blue whirl of the patrol cars. Then there's the incessant *thump-thump-thump* of the helicopter's blades slicing against the wind, not to mention the sounds of the bloodthirsty media, jostling for primetime real estate against a growing crowd of gawking bystanders.

There isn't much to Katherine McNabb that I haven't already seen. The most surprising thing to me is the fact that there isn't a single bullet hole or scratch on the SUV's body, which is peculiar when one takes into account the victims' causes of death.

I shine the Maglite's beam into the SUV's blood-covered cabin. On the dash is a picture of McNabb along with a younger woman with curly blond hair who resembles her. The woman is either a sibling or her daughter. On the floor are the contents of McNabb's purse, which consist of a work ID, a few cosmetic items, a tampon, and an open wallet. I call out to Lions, who's on the other side of the vehicle.

"What's up?" he replies, appearing at the passenger side door.

"Do you mind checking the glove compartment?"

"No problem."

He reaches into the vehicle and pops open the compartment. To our surprise, Officer Richardson's service sidearm comes rolling out and falls onto the blood-soaked floor. "I'll be damned," Lions says, stooping down to examine the gun. He sniffs the air around the muzzle and comes back up shaking his head. "Poor bastard didn't even get a shot off."

"Looks that way," I say. "Let me know when you're ready to compare notes."

I duck my head back out of the cabin of the SUV and find Maggie Westhall, the head medical examiner, staring up at me. She's a person with Dwarfism, measuring in at three feet and five inches. For years, she had long blond hair, but it has since been dyed black and cut into a short, stylish bob. "You and Fred still playing with yourselves, or can a real woman cut in?" she asks, smiling. Her eyes are the color of a full moon, bright and slightly blue.

"Hey Mags, how's it going?"

"I was sleeping before this came in, and the CPD machine demanded my presence." I nod. Mags is at a point in her career where she doesn't normally have to come out to a crime scene, bodies come to her. "So, what are we looking at?" she asks.

"So far, double homicide. A civi and one of our own."

"It's going to be a long night," she says, pulling on latex gloves.

"Mags, you just hit the nail on the head, but I'm sorry to say that you won't be able to put the vics on ice until forensics finishes with them."

Mags looks at me, her doughy hands on her hips. "Are you telling me they dragged me out of bed and forensics hasn't even had their turn on the ride?"

"Yep, 'fraid so, Mags. Captain Haggerty wanted to make sure we got a good look before anyone did a thing. You know, fresh eyes and all."

"Shit!" she snarls with a dead tone, pulling off the gloves. "Well, I guess I'll grab a cup of coffee. I see they brought in one of those new high-tech mobile command centers... I wonder if they have an espresso machine?"

I watch Mags leave, then turn back to the SUV and count the yellow cones. Still eight in total. Five of them, starting with the number eight, are near the driver's side door, spaced about six inches apart from one another. The trail counts down and ends at the number four, then picks back up, 40 feet away, across the street where the last three cones have been placed, ending with the number one. I stand there for a few seconds, examining the distance between them.

"You find something?" Lions inquires, rounding the back of the hatchback.

"Not sure. Tell me what you see when you look at the markers."

Lions scans all eight cones. "Nothing. What do you see?"

"I see distance between shots. Three there." I point across the street. "And five here."

"So what? Maybe the asshole got the drop on them, then really unloaded once he was up close."

"Maybe, but it doesn't make sense. There's no damage to the vehicle, and Richardson wasn't even able to get a shot off."

Lions shrugs. "Maybe forensics can shed some light on this one."

"Yeah, maybe so."

"By the way, did I hear Mags over here?"

"Yeah, she went to grab a cup of coffee at the mobile CC, while she waits for her time at the wheel."

"How about we do the same? That way we can really compare notes."

"Might as well. Forensics is in the driver seat now."

When we approach the mobile command center, which is a rectangular mobile home turned into a high-tech communications hub with an extended trailer, we find officers of every rank standing around a large coffee dispenser set up on a folding table, trying to keep warm while scarfing down donuts.

"Hey Thomas," one of the uniformed officers, a jolly Santa Claus looking man calls out to another uniform, as he sips his coffee. "I hear you caught a zit at last call. Heard he swallowed a whole dope pack."

"Dumbass watched too many movies," the other officer says. "Somebody should have told him what happens when you swallow twenty bags of coke. Medics had to pump his stomach before he OD'd."

"Well, at least that's one zit popped," the jolly officer laughs into his cup.

Once we have our coffees in hand, Lions and I enter the MCC. Inside, there are flat screens mounted all over the walls with versatile keyboard shelves mounted to an elongated plastic counter, which has a built-in computer system that controls everything from the headlights to the air conditioning.

We retreat to a section in the back of the extended trailer that houses tables and chairs. We find Mags sitting alone at a table. At another table three M.E. techs sit, waiting for her to give the word to go to work on the bodies.

Mags looks up from her cup. "Are we up?" she asks.

"Almost," I say, scanning the room and finding a table in the back corner of the small space. "I'm sure forensics will let you know." We move past her to our seats. "So this is what I think happened," I say to Lions. "The shooter comes from the westbound side of Franklin. He's more of a shoot-first, ask-questions-later type of asshole. Maybe the first two shots hit McNabb, and before Richardson has time to react, the asshole is on him, letting loose like a madman."

"Maybe," Lions responds. "But if that's true, why did Richardson grab his badge instead of going for his piece?"

"Maybe he froze up. Maybe he was thinking that if he flashed his badge, he could live through it... You know, scare the asshole off."

"I guess somebody in the academy should have told him that these streets don't respect the badge."

"Yeah, I guess so," I respond, knowing that that *somebody* should've been me.

The door to the trailer opens and Captain Haggerty sticks his head in. "Lions! Calhoun!" He calls us over to him. "Now that you've seen the bodies, how do you want to play this, Fred?"

The fact that Captain Haggerty addresses Lions instead of the both of us is a clear reminder that Lions is the lead investigator on this case.

"We're playing it as a homicide, Captain."

Captain Haggerty frowns. "I know it's a homicide, but I gotta give Estrada something to give to the press. How do you want to play the information game?"

Lions looks at me, then back to the captain. "We're um...going to call it a robbery homicide for now."

"Good, we can sell robbery-homicide." The captain turns to go, then turns back to us. "Oh, and before I forget... There's going to be an official press conference at O-nine hundred hours, down at headquarters. Get cleaned up. You're going to be on

14

TV."

"The fuckin' circus," Lions tosses his coffee into a trashcan. "Frank, you know what this means, right? You owe me twenty bucks."

Chapter 3

We stand in the bullpen of cops near the MCC, watching as Adriana Estrada stands before the bright lights of the media's cameras, readying herself to reveal to the rest of the city the horrible news that will become the topic of today's coffee breaks.

Estrada is a short but bold woman with a smile that can disarm the most dangerous criminal. It's rumored throughout the department that she's a black belt, though no one knows in what, and no one wants to find out.

I can only imagine how the crime scene looks on TV. The whirling emergency lights in the background, along with the yellow tape cordoning off the scene, make it look like a Hollywood set. But there's no glamour in a killing, or in the job of apprehending a murderer.

"You think The Zookeeper can handle 'em?" Lions asks as he leans back on a squad car. Estrada was nicknamed "Zookeeper" as a term of endearment by members of the department. It's believed by many on the force that the media are a bunch of wild animals biting and clawing for the next big story, and as the department's official spokesperson, she's the zookeeper who feeds them bits of information and keeps them in order.

"Maybe," I say. "But this beast is going to grow legs before the day ends."

I eye Detective Jeff Bishops and his new partner Tim Michaels maneuvering their way towards us through the crowd of officers. There's a mutual hatred between Bishops and me, because I'm the son of a cop-killer, and he's done his best to make sure I don't forget it.

"Fred," Bishops utters, extending a thin white hand to Lions, his old partner. He's wearing a blue pinstriped suit with dark shoes. His black hair is cut short and has started to gray on the sides.

He shakes Lions' hand. "Calhoun," he says in a melancholy tone, refusing to look in my direction with those black eyes of his that are deep-set in his slender face. There's no love lost between us.

"Bishops," I reply, turning to greet Michaels with a partial smile.

Michaels is a cheerful guy, maybe too cheerful for the job. He has sandy-colored hair that is sculpted into a perfect wave of curls on his head. And unlike Bishops, Michaels loves wearing Hawaiian shirts, even in the winter. Hell, his eyes are the color of an exotic blue sea, and yet he is a Chicagoan through-and-through. During football season, Michaels bleeds orange and blue for the Bears—during baseball season, he bleeds black and white for the Sox.

"You guys got called in, too?" Michaels asks, showing his white, seashell-colored teeth.

"Even better," Lions says. "We got *the* call."

Both men whistle, not because they don't want the case, but it's a natural reaction to the fact that a case such as this means that all eyes are going to be on it, from the mayor on down to the loneliest patrolman—which means this case has to go on the books as solved, or it's going to live with us till the end of our careers.

Bishops points to a growing crowd of officers gathering around a remote monitor. "I see The Zookeeper is about to go to work."

"Yeah, she's gotta give the people what they want," Lions replies, pulling a lighter from his pants pocket. He flicks it and the flame leaps to life, then quickly dies.

"Well, we'll see you around. Gotta find the captain and get the orders." Bishops walks off with Michaels following. If Lions isn't going to tell him that the captain is in the MCC, then why should I?

"That guy can be a dick sometimes," Lions says, once Bishops is out of earshot. Surprised, I turn and look at him. I've never heard Lions badmouth another man, especially an old partner.

"What?" He looks back at me, still flicking the lighter. "You thought I chose to be your partner out of pity? Shit, I couldn't take his attitude anymore. I was shooting to have Michaels as a partner, but the captain thought it best if you had someone that you could relate to. Like I know what the hell that means. Just 'cause I'm Black too doesn't mean we can relate."

I shake my head and lean back on the squad car. I have to love Lions for his truthfulness. We watch from a distance as Estrada stands tall in front of the video cameras and various sized microphones that are being shoved in her direction. Her shadow silhouettes the crime scene as if it's a magical veil cast over it to hide the incident from the rest of the world. Her voice erupts from the monitor to the right of us where every officer now stands in uniformed silence.

"At one o'clock this morning a call came into Emergency Services reporting gunshots fired. Upon the arrival of officers, two victims were found. One was an off-duty police officer, the other was a civilian. At this time the names of the victims are being withheld until their respective families can be notified. Investigators are still conducting their investigation, and as of now, all we know is that this incident is a robbery turned fatal." Estrada takes a breath, not for herself, but for the media, so that they can rattle off their questions.

At that exact moment, the door to the MCC bursts open and Captain Haggerty steps out onto the stoop. "ALL RIGHT YOU HOUNDS!" he barks, his voice demanding the respect and attention of every man and woman with a badge. "I know you've been waiting for orders, and here they are." Our ears perk up and our eyes grow wide. "As you all know, one of our own has fallen this night. Whether he was in uniform or not, it doesn't matter. He was one of us." The captain looks out over the crowd.

The fact that he mentioned Richardson was out of uniform means he's signaling to the rest of us that there's going to be a battle with upper brass and the city over survivor benefits—a battle that won't officially begin until we've found Richardson's killer.

"Somewhere out there a cop-killer is walking free, breathing air, and laughing about the evil deed he has committed. I want this asshole found, tried, and locked away for the rest of his life. I want every officer to hit these streets, to put a vice-like squeeze on every hustler, pimp, prostitute, crackhead, gangbanger, weed smoker, and drug dealer, until someone either gives up this asshole or gives up information that will lead to his arrest. I want a message sent to the streets that we won't tolerate the killing of law enforcement in this city. Now get out there and find this asshole!"

Every cop breaks formation like good soldiers and scatters

off to their cars, ready to carry forth Captain Haggerty and the upper brass' message that killing cops is bad for business.

Now that the hounds have been unleashed, Lions and I set off for the crime scene. By now, we're sure that forensics has collected enough evidence and photographs for us to start piecing together the puzzle.

"Lions! Calhoun!" The captain calls after us as he makes his way through the dwindling crowd of officers. "Where do you two think you're going?"

"Back to the scene," I say.

"Don't worry about the scene for now. I have Bishops and Michaels coordinating the bag-and-tag. I just got word that Richardson is the one who made the call to Emergency Services before he was killed. He gave us something to go on, but we're not releasing it to the media until the press conference downtown. By that time, whatever he gave us will have hit roll call and be on the streets with our boys. Lions, I need you to go down to Emergency Services and get that operator's audio."

"What about me, Captain? What am I going to do?"

Captain Haggerty smiles and puts the stub of his cigar in his mouth. "You're going to question the first responding officer."

"And who would that be?"

"Officer Smith. You remember him, don't you? You broke his nose last year."

Chapter 4

I stare across the small aluminum table at Officer Smith. His black hair is tucked neatly under his officer's cap, which he removes when he takes a seat. I can see that his eyes are still ablaze with hate for me as he scrunches his furry black eyebrows together into one long unibrow.

He taps his calloused fingers against the table, and in a way I'm grateful, because it keeps me from looking directly at the misshapen mound of cartilage over the bridge of his large hook nose--where I broke it.

I decide to try and clear the air by letting him know that we don't need to be at each other's throats. In spite of everything, we both bleed CPD blue. "So, where's your partner, Richter?" I ask gingerly.

"He's nursing a desk downtown until DOPS clears him on an OIS."

The fact that the Department of Professional Standards hasn't cleared Richter in an officer-involved shooting is a clear signal that the situation is drastic—for both the department and the city.

"He shot a kid," Smith says, staring at me with dark piercing eyes as if he just read my mind. "And not just any kid. A *Black* kid."

The way he says "Black" makes me feel as if I'm the one being questioned, because of the color of my skin. I sit forward in my chair. "And what's *that* supposed to mean?"

Smith sneers, looking off to the side. "You know what it means. Richter's white and the kid's Black. Whatever soapbox preacher or corner reverend they can get will be pulling the race card from here to Mississippi."

I say nothing, because what can I say? It's the truth. Every cop knows how the game of "serve and protect" is played. Richter rolled the dice and hit craps. "Well I'm sure that DOPS will find he was justifiable in his actions. Plus, he's got you to testify on his behalf." This time it's Smith's turn to say nothing as he drops his head. I realize then that he hadn't actually been with Richter during the shooting.

Clearing my throat, I open my notepad to a fresh page and start in on the questioning that has brought us together. "From the beginning, can you tell me what you saw when you arrived on the scene?"

Smith stops tapping the table and sits up in his seat. "At about twelve-thirty I got a call from Emergency Services that there'd been shots fired in the vicinity, and there might be a victim in distress. When I arrived on the scene, I found both victims on the ground. It was apparent that they were both DOA, so I halted the arriving EMTs and started cordoning off the scene for investigations."

"Thank you for doing that. You probably saved a lot of crucial evidence. Now, despite the EMTs, were there any other vehicles you might have seen fleeing the scene?"

"None. I made sure that the residents who wanted to move their cars didn't. Can you believe one woman told me she didn't want the blood to ruin her new paint job? The nerve of that nig—" He stops short of saying what I know he's going to say.

The room grows quiet. I sit back in my seat and wait. I want Smith to understand what his mouth almost got his ass into. "Okay, Officer Smith, I need for you to take a few minutes and really think back to after you taped off the area. Was there anything out of the ordinary? I mean, anything that grabbed your attention for whatever reason?"

Smith takes a second. He's biting his bottom lip while looking down at the table. I can tell he's reliving the moment in question, looking at every angle as if he's there again.

"Wait," he says. "Now that I think about it... I got a call about the silent alarm over at the Conservatory across the street going off around the same time I arrived on the scene. After coming across the bodies, I paid it no mind and went about preserving the scene."

I nod as if I understand his reasoning. "Did the alarm go off while you were on the scene or before you arrived?"

"It had to be before, because I was in route to the scene when I heard the call about the alarm come in over the radio."

"You sure?"

"Yeah, I'm sure."

I rise from my seat and extend my hand. "Thank you, Officer Smith, for your help."

"Yeah, don't mention it," he replies, shaking my hand. "I hope you find the fucker, and he puts up a fight, so you can put one right between his eyes. I may not have known Officer Richardson, but he was one of us—that's all I need to know."

* * *

I wait until Smith has exited the MCC before I sit back down and go over his statement. The fact that the Conservatory's silent alarm went off before he arrived on the scene has my gut churning. What does it mean? I have no idea, but I'm determined to find out.

I close my notepad and head out to the crime scene.

There are still news vans parked all along the perimeter of the small street, with reporters and their crews readying themselves for the early morning shows. Forensic techs and photographers are busy working the scene, while Bishops works the bag-and-tag of evidence, and Michaels catalogues everything.

The bodies have been removed, but I've got a clear image of Katherine McNabb and Officer Richardson burned into my psyche. With the media still nosing around, waiting for any tidbit of information to come out of the makeshift camp, I decide to do a few door-to-doors as a means of masking my actions. I don't need news cameras following me from the crime scene to the Conservatory. Plus, in all the excitement of collecting evidence, I'm sure that Bishops hasn't done the due diligence to put someone in charge of questioning possible witnesses.

The first door I come upon is white with a semi-circle of glass at the top that's separated into three panes. The mailbox mounted to the front of the small brick home reads: JOHNSON. I ring the doorbell and wait for someone to answer. I check the time on my watch: 4:00 a.m. Waking people up at a time like this doesn't bode well for the investigation. A few seconds pass before a dark face appears at one of the panes of glass in the door. A huge man whose eyes are bloodshot.

"Yeah, who is it?" he asks.

I show him my badge. "I'm Detective Calhoun. I want to ask you a few questions about the shooting that occurred outside your home."

"Man, I'on know nothin'. I was asleep." The red-eyed giant disappears back into the darkness of his home. I nod and turn away from the door, knowing this is just the beginning.

The next door I come across is inside an apartment building of ten units. I have to remember to request patrolmen if we're ever going to get the questioning done in a timely manner. I knock but don't receive an answer even though I can see a person's shadow pass over the peephole.

I turn away. What can I expect from residents that understand the unwritten law of the streets: if you don't see anything, then you can't say anything. And if you don't say anything, then you live a longer life.

I can't fault anyone for being afraid and not wanting to talk to the police. We are the frenemy of society's less privileged.

After four more "I'on know nothin's" from behind closed doors, I decide it's time to make my break for the Conservatory. I take the apartment building's gangway and follow it to the back, then out into the alley. I head south until I hit Lake Street.

The Garfield Park Conservatory is on the west side of Central Park Avenue. It's a football field size greenhouse with concrete stairs that lead up to the entrance. When I reach the top of the stairs, I turn and stare across the way at the caravan of news trucks. There are streetlights aligned on the street, and yet, the darkness from the park's lagoon to the right of the building seems to be a deep pit, waiting to devour the world.

I turn back to the entrance, which consists of four doors made of glass and steel. The lights are off inside, save for the yellow luminescent fixtures attached to the gray concrete medians between each door. The place looks like a gothic haunted house. Down near the lower part of one of the doors, the glass is cracked into a million pieces. I bend down to examine it, and I can smell the exotic plants inside.

"Thought that was you," a familiar voice says from behind me.

I turn and find Arnie Ratcliff standing on the stairs, staring down at the hole in the glass door. "What ya want, Arnie?"

He adjusts his black-rimmed glasses and runs a hand over his balding head. "The same thing every reporter out here wants... A lead, a comment on the murders."

Arnie works the murder beat for the *Chicago Tribune*. A year ago he gave up the name of a source in the murder of my mentor, and in exchange I give him an exclusive interview with my incarcerated father. Word on the street is they're developing a memoir and Arnie already has a publishing deal in the making, but for me, that chance encounter has become the proverbial deal with the devil.

I look out over the drove of reporters, then back to Arnie. "You'll get it when the rest of your horde gets it."

"From The Zookeeper? Come on, Frank. I thought we went back farther than that? Besides, what's it gonna hurt for you to comment on the investigation?"

"Like I said, Arnie, I've got nothing to say."

"Okay fine, no comment. Mind if I ask what brings you over to the conservatory?"

"Just checking up on a few things. Turns out it's nothing."

"What's nothing?" He sniffs the air as if the scent from the exotic plants inside the conservatory allures him.

"This here is nothing. Just part of the routine investigation. See?" I move to the side so that he can see the small hole in the door. I'm not really convinced that the silent alarm is coincidental, but I have to play it cool around Arnie. I don't need him to start writing about this in an article that my suspect could possibly read. "I'll see you around, Arnie. Gotta get back to the investigation."

"Yeah... See you around, Frank."

I leave Arnie with his thoughts as he paces back and forth in front of the conservatory's door.

As I cross the street and round the hub of media hounds, I see Lions' car pass between the posted patrolmen and their wooden barriers and pull into the protective circle of the investigation. He hops out of the car holding a white computer disc, his lips fixed into a frown.

"Is that what I think it is?" I ask.

"Yep, and it's not pretty."

We both enter the MCC, which is damn near empty except for a female officer manning a computer terminal used for coordinating the evidence intake.

Lions and I take a seat at an open terminal. He slides in the disc. There's a second or two of dead silence, and then the voice of a female operator comes out of the external speakers.

"911. What's your emergency?"

"A robbery. Three men. A maroon car fleeing west."

"Sir, I'm getting you help. Are you still there? Sir?"

BOOM!

Lions and I look at one another, then turn to look at the officer manning the computer. At the sound of the gunshot, the officer stops typing and is as shocked as we are.

We turn back to the terminal and replay the audio once more, listening for any distinct names or sounds that can give us a more definitive description of our suspects. Each time we hear the report of the gun is a sucker punch to the stomach. At some point, I look over at the officer and find her terminal empty. She stepped out without us even noticing.

I slump down in the chair. "Jesus, Fred. At least now we know why there's only a single shell casing next to his body."

"Yeah, the poor bastard never had a chance."

We sigh and shake our heads in disappointment.

Chapter 5

"**S**o how'd the questioning with Smith go?" Lions asks as we head south on the Dan Ryan Expressway to Officer Richardson's apartment. At five in the morning, the roads are nearly empty.

"How do you think it went?" I reply, staring out at the road.

"That bad? I actually thought you boys might pick up where you left off."

I smile. A year ago, Lions stood his ground with me inside my uncle's restaurant against Smith and a handful of uniforms after they came for my head. "It actually wasn't that bad. I think Smith is over it. He even gave me a 'good luck' on catching the asshole." Lions chuckles and shakes his head. "What? You think I'm lying?"

"Listen, Frank," he says. "Just because Smith is all team spirit doesn't mean he's forgotten what you did to him. You can see it in his eyes—a man like him is always looking for blood. Don't let your guard down or you'll be sure to pay."

"Are you serious, Fred? Come on, man!"

"Hey, all I'm saying is: once a uniform, always a uniform."

"I guess the same could be said for us old bloodhounds."

"Who you calling old?" We both chuckle, knowing that laughter is our only salvation.

29

I continue to stare out the window, watching as the last of the night passes away. A semi-truck speeds past us into the unknown, heading for a world that is far from here—a world that I'd like to believe isn't plagued by death. But in my heart, I know it isn't true.

Heading into the darkness is the true duty of every cop but having the constitution to stare into that darkness day after day, without it consuming you, is what defines a homicide detective. Our mission is to hold tight to the torch of justice in order to catch killers that would blanket the world with that darkness.

* * *

Officer Richardson's apartment is located off 47th and MLK Drive, in the historic Bronzeville district, on the top floor of a three-story Victorian brownstone. Before we can enter the apartment, we have to buzz the building's superintendent to let us in. Once we explain that Richardson is dead, he loses all color in his puffy russet face, and allows us to enter.

The apartment smells of a Berry or Wild Island Breeze fragrance that has been captured and stuffed into an aerosol can. Next to the front door, a key rack hangs with a Ford Focus key dangling from one of the hooks. I fish the key off the hook. "Let's hope the car is downstairs," I say to Lions.

We fan out into the living room. There is a sixty-inch television mounted to the main wall, above a cherry red entertainment center, housing the latest PlayStation, an Xbox 360, and even a Mac Mini.

"Damn," Lions says, putting on a latex glove. "A rookie can afford shit like this?"

"Gotta remember who his brother is," I say, rounding the

white sofa. I scan the covers of the *Essence* and *Jet* magazines Richardson has collected on the dark coffee table. In the other corner of the room is a glass dining table surrounded by four chairs.

Lions has already turned away from the living room and is moving down the hall to the bedroom. I run a finger across the edge of the table. There isn't a speck of dust.

"You find anything?" I yell back towards the bedroom.

"Nothing! Just some boxing gloves and a gym bag."

Hearing Lions mention boxing gloves brings to mind the first time I actually met Richardson, at the Garfield Park Golden Dome Recreational Center. Richardson was mentoring young Black boys on how to be men through the art of boxing. After our first encounter, I started watching him on numerous occasions sparring with street kids who'd maim and kill at the slightest wrong look. But through the jabs, the hooks, the reckless punches and vulgar language, he never yielded and never gave up on any boy that had the courage to step into the ring. He was a champion and possibly the closest a cop had ever gotten to knowing those that ran the streets.

"Found something!" Lions yells from the bedroom.

I step down the narrow hall and turn into the bedroom. Lions is down on one knee. In his right hand he holds a Glock nine-millimeter. He removes the clip and pops the round out of the chamber, then hands the gun over to me.

The Glock is heavy, as if a full clip is still in the handgrip. I turn it over in my hand, looking for the serial numbers along the muzzle, expecting them to be filed off, but they aren't. I'm relieved because I feared the gun was a 'drop down,' the kind of illegal gun a dirty cop leaves at a scene to justify a slaying or an arrest. I'm also relieved because it would've meant that the worst practices, used by a very select group of officers, were being taught early on to the newcomers.

"That's not all I found," Lions states, reaching his hand under the bed and pulling out three bulletproof vests and a shotgun.

"Jesus. What the hell is all this?"

Lions rises slowly, pushing himself up using the support of the bed. He places a hand on the small of his back and groans. "Looks like our rook was planning to go to war."

"Yeah, it looks that way. Or maybe these were for someone else."

Lions smiles. "Someone like Prince Paul? You think this double homicide has anything to do with him?"

"Who knows? Truthfully, I don't think so, but one can never be certain in this world." I start unloading the shotgun.

"Who you telling? I was dating this woman once that I thought I could see myself marrying. Then one day she says she wants to add another person to our relationship. At first I was alarmed, but you know, I'm willing to hear her out. Then she tells me she wants to add a woman to the relationship."

"Sounds like you got every man's dream." I continue pumping the gun to unload it.

"Exactly what I thought. I was lost for words and had a huge smile on my face. But then she says the woman she wants to bring into the relationship is none other than my sister. Can you believe that?"

"So what did you do?"

"What any man would do: I walked out on the bitch and I haven't seen her since."

"These things only seem to happen to you," I say, shaking my head. "Can you call this in, and I'll head downstairs to start looking for the car?"

32

"Sure thing."

I leave the apartment and head down the stairs. *What the hell had Richardson gotten himself into?* Outside, the first light of day is just beginning to break through the crust of gray clouds covering the Chicagoland sky. I don't have to go far for the Focus because it's parked on the side of the building in a vacant lot.

A Hispanic woman wearing short shorts jogs past me while holding the leash to a slobbering, vicious-looking pit bull. I'm thankful that Lions is still upstairs because the pit bull looks as though it isn't allowing a soul within five feet of its waxed-leg goddess.

I wait until the jogger and her dog are halfway down the street before I go to the driver's side door of the Focus and open it.

The car is immaculately clean for a guy's car. A cardboard air-freshener shaped like a pine tree hangs from the rearview. I lean over the driver's seat and open the glove compartment. All I find is the registration and insurance card. By the time I decide to climb into the backseat to search under the cushions, Lions is coming out the front door of the building with his pager in his hand.

I duck my head as though I haven't seen him and dig my hands down in between the seating. Nothing but a golden Sacagawea dollar. "Dammit!" I punch the cushions. Lions taps on the window and nods his head up and to the side. I open the door and step out of the car. "What's up?"

"Captain wants us to make roll."

I nod. "Okay, just let me check the trunk. Someone coming for the vests and guns?"

"Yeah, Evidence Control's got it covered. I told the super to keep the place locked down until they arrive."

"Good, good," I say, heading for the trunk. I jam the key into the lock and pop it. The trunk opens only a few inches and then a blue tarp spills out over the bumper and license plate. I look at Lions and he at me. I place a finger under the already bouncing trunk lid and push up on it. The trunk flies open and more of the blue tarp falls out. Lions grabs a small corner of it and I do the same. We slowly pull back the tarp, only to find old tent poles housed inside beaten-up green and red nylon bags.

"Fuck me, Beatty," Lions says, crossing his heart. I laugh hard, feeling that sense of despair that we both felt wash away. We refold the tarp and close the trunk. "Come on," Lions says after we're done. "The Captain's going to spit fire if we miss roll."

"Yeah I know," I jump in the car. "By the way, who's Beatty?"

"What?"

"Back there at the car you said, 'Fuck me, Beatty'."

"Oh *that*," Lions says, pulling out into traffic. "That was the name of the sister-fucker."

Chapter 6

It's six o'clock in the morning and roll call is already underway as we step through the steel and glass doors of the Area Four precinct house. O'Malley, the desk sergeant, buzzes the door and we walk on back while passing a white male who's handcuffed to a bench on the side of a holding cell. He's covered in scars and smells like week-old piss. His eyes register nothing but a glossy stare, and his pock-marked face tells the story of his acquaintance with meth and their inseparable friendship.

Lions pushes open the squeaky door to the roll call room and a few officers turn their heads to peer at us, wondering who'd be stupid enough to interrupt Sergeant Ronald Newton's soapbox moment. Newton's headed up morning roll since the beginning of time. He came up through the ranks along with my father so the loathing between the two of them has naturally been passed on to me. He's a skinny white man in his late fifties with dull gray eyes, and an even duller personality.

Lions and I slide into place along the back wall and listen to Newton run through his checklist of "officer expected duties." No one can fault the Sarge for the sometimes-cynical list of B.S. that patrol officers have to deal with, because we all know it comes from the upper brass and works its way down the chain of command.

Newton slits his eyes at us and continues. "As you all know, we lost one of our own early this morning. I've been told that Detective Lions will be sharing some information about the investigation. But before I bring him up, I want to impress upon everyone that as officers of the law and of this city, we will be stepping up our efforts to enact more community policing."

There are a few grumbles. Someone asks, "How are we supposed to police a community that hates us?"

Newton doesn't respond and pretends as if the question is all part of the act. Then he looks over in our direction. "Detective, if you will," he says to Lions.

Lions pushes himself up off the wall and steps in between a few seated officers to reach the podium. He clears his throat, thanks Newton, then turns his attention to the patrol officers in the room. "As the Sarge said you already know what went down, so I won't go into detail. But before Officer Richardson was killed, he gave an emergency operator a brief description of his attackers. He told the operator with his last dying breath that it was a robbery involving three suspects in a burgundy vehicle. At this time, we don't have a make on the vehicle, so all I can say is to keep your eyes peeled for any type of burgundy vehicle if you're patrolling near the area of the crime."

"Thank you, Detective," Newton says, returning to his sacred place behind the podium.

I follow Lions out of the room and down the gray hall. "Now that that's done, we gotta do the notify before the press conference," he says to me.

Coming down the hall are five narcotic detectives wearing black bulletproof vests, blue jeans, and black military style boots. The men walk shoulder-to-shoulder, spread out, as if they own

36

every inch of the narrow hallway. Notoriously known on the streets as the Goon Squad, they're led by Lieutenant Daniel Gore, a large man whose broad chest must measure at least two feet across. He wears a blue and orange Chicago Bears cap backwards on his head. His eyes are wide and black like licorice and his face is red and meaty, as if he swallowed a chicken bone and is choking on it. Gore and his men are the last remnants of the now defunct Special Operations Section, which was shut down after a few officers were caught stealing from drug dealers and evidence control to sell back to the very dealers they were supposed to be arresting. The whole incident created a huge media stink for the department, and after damage control, Gore and his men are all that's left of SOS.

"Detectives," his voice projects clear down the hall.

"Lieutenant," I say nodding my head.

"Don't worry," Gore says as the other men fall in behind him. "We're going to do our best to help you catch this asshole. I already got Detective Ramirez here hitting all of our CI's to see if any word of it has made it to the streets."

"Thanks," I say.

"Yeah, we appreciate it." Lions nods as we continue on our way.

The fact that even narcs are getting into the mix means we're at war, even if the streets haven't yet taken notice.

"Say," Gore calls after us. "If we get a lead, you boys will be the first to know. By the way, Newton still on his soapbox?"

"Oh yeah," I say. "He's going for the full sermon this morning."

* * *

37

At about seven, we pull up in front of the McNabb residence in the Franklin Park Neighborhood, near Lake and Ashland. As we get out of the car, I look up towards the building's roof and can see the tip of an old water tower jutting into the air like a rocket ready for takeoff. The brick structure looks like it used to be a dry goods warehouse that's been converted into lofts.

"I might be in the wrong line of work," I say. "When did social workers get a raise?"

Lions hunches his shoulders, then we proceed towards the lighted entrance and ring the doorbell to the McNabb loft. We wait a few seconds and then he rings it again.

"So how do you want to handle this?" he asks, his eyes glued to the ground. I can tell this is the one part of the job that he hates. Hell, every cop hates it, because you have to look into the eyes of a total stranger and tell them that one of their loved ones has been taken from this world. The best you can do to ease their pain is to tell them you're going to do everything you can to catch the killer.

"How about we just play it like tennis? I'll serve and then we'll move back and forth as we see fit."

"Sounds good to me."

Lions closes his coat, blows into his hands, then presses the doorbell once more, this time mashing it down.

A few seconds later, a female voice comes squawking out of the intercom. "Y-Yes? Who is it?"

"Um, ma'am, my name's Detective Fred Lions, from Area Four. I'm here on official police business. Can you please buzz us in?"

"What is this about, Detective Lions?"

"Ma'am, I'd rather not say over the intercom."

Silence.

Buzz.

We take the elevator up to the second floor and follow the exposed brick wall to the entrance of the McNabb loft. When we reach the door, it opens a few inches. I can see the links in between the security chain and the doorjamb even though I can't yet see the face of the person behind it. "Badges," the female voice demands. I flip open my wallet and hold it up to the door. "I thought you said your name was Detective Lions?" The voice from behind the door asks.

"Sorry, I'm Detective Calhoun, Lions is my partner." I point behind me as I move back from the door and allow Lions to take my place with badge in hand.

After showing our identification, the woman closes the door, unlatches the security chain, and reopens it while standing with one hand on her hip. She's short, possibly twenty-three or twenty-four years of age, with frizzy blond hair and pastel-pink cheeks. There's no denying she's the woman I saw in the photo on Katherine McNabb's dashboard.

"How may I help you de-tect-ives?" she yawns while still wiping the sleep from her eyes.

"Does a Katherine McNabb live here?" I ask.

"Yes, she's my mother. I'm Katriona McNabb, you can call me Kat."

I unconsciously nod as if I've known this all along. "May we come in?" I ask, even though I'm already making my way into the apartment.

"What's this about, Detective?"

"Can we sit?" I ask, moving freely into the living room. As we cross over to the black couch, I notice the large bay window that gives anyone coming into the loft a breathtaking view of the city's burning-bright skyline. I'm sure it was the selling point for the place. The loft is all exposed brick save for a painting here and there covering the bare walls. There is a winding metal staircase that leads up to where I figure the bedrooms are. To my right is a stainless-steel fridge, a matching stove, and black polished cabinets. To my left, a flat screen TV is mounted to the main wall. Beside the couch, there is a black La-Z-Boy. An ancient-looking white and red rug covers much of the hardwood floor.

Lions moves in behind us, taking a backseat to the tragedy I'm about to unleash on this poor young woman.

Once we sit, with Lions continuing to stand, I take a deep breath and turn my attention to Katriona McNabb. There's no good way to go about this. "Kat, I'm here because we found your mother."

"What do you mean you *found* my mother?"

"She was murdered early this morning during an attempted robbery."

"No," she shakes her head. "You must have the wrong McNabb. My mother is upstairs." She points to the staircase as if she has the power to make her dead mother appear.

"Are you sure?" Lions asks.

Kat whips her head around with eyes narrowing like a guillotine. "Yes, I'm sure. I'll prove it."

"Ma'am—" I begin to say, but before I can finish my sentence Katriona McNabb is running up the staircase, yelling for her mother to awaken from her deep sleep.

I look to Lions, who shakes his head. I stand and move over to the staircase, about to ascend when Kat starts walking back down. Her face has gone white and her mouth hangs slightly open, as she stares off into a place where only her mother exists. When Katriona hits the third step from the bottom, she stumbles and falls into my arms, then instantly begins to weep.

I hold her like I've held so many parents whose children have preceded them in death. Her tears are followed by deep, breathless sobs. "I'm so sorry," I say, watching as the young woman turned little girl curls into my arms.

"I'm so, so sorry," I continue to say, as I brush her hair with my hand, knowing all too well that my words are a bitter sweetness in a rather routine day in the lives of men like me, who live alongside death.

Chapter 7

"   hate to ask this, but when was the last time you saw your
     mother?"
          Katriona wipes the tears from her puffy pink cheeks
and looks into my eyes. "I think it was around ten-thirty last
night. She went to sleep right after the news. We always watch
it together." She starts crying again. The memory of the last
time she saw her mother alive is heartbreaking.

"So you didn't see or hear her leave?" Lions asks.

"No." Her mouse-like *no* makes it feel as if she's apologizing
for not knowing her mother's actions.

"It's okay," I gently rub her head. "Do you know why your
mother might have left the apartment so late at night?"

"No."

"Did she have any known friends or associates in the Garfield
Park Area?"

"Wait." She pushes back and looks up at me. "Is that where
you found her?"

"Yes," I say, trying to keep my voice at an even pitch. "Why?
Did she know someone in the neighborhood?"

"Not that I know of personally, but she had a lot of clients in
that area."

"You mean foster kids?"

"No, I mean clients."

I shoot Lions a look. "What kind of clients?" he asks her.

"Homebuyers. My mother was a real-estate agent in that area."

"So she was a social worker by day, and a real-estate agent by night?" he says.

"I guess you could say that. She really wanted to help those poor kids, but she also wanted a better life for us."

"Did your mother keep a list of her clients?" he asks.

"Yes, I believe so."

"Can you get us a printout?" I ask.

"I think so," she says. She turns towards the stairs, then pauses and stares blankly at her feet.

I move to her side and wrap my arm around her shoulder. "It's okay. We can get the list later." I lead her back to the couch and we sit. Tears begin to run down her cheeks as she leans her head on my shoulder. "Is there anyone I can call to be with you during this time?"

She looks up at me. Her face is serene, beautiful, and I can't help but think that the slight smile of bravery she's trying to express is a reproduction of Da Vinci's *Mona Lisa*. "My mother is all I had," she says.

"Okay, I'll call to check on you periodically, if that's okay with you?"

She nods. I hug her a little tighter. "I promise I'm going to find the person responsible for this." Lions gives me a hard look. I hold his stare while I whisper into her ear, "I promise."

* * *

After we're out of the McNabb loft, Lions turns to me with that bug-eyed stare of his. "Frank, what the hell was that?" he says.

"What?"

"You know what. Promising that girl that you're going to find her mother's killer."

"Come on, Fred, you saw how she looked. She needed something."

"Yeah, but not *that*, Frank. I thought you of all people would know not to tell a victim's family what you just told that girl."

"What can I say? She needed hope."

Lions steps in closer and stares into my eyes. "Hope is one thing. You're promising a miracle, and from where I'm standing, neither one of us looks to be the Son of God."

Chapter 8

It's a ten minute drive from the McNabb residence to my home, but with the uncomfortable silence sitting between me and Lions, it feels more like half an hour.

The sun hasn't yet broken through the gray clouds that cover the sky, but it's morning all the same. School kids run up and down the street as crossing guards stand at intersections wearing neon-orange vests, as if that's all they need to stop the flow of traffic. The city's baby blue garbage trucks crisscross between alleyways, followed by the sluggish rusting pickup trucks of junk collectors.

I'm not about to apologize to Lions for what I said. Katriona needed to know that someone cared—that her mother's death wasn't just a number in the city's homicide rate.

When we pull over to the curb, I get out without saying a word. Lions rolls down the passenger side window. "I'll swing back in thirty. Be ready—we can't be late."

I half salute, then turn and stroll down the sidewalk to my home. Standing on the porch with their backpacks in their arms are Jamal and Janai, my girlfriend Gloria's kids. A year ago, Jamal was something of a chubby kid, but now he's as skinny as a skewer, with lanky arms and long legs. He's wearing a red Bulls jersey with a white headband. His sister, the ever-present little woman, is dressed in a navy blue dress with a white collared shirt. Her thick black hair is sculpted into several shimmering braids.

"Hey Frank," she says to me as I step into the gated yard.

"Hey kids." I smile, turning on the charm.

"Mister Calhoun," Jamal says, deadpan. Ever since his mother and I started dating, he's done his best to keep our relationship as cordial as possible, despite his natural contempt for me. I can't fault him though. After all, he was the man of the house before I came along. I'm sure he believes that it's only a matter of time before things return to the status quo.

"You're looking clean, Jamal," I say. "Shouldn't you be in your school uniform?"

"He thinks the school won't send him home," Janai says.

"Shut up, stupid," he scolds her.

"You're stupid!" the little girl counters.

"All right you two. No one's stupid, you hear me?"

"Whatever," Jamal says as he steps down the stairs. "Janai, you coming?"

The little girl gives me a hug. "See you later, Frank." She bounds down the stairs and follows her brother off to school.

I stand on the porch, watching as the kids disappear into the gray morning. I can't help but wonder how long Jamal and I will be at war for his mother's affection.

Chapter 9

I n exactly thirty minutes, Lions pulls up in front of my building. I get into the Brougham and throw on my seatbelt. We've both changed clothes since our last encounter. He's wearing a pair of dark gray pants along with a white collared shirt, a blue and gray tie, and a blue blazer with a miniature gold detective's badge pinned to the lapel.

"You ready for this?" he wants to know.

"If I told you I didn't want to go through with it, would it matter?"

"Nope. Our fate is sealed."

"Then, I guess I'm ready," I say, plucking a stray piece of lint off my black blazer. I'm also wearing a white collared shirt, but with a blood red tie and black slacks.

"Then it's off to the big top."

Lions pulls away from the curb and heads down the street. He hooks a left on Austin before jumping onto the 290-expressway heading east. The morning rush hour traffic is just starting to back up near the Dan Ryan exchange, so we jump off at Taylor Street and head south past Little Italy and the Maxwell Street area.

We sit in silence for a while, taking in the calm before the storm. We race through the outskirts of University Village, the new gentrified cardboard cutout that the University of Illinois at Chicago built to replace the rundown row houses and project buildings that once made up Old Jew Town. The only relic to stand the test of time is the Maxwell Street Polish and Burger Shack, which has expanded and now has two walkup windows.

"After the press conference, I figure we should do the notify on Richardson," I say.

"And how are we supposed to do that? You think the last known address on Prince Paul's rap sheet is actually going to be his current one?"

"Maybe. If not, then we try that club of his on Madison."

"Richardson doesn't have anyone else?"

"I don't think so. I think it was just him and his brother."

"I wonder what that's got to be like."

"What what's got to be like?"

"You know... Having your brother as a criminal."

"Well, I'm sure it wasn't that hard. They were brothers after all."

"Yeah, but brothers with two different points of view when it came to seeing the world. It makes you wonder what Richardson would have done if he'd had to arrest his brother. Now *that* would have been something to see."

"Probably. But then again, would you have really wanted to see that?"

"I know a few officers who'd pay well to see it." Lions smiles as he stops at a red light.

I allow the silence to settle in between us again as I give his words some thought. The fact that I had to arrest my own father for the murder of my half-brother is a chilling comparison to the speculative incident that Richardson might have had to face.

"Ay, Frank. You okay?" Lions asks.

"Yeah, Fred. I'm good. Just thinking about the hand that life deals us sometimes."

"Well, if you see the dealer, tell him I need a new hand. I'm ready to throw mine in."

I sigh. "Aren't we all?"

Chapter 10

T he headquarters of the Chicago Police Department is in a seven-story brick building with a top floor made of glass and steel. Its square windows, sectioned off in rows of three, look out over the city in every direction. I guess there's something mythological to its design—guarding all the gates from unknown enemies.

Lions parks his car in an empty spot in the public parking lot, then we trek over to the building's main entrance. Inside, the place feels more like a Macy's department store than a police station. There are surveillance cameras everywhere.

A female officer sits inside a bulletproof booth. She's busy reading a magazine when we approach. "How can I help you?" she asks us.

"Detectives Lions and Calhoun. We're here for the press conference," Lions says.

The female officer glances up from the article she's reading and looks us over, then asks for our badges. We flip them out, then return them to our pockets.

"Um... I need to actually *see* them," she says snidely, sitting up straight in her chair. Her hair is dyed black cherry, and it makes her thin eyebrows and puffy face look even more serious than the attitude she's giving us.

We slide our badges under the opening in the glass. The officer runs them under a black light. After she's verified who we are, she returns our badges and says, "The press conference will be held on the fifth floor. Please step forward through the scanner one at a time. If you have any weapons, drop them into the chute before proceeding."

We do as we're told before passing through a biometric scanner. On the other side, two officers await us with our weapons in hand.

After re-holstering our guns, we take an elevator up to the fifth floor and find Captain Haggerty waiting in the hallway. "Detectives, right this way." He leads us into a small conference room that's been fumigated with what smells like apple cider.

Sitting at a long rectangular table are three other men. The first to look up from their conversation is the Chief of Detectives, Bill Gladstone, a staunch man with green eyes and red hair. He wears his Irish pride like he wears his badge—over his heart. Sitting next to him is the Deputy Superintendent of the Bureau of Investigative Services, Michael Thorn, a once All-American athlete with a now sagging body that looks pressed against the outline of his suit coat. Next to the two men and sitting at the head of the table is Superintendent Johnny West, a former FBI agent, and only the second person in CPD history to make the top brass without coming up through the ranks.

West rises from his seat and greets us with handshakes. I happen to like him, even though most in the department wouldn't spare the spit in their mouths if he were on fire. Their major complaint being that he isn't one of us. But like the mayor, I'd like to think that having a superintendent who isn't one of us might make a difference in changing a city that has always drawn lines in the sand between us and them.

After we dispense with the pleasantries, we all sit and wait to hear what our newfound savior has to say.

West looks around the table, locking eyes with each of us, ensuring he has our undivided attention. "The media is going to be feeding off this story as long as they can. We need to throw them a bone in order to keep them happy, but just enough, not too much. I don't want the scum that did this to start lying low. We need him out there thinking he's accomplished something. Give him some room so he can start talking, and then he'll hang himself. Now before we go out there, have we notified the victims' next of kin?"

Everyone turns to look at me and Lions. "Technically, sir," Lions says, "yes and no."

"What do you mean, *technically*, Detective?"

"Well, sir, we were able to notify the female vic's family... But at this time we are unable to contact the next of kin for Officer Richardson."

West narrows his eyes. "And why is that? By my watch, it has been well over eight hours since the crime occurred."

Gladstone clears his throat. "If I may, sir, Detectives Lions and Calhoun have been working the scene since early this morning. They've also taken it upon themselves to do the notifies. I believe that the detectives would have notified Richardson's family if they had had time to."

"Okay," West says, holding up his hands. "Is there any way we can get a uniform over to Richardson's family in the next fifteen minutes?" Everyone is silent. "Okay, people... Can we or can we not notify this slain officer's family?"

It's Thorn's turn to speak. He clears his throat and begins in that gruff voice of his. "The reason we can't notify Richardson's family is because we don't know where his next of kin resides. It has been brought to my attention by Chief Gladstone that Officer Richardson's next of kin is a notorious gangbanger and drug dealer who goes by the name of Prince Paul."

West closes his eyes and takes a deep breath. When he opens his eyes, he looks directly at me and Lions. "Does this Prince Paul have anything to do with the murders?"

Lions looks to me and then back to the Superintendent. "As of right now, there's no connection."

"Then I'd be right to assume that we're still looking at this as a robbery-homicide?"

"Yes, sir," Lions says.

West claps his hands together. "Good. Then our plans for a press conference will go on as scheduled. We'll keep this little-known fact about Officer Richardson's brother out of the press. The department doesn't need to take another hit when one of our own has just fallen."

Everyone nods in agreement except me. What the Superintendent is proposing sounds logical, but in my heart, I feel as if the department is trying to create distance between Richardson's murder and the fact that his brother is a drug dealer, so that when the shit hits the fan, they can duck for cover.

"Sir," I say. "What about Officer Richardson's brother? What about our duty to notify the next of kin?"

West looks to the Deputy Superintendent. "What's been done has been done, Detective. Our job now is to pick up the pieces and catch the scum responsible for this."

"But, sir, what we're about to do is inhumane. We haven't even had a chance—"

"Detective!" Deputy Superintendent Thorn interrupts me. "This is non-negotiable."

The room goes silent, then we all stand and watch Superintendent West exit. Once he's gone, Thorn turns on the full wrath. "Chief Gladstone, I would advise you to get your detectives on board with the Superintendent's game plan. I am well-aware of their career jackets, and I won't have any rogue detectives running around on my force doing as they see fit." Thorn cuts his eyes at me before he leaves the room, and I know that the last part of his statement is meant for me.

"Dammit, Calhoun!" Gladstone yells. "I can only go to bat for you guys if I know you're willing to play the game. What was that shit about being inhumane? You think this is how the Superintendent wants to play it? He has no choice. We're already battling a public that wants to crucify us for an OIS, and now this. You have to understand the position that puts the department in. We have to try and control the flow of information as long as possible. When this shit gets out about Prince Paul being Richardson's brother, things are never going to be the same."

"I'm sorry, Chief. I wasn't thinking."

"No, you weren't," Gladstone turns to look at Captain Haggerty. "Joe, you said he was ready—that the hit the department took for his father was a one-off. But from where I'm standing, he's trying to destroy what's left of his career." Gladstone storms out of the room.

The fact that the upper brass chooses to talk about me as if I'm not even in the room is really starting to piss me off. Who are they to stand in judgment?

Captain Haggerty sits down, sighs, and removes his burned out cigar stub from his jacket pocket. He looks it over as if considering lighting it, then he puts it back in his pocket. "Well, you heard the man. It's time to either shit or get off the pot. What's it going to be?"

Chapter 11

The press conference is held inside a chair-filled room where reporters jostle for the perfect angle while their cameramen work to get the empty podium into their lenses.

Lions, Captain Haggerty, and I stand to the left of the stage while Deputy Superintendent Thorn and Chief Gladstone stand to the right. Photographers are already snapping pictures even though Superintendent West hasn't yet taken the stage.

"Fuckin' circus," Lions says under his breath. "I hope the Superintendent plays it by the numbers. It'll make things go a lot faster."

"Yeah, I hear you, partner." I whisper back. "All this time wasted, and we could've been out on the streets."

"Well, you're not. So pipe down," Captain Haggerty commands.

Half a minute passes before Superintendent West approaches the podium. The room goes live with camera flashes and then he waits for the media to calm down before he addresses the crowd. "Today is a sad day in the department's history because a fellow officer has fallen. Not only did we lose a friend to the city and its citizens, but a mother and father have lost a son. At approximately 1:30 a.m., officers responded to shots fired in the

55

3300 block of Central Park Avenue. Upon arrival, they discovered first-year Officer Tavares Richardson and a female companion, now known as Katherine McNabb, had been fatally shot. At this time, we do not know the full extent of Officer Richardson and Ms. McNabb's relationship, but we believe this to be a robbery-homicide, in which both victims were in the wrong place at the wrong time."

I allow Superintendent West's words to fall on deaf ears. Since when are the words "wrong place and time" a justification for murder? I know that's not what he's implying, but that's how it feels. Truthfully, I'm still not sold on the upper brass' choice to release Richardson's name to the media. They're treating his death as if he was a politician who got caught with his mistress on Election Day. But as long as the department is covered, who gives a damn about the casualties?

"This is shit," I whisper to myself.

Captain Haggerty leans in towards me. "And what did you think you were going to be shoveling when you became a detective? Bricks of gold?"

"No, sir, but I—"

"Detective, be mindful of your next statement." I bite back my words and swallow hard. "Congratulations—you've just learned how to swallow shit."

I turn my attention back to the pack of media wolves closing in on the podium. They don't give a damn that an officer has lost his life. To them, he's just a headline until the next catastrophe strikes. But to me and every man and woman wearing the uniform, he's our brother-in-arms. No, he's more than that—he's a saint amongst society's damned, who's been baptized in the muck-filled waters of Lake Michigan and reared in the teachings of a fraternal order known unto every officer in this city as the Blue Religion.

In essence, one could sum it up with The Three Musketeers' motto: All for one, and one for all. When you boil it all down, it means that every officer—no matter the pain, the sorrow, or the risk of fatality—is willing to lay down their life to serve and protect those in need. That's what the Blue Religion is all about.

Looking out over the crowd of reporters, I can't imagine any of them understanding that code. Suddenly, I feel sick to my stomach as I realize that the gatekeepers of our department have forgotten the cardinal rule: you're only as good as the partner that backs you up.

Chapter 12

After the press conference, I tell Lions that I'll meet up with him at Uncle Skeet's Diner within the hour, because I have errands to run. I'm glad he doesn't press me for more information, because I'm determined to make the notify on Officer Richardson. I don't give a damn that Prince Paul is a suspected murderer and drug dealer. All I care about is doing the right thing for a fallen comrade.

When I pull up to the curb of The Pocket, Prince Paul's billiards nightclub on Madison near Central, I realize the building has been painted all black instead of the brown brick it once was. The long neon sign that once blazed hot pink with the word CHATEAU has been replaced with a neon pool table with the name of the establishment spelled out in white.

I bang on the dark door three times but get no answer. I go around back to the receiving door and ring the bell. I wait a few minutes, but still no answer. I return to my car and sit outside the business for a whole fifteen minutes but never see a soul enter or exit the place. I start to wonder if Prince Paul knows about his brother's death. And if so, does he also know who might be responsible? Then again, a street hustler like him isn't likely to watch the news or read the paper. If such wishful thinking is true, then I still have a shot at notifying him before some dumbass unknowingly spills the news.

I start up the car and bust a U. There's only one person I know who can possibly give me a bead on Prince Paul... If not a key to every home in the city.

***

Buddy Heim throws open his front door wearing nothing but a wife beater and blue-and-black checkered boxers. He has the frame of a praying mantis—skinny but built strong. His once large Afro has been cut down into a low fade with waves surrounding his head.

"Preacha," he says, yawning.

"Hey Buddy, how's it going?"

"Shit, it's early as hell. It's like what––eight?"

"It's eleven o'clock."

Buddy chuckles. "Well, you know me... I'm more of a nocturnal kind of guy."

"Yeah, I know."

The fact that Buddy is a master thief doesn't sit too well on my moral compass, but as a confidential informant, he's the lesser of two evils when it comes to working homicide. He lets me in, and I follow him down the hall of his apartment. The walls are bare, save for the dirt, which has built up on the bottom panels of the walkway.

"You want some breakfast?"

"I'm good, Buddy. I came by because I need to find Prince Paul."

"Prince Paul? I'on wanna have nothin' to do with that dude."

"Why's that?"

"Shit, you ain't heard?" he says over his shoulder. My

stomach churns. I guess the cat's out of the bag. "Paul's been upgraded."

"Upgraded?"

We enter the apartment's living room. In the middle sits a workbench with a key cutter, a few assorted keys, an array of metal lock picks, and a small putty like substance that I suspect is C4. I remind myself that Buddy is the lesser of two evils.

He pulls up a stack of plastic milk crates and offers me a seat. "Yeah, man," he says. "Paul is calling it for all the GDs on the West Side now. He got bumped up to Gov."

I sit down and relax a little. Word hasn't yet hit the streets about Richardson's death, which means I still have a chance to find him first. "I get that you don't want to have anything to do with Paul, but I do. Do you know how I can find him?"

"Listen, Preacha, right now Paul's a ghost—he disappears and reappears at will. When he does reappear, trust me... You don't want to be in his line of sight, you feel me?"

The fact that Buddy is wary of Paul's new status as the Governor of the Gangster Disciples has me worried. As a career criminal who's done a nickel down in Joliet Penitentiary for armed robbery, and possesses the street-smarts not to return, I find it hard to believe that even he is ducking for cover. If Paul's newfound power can force a man like Buddy Heim off the streets, I'm afraid to think of what he may do when he finds out his brother is dead.

"So what you lookin' fa Paul for?"

"Just something I need to talk to him about," I say nonchalantly.

"Ay," Buddy throws up his hands. "You don't have to tell me. The less I know, the better I'm off."

"You know what, Buddy, you might just be right about this

one." I stand up. "Just so you know, the streets are going to be hot the next few days. There's gonna be a lot of patrols coming through. The gloves are gonna come off. You should take a vacation or at least lay low for a while."

"Damn, that bad, huh?"

"Let's just say it's gonna be judgment day soon and every soul's gotta pay their pound of flesh."

Chapter 13

After leaving Buddy's place, I jump into the car and head down Congress Parkway towards Kilbourn Avenue. At the corner, four uniformed officers have five young hustlers on their knees with their hands behind their heads and their jeans pulled down to their thighs. One of the officers nods as I pass, but that recognition can't quite wipe away the embarrassment I feel for these young Black men. *A pound of flesh is just the beginning.*

I turn left at Kilbourn and take it up to Harrison, then catch the on-ramp at Kostner and ride the 290 expressway east towards Western before getting off. The rows of new three-story townhomes that have replaced the sixteen-story project buildings are something of a refreshing sight. The fact that the city is trying to make the area one of "mixed income" is going to be a hard-learned lesson in urban redevelopment that is sure to fail.

I park the car outside of Skeet's diner on Western and Madison and enter. The place is as long as a bowling alley and about three lanes wide. The lunch crowd of cops, pawnbrokers, hustlers, and business owners is just starting to settle in.

Having not made any headway in finding Prince Paul, I've decided to meet Lions for brunch so that we can go over the

M.E.'s findings. It's more of a formality, given that we both know how the victims died, but we're hoping that the forensics report, coupled with the M.E.'s findings, will give us a clearer picture of how it all went down.

Lions is sitting at a square table that houses four chairs. Next to him are two tables, which have been pulled together to accommodate six patrol officers. A waitress the color of banana bread, and another, the color of a pinto bean, maneuver around the place, taking orders and refilling coffees.

"Hey, Philicia," I say, cutting in between tables. She's the black coffee to my Uncle Skeet's French vanilla. She's the first steady girlfriend I've seen him with in a long time. I like her. She gives my Uncle Skeet balance. She stands at the S-shaped counter with her hands on her hips, looking long and dark like the shadow of an eclipse, giving one of the regulars a mouthful on his tipping habits.

I take a seat at the table. Lions is busy working sugar into his coffee when he looks up at me and raises an eyebrow. "How'd the notify go with Paul?"

"Should've known you'd know. Couldn't find him."

"Yeah, I thought so. A man like Paul doesn't leave too much of a trail."

"No one can say that I didn't try. How'd the visit with Mags go?"

"Pleasant as always." He pulls the reports out of a brown accordion folder sitting on a chair next to him and places them on the table. Two legal-size gray files, each labeled with their respective departments.

I pick up the folder from the M.E.'s office and read the first few pages in silence, pouring over the opening procedures of Mag's report. I close the file and lay it back down on the table.

"Seems like Mags is on point with her autopsy. Any juicy info in the forensics folder?"

"A few pieces." He opens his small leather-backed notebook and starts reading. "The bullet that killed Richardson was fired from a .32 Smith and Wesson. McNabb was killed with a nine-millimeter, which possibly gives us two shooters."

"Just like we suspected."

"Yeah, and that's not all. Forensics counted the shells-fired from the Glock and came up with eight. So far they've only recovered five: four in McNabb, and one in Richardson. The other three are unaccounted for."

I lean in close. "That means that three of the rounds either went missing in action or the gunmen fired them at someone else."

Lions smiles. "My thoughts exactly." He opens up the forensics file and pulls out three photos. He places them down on the table. One is an aerial view of the crime scene with both bodies face down on the ground. The second photo is an eye-level shot with all eight of the yellow triangular markers in succession. The third photo is a close-up of markers one through three.

"I had the tech boys measure the distance on the spent shells. Turns out nine-millimeter shells fly to the right and land approximately ten feet behind a shooter." He points to the third photo. "These three casings here all point towards the west of the scene."

"West? But there's nothing there but a street."

"Right, so my guess is someone saw this going down and the assholes let a few loose to try and scare them off, maybe they even went as far as to pursue. But as of now, it looks like we might have a witness."

I sit back in my chair, absorbing the information that Lions has imparted. Three shots were fired westbound, which means that the bullets would have had to cut across the darkened park and crisscrossed into traffic. At that time of night, in that part of the city, I couldn't see a reason why a heated gunfight hadn't erupted. Plus, any real robber cares more about saving their own hide than about scaring off witnesses. Something wasn't adding up, but I had to buy into Lions' theory. It was the best one we had.

"Little Cornbread Snatcher!" my Uncle Skeet says as I turn to see him approaching our table from the kitchen. As my father's old partner, he's been my uncle by default since retiring from the force some twenty odd years ago. I stand and he wraps his long arms around my body and embraces me in a bear hug. I love my uncle with his yellowish complexion and dark curly hair. He's a cross between Billy Dee Williams and Chico DeBarge, except he has a small angular nose that makes him handsomer than either of them. When he releases me, he takes a step back and gives me a once over. "Boy, you still growing or is that new woman of yours just feeding you good?"

"A little of both, but I guess the same could be said about you."

"Now watch it." He throws up his guard. "You ain't too old for me to kick yo ass."

We start sparring. A few customers watch us, more interested in being entertained than enjoying their meals. I duck under a long hook and we hug again. "Unc, you remember Fred Lions, my new partner?"

"Fa'sho. How ya doin' Fred?" They shake hands. Uncle Skeet was a beat cop his entire career, and as such, the streets have been in his blood as much as being a cop has. "So, what'll it be for two of Chicago's finest?"

65

Suddenly, someone yells out my name. "Calhoun!!!" Everyone turns and looks at the door, but I don't have to look. I know the voice. Its intensity smacks me clear across the face, and I instinctively want to go for my gun, because I know it belongs to a man who has sent many to their graves.

Chapter 14

Prince Paul stands in the restaurant's doorway flanked by an enormous gorilla-looking man and two cocky teens: one light-skinned, about five feet tall, the other six-foot and dark. Paul is taller than all three—light-skinned, and sporting dreads instead of his customary cornrows. His tattooed arms of devils with pitchforks are covered up by the sleeves of a black jacket. All that's visible is the tattoo on his right hand of a smiling baby girl.

"Is it true?" Paul's voice splits the room in half. I stand up from my seat. My attention instantly goes to the table of officers who are trying to assess the situation. "Is it true that my brother's dead?" Paul says as he maneuvers around a table where a bald Black man sits, a white-gold chain dangling around his neck. Paul inadvertently bumps the man as he passes.

"Ay, muthafucka, watch where you goin'!" the man yells. Before Paul can turn to give a response, the gorilla lifts the man up out of his seat by his head and throws him out the door, face-first towards the pavement.

Several officers move into action, but before they can make it out of their seats the two teens draw their weapons—a .45 and a baby Uzi. The teens' lack of hesitation tells me they're trained to kill. Women scream, dishes hit the floor, and everyone except

67

me dives for cover.

"Nobody draw," I command the uniforms. I throw up my hands so Paul and his goons can see them clearly.

"Nigga, you crazy coming into my business—"

"Uncle Skeet, let me handle this."

Paul's nostrils flare as he approaches me. "Is that my brother that the news is reporting as dead?"

"Listen, Paul, tell your boys to put the bangers away and we can talk about this outside."

"I asked you is it true? Is that my brother?"

Half the room is scared shitless. The five or six of us that aren't just wonder when it will all be over.

"If I told you that was your brother, then what? You need to think before you do something stupid. Because that information is going to be irrelevant if you're dead."

Paul bites his bottom lip so hard he draws blood. "Aight, D-Lock, let's move." The dark teen holding the Uzi turns and heads for the door, with me in tow.

I look back at Lions. "I'll be okay, Fred. Just make sure the unis don't call this in."

"Sure, Frank. I'm all over it." He calmly sits at the table.

D-Lock keeps his gun raised until we're out the door and safely in the back of Paul's black Escalade. The gorilla is the driver. D-Lock is in the passenger seat, and the other kid sits in the second row. I wait until we're far enough away from the restaurant, heading west on Lake Street, before I open my mouth.

"Paul, I'm sorry you had to find out like this. I came by your club, but I couldn't find you."

Paul stares out the window, lost in a place that I know all too well, and we drive in silence for a while. "Doesn't the department have some type of protocol about notifying family members of dead officers first?" he says without looking at me. "Yeah, we usually do, but when they found out you were Tavares' brother, they decided that notifying you was at the bottom of the list."

Paul bites his lip and draws blood again. He nods. "That's how they want to play it?"

"Listen, Paul... I'm sorry. I know how you feel but—"

"How'd he die?"

"I'm not sure you really want to know that right now."

"How did he die?!!"

"A shot to the head."

Paul nods, accepting the violent act as if it had been preordained.

We turn off Lake Street and onto Kildare, heading north through an industrial park covered with soda pop bottling warehouses called The Strip. During the day, it's mainly used by uncles taking their nephews out for their first driving lesson. At night, it becomes a workingman's motel where whores service their johns in the backseats of cars.

The putrid smell of decomposing waste and trash from the West Side garbage facility at the end of The Strip stifles the air inside the vehicle, but it doesn't affect Paul as he continues to stare out the window. "You working my brother's murder?"

"Yeah, me and my partner."

"You got any leads?"

"Nothing. As of now, it's still fresh."

Paul finally turns and looks at me. "You wouldn't be lying to me, would you?"

I have to choose my words carefully. Cop or no cop, I'm riding with murderers who value my life about as much as they do a spit in the wind. "And why would I do that? I want to catch who killed your brother just as much as you do."

I hold his stare. My words are sincere. I know what it means to bring a sibling's murderer to justice. The scent of trash grows stronger but lowering the window won't help. Plus, I'm reluctant to make any sudden move for fear that D-Lock is itching to put his Uzi to use.

Paul turns and looks back out the window, staring at rows of Pepsi-Cola delivery trucks pulling away from the doors of a warehouse's dock. "Can I see him?" he asks.

"Sure. The Medical Examiner's going to need you to make the I.D. in order to release the remains."

We pull up in front of the Waste Management treatment center and the gorilla throws the truck into park. The two teens look forward, but I can see D-Lock in the front passenger seat stroking the barrel of the baby Uzi. I take a deep breath and try to relax, even though my heart won't let me. If a bullet is coming, it's most likely going to come from the light-skinned shooter, since he sits in front of me in a seat to the left, which means that if he turns to blow my brains out, he's got a clear shot across the seat before I can reach for my own piece. Never mind that Paul could cut my throat with a razor blade before I have time to blink. Funny how the mind calculates the different ways you might die but can only come up with one solution as to how to survive: fight.

I bend forward, faking a cough as I inch my hand towards my piece. The buckle of the holster is still over the hammer. *Fuck, I'm as good as dead.*

Paul continues to stare out the window. "When we were kids," he says, "me and my little brother use to come down here and break into trucks. We'd wait until the garbage plant started up its furnaces because then everyone on the warehouse docks would go inside to finish up their work. They'd leave stacks of can pops and two liters out for anyone to grab. I guess the employees figured if someone could withstand the stench from those smokestacks, they deserved a can of hot pop."

Paul sighs and nods his head as if he's reliving the moment. He calls out to the gorilla. "Ay, yo, Big Homie... To the Medical Examiner's office."

Chapter 15

P aul and I ride the elevator down into the tombs of the Medical Examiner building. We leave Big Homie, D-Lock, and the other kid, who I nickname Smooth because of the way he drew that .45 out of his pants with ease, back in the truck.

"You know what's crazy?" Paul says. "I always thought it would be me to go first. You know, out here fuckin' with this street shit."

I don't know what to say to that. Unlike Richardson and Paul's relationship, my half-brother Blue and I were best friends who never knew that we shared the same father. It was only on the eve of his death that I learned the truth, after arresting my father for his murder.

"I never thought he'd go out like this. Shot dead on the streets just for doing his job," Paul says, looking down at the floor.

"Well, that's not entirely true." He looks up from the floor with questions in his eyes. "Your brother wasn't in uniform when he died."

He stares at me, searching my face for answers, then his eyes grow wide. He pushes me up against the wall of the elevator and takes hold of my shirt. "Are you saying that some nigga just up and nailed my brother for no reason?"

"Maybe someone had a reason."

"Are you saying this is because of *me*?"

"I'm not saying that. But I'm not the only one that knew you two were brothers."

Paul releases me, then turns to punch the adjacent wall just as the elevator doors open. We walk down the empty white corridor in silence until we come to a barren wall where a glass partition has been set into it. Covering the glass is a white curtain that can be pulled back from the other side, and next to it is a small intercom.

"You sure you're ready for this?"

"Yeah," he sniffles. "Open it up."

I hit the intercom and give the technician on the other side the okay. The curtain is thrown back, exposing the corpse of Tavares Richardson from the neck up. The exit wound where his left eye should be is nothing more than a gaping black hole. His lips are chapped and purple. Paul stares at his little brother for no more than a few seconds. "Close that shit, man," he whispers finally.

I buzz for the curtain to be closed, but the damage is done. Paul rests his head on the wall and slams his fist against it. With each thump of his fist a wounded howl, like that of a wolf caught in a trap, echoes down the hall. I take a step forward but stop. *Even a wounded wolf can still be a danger.*

Paul slides down the length of the wall until he's on his knees in a position of prayer. I stand there, bearing witness to a thug's cry. For the first time in my life I wonder if there is, in fact, a heaven for a G.

Chapter 16

After Paul composes himself, we start back down the hall.

"Since Tavares wasn't in uniform, does that mean he doesn't get a departmental funeral, or would that be void anyway, because I'm his brother?"

"I don't know, Paul... That's up to my bosses and the city to decide."

We come to the elevator and I hit the button for us to travel topside. "I understand political shit," Paul says. "But there's political shit on these streets, too. For instance, did you know that Alderman Reynolds of the 26th Ward was trying to get families in K-Town to sell their homes to these crooked-ass developers who were just gonna bulldoze everything and move all the Black people out to some unincorporated suburb, like they did everyone in the projects? Just so a new generation of white kids could move back into the city... Well, we put a stop to that."

The elevator opens and I hit the number one on the panel. "And who's we?"

Paul smiles. "Growth and Development. We're beyond that street shit, even if some in the organization haven't yet gotten the memo."

Growth and Development is the new political calling card of the Gangster Disciples. It was initiated by their Chairman of the Board, Larry Hoover, from his cell in a federal maximum-security prison, after a new generation of members started to fall by the wayside and disregard the laws that originally built the organization into a national powerhouse. Plus, it doesn't hurt the gang's image. I guess they figured if Willie Lloyd and the Unknown Vice Lords of Lawndale could create a political party and be awarded federal funds, then why not the Gangsters? Using the new moniker, they backed the Chicago democratic machine and placed highly skilled members into positions of authority. They used the Al Capone blueprint to ensure their reach touched everything politically connected in and around Chicago.

We ride the elevator up in silence. I can't help but think about what Paul said about politics in the streets. From my time as a missionary preacher, I know that street politics is usually won with a gun, and some poor soul ends up in a body bag.

"Paul, I gotta ask you something," I say, whispering.

"I'm listening."

"I need to know that you're going to leave your brother's investigation up to us."

Paul runs a thumb under his chin, the tattoo of the smiling baby looks as if she's smiling at me. He grins. "What makes you think that I'm not?"

"I just got a feeling. Call it street intuition."

He chuckles. "You know what, Frank? Sometimes I wonder what our lives would have been like if we weren't always fighting each other as kids."

I pause, as if giving his words some thought. "I'm telling you now, Paul... If any bodies should drop in the wake of your

75

brother's death, I'm gonna come for you with the full strength of the department behind me."

The elevator doors open. Paul steps off, then turns to look at me. "Is that a threat, Officer Calhoun?"

"It's *Detective*. And no, it's not a threat—it's a promise."

"Good. Because all I can promise is that if you don't catch whoever did this, I will. Even if I have to go to war with the Chicago Police Department to do it."

I watch Paul walk away. He's as much a man on a mission as I am. Within those few seconds, a thought crosses my mind—a memory of the first time Paul introduced me to his brother. We were sitting in a car outside the Golden Dome Recreational Center in Garfield Park.

I remembered turning to Paul and saying, "The Dome? That's where we're going? I never thought of you as a person that visited The Dome."

Paul smiled that sinister grin of his. "When I was a shorty, I used to play chess there every Saturday. Now I use what I learned inside The Dome out there on the streets."

Paul's statement now blares red in my mind, because I'm afraid he may be a psychotic strategist who is ready to go to war and sacrifice all his pieces to win.

Chapter 17

Upon leaving the M.E.'s office, I call Lions and explain how my little trip with Paul has led him to do the I.D. on his brother. We decide to meet back at Area Four headquarters on Harrison and Homan. Since it's a straight shot up the street, I catch a bus back.

When I enter the detectives' division on the second floor of the two-story building, Lions is sitting at his desk typing out a report using both of his index fingers. "I gotta be the last generation of detectives to actually use a manual typewriter," he says with a snort.

I take a seat at my desk, which is parallel to his. "So how'd the unis take it when you told 'em they wouldn't be pursuing Prince Paul?"

"How do you think they took it?" he says. "One of 'em even tried to recite city code violations to me. Like I haven't been around the block enough in my fifteen years to know the damn thing by heart." He shakes his head. "Good thing your uncle stepped in and made it clear that to go after Paul would put your life and possibly other lives in danger. The unis respond well to one of their own."

"Thanks for backing my play. I know it's not what you would have normally done, but the guy was just hurting."

"Paul is a loose cannon. Hurting or not, he got a reprieve. He might not be so lucky next time."

"I think he knows that." Lions returns to his two-finger typing. "What are you working on?" I ask him.

"Evidence list. Michaels sent over the first round of bag and tags. Looks like they're going to be out there the whole day. He says it's been a little piece of hell trying to sift through what might be trash and what's evidence. It's about time somebody else gets fucked on this case," he spouts, clicking away with his index fingers.

"Who you telling?"

Lions looks up from his report. "Don't look now, but the captain's headed our way."

The collar to Captain Haggerty's pinstriped shirt from this morning's press conference is unbuttoned and his sleeves are rolled up, revealing a cherry bomb tattoo on his right forearm.

"Fucking vultures! We give 'em a press conference... We even give 'em a media spokesperson... But somehow they still find a way to get my direct line. How's the investigation going?"

Lions stops typing. "Well, sir, as of now we haven't made much progress, even though we have officers on the streets looking for the maroon vehicle that Officer Richardson reported before his death."

"Anything come back from forensics on the shell casings?" he asks, hands on his hips as if he's waiting for the good news to hit.

"Nothing. Casings were clean. The assholes probably wore gloves."

"Assholes?"

"Yes, sir," I chime in. "We think that there might have been more than one shooter. The female victim was killed with a

Glock nine-millimeter. Richardson was killed with a .32 Smith and Wesson."

"Okay, I'm following." He folds his arms over his chest. "But what keeps this from being a shooter with two guns?"

Lions and I look at one another. "That's a possibility," Lions says. "But we just don't see the killer unloading four shots into McNabb and one into Richardson and then switching up guns to finish the job. Plus, we've got three other shells from the nine, which leads us to further believe that there were two shooters."

The captain nods his head, contemplating our reasoning. "Okay, let's say we have two shooters. What now?"

I clear my throat. "The way we see it, Richardson and McNabb were sitting inside the vehicle when the first shooter got the drop on them, maybe he was pretending to be drunk—"

"Or maybe the asshole just unloaded," Lions adds.

"Yeah, that too. Anyway, the killer moves in fast once he has them in his sights. His partner is probably either sneaking up on the other side of the SUV or coming out of one of the gangways from an adjacent building. The partner sees Richardson with his phone and badge and does him right then and there."

The phone in the captain's office rings. "Goddamit! I swear it better be important. Keep working, detectives. If you need anything, let me know."

"Speaking of which, Captain... We could use some extra bodies down at the site to do door-to-doors."

The captain's phone continues to ring. "Okay, I'll get you what you need." He rushes back to his office.

"You know something," I say to Lions as I sit forward in my chair. "I've been thinking about those three missing bullets."

"Yeah, what about them?" Lions hits a letter on the keyboard.

"I didn't think about it until now, but when I interviewed

Smith, he said something about the silent alarm going off at the conservatory."

"Yeah, so what?"

"I went over and took a look. Nothing seemed out of the ordinary, but there was a hole in one of the glass panes of the door."

"A hole?"

"Yeah, I didn't have time to look at it closely because Arnie Ratcliff came nosing around."

"That old news whore still calling you?"

"Nah, I guess he found something juicier to write about other than me and my father. But anyway, I think we should at least check it out."

"Okay," he hits another key. "I'm game."

We get up and head for the door. As we're exiting, Daniel Gore enters wearing his trademark Kevlar vest, dark T-shirt and dusty jeans.

"Hey guys, you heading out?" he asks.

"Yeah, back to the scene. You know how that can be," I say.

"Tell me about it. I was dropping in to see if anything new had come in that my team and I should be on the lookout for."

"Nothing new. The asshole still has breathing room," Lions says.

"I understand. We're hearing a lot of chatter on the streets. Nothing solid, but the way things seem to be moving, hopefully we'll catch something that you guys can use."

We thank Gore for his help and head out the door.

Chapter 18

The Garfield Park Conservatory is an immaculate building. At night, all I could make out of the structure were obscure angles of steel and concrete, but in broad daylight, a wave of shimmering blue glass is outlined by strands of steel beams that form an elaborate roof over the hundred-year-old greenhouse.

A guy wearing cut-up jeans and an old Nehi grape soda pop T-shirt stands at the broken glass door, measuring its length with a tape measure. We walk past him and into the lobby. The scent of potting dirt and rare blossoming flowers clogs the air.

A woman sits at a dark wooden kiosk set up at the end of the lobby with a phone cradled to her ear. On the left-hand side is a door labeled GIFT SHOP, and another one labeled CLASSROOMS. The woman throws up her index finger as we approach, drops her head, and returns to her conversation. Behind her are four glass and steel doors that showcase the sprawling foliage of exotic plants sprouting right up out of the floor as if God had touched this very patch of land with His own hand.

"Haven't been here since I was a kid," Lions says, looking around and nodding his head.

"I know. I can't even recall coming here, even though I know I visited on a school field trip."

On the right wall is a floor plan of the four-and-a-half-acre greenhouse in all its glory. Sun shines down through the glass roof, making the room feel at least ten degrees warmer than it actually is.

I tap Lions on the shoulder and nod at the closed-circuit camera right above our heads. "You think they've got these all over the place?"

"We're about to find out."

The receptionist hangs up the phone. "How can I help you, gentlemen?" she asks with a blood red smile. Her black hair is streaked red, and her right eyebrow is pierced with a small hoop. An upside-down cross is pinned to her left nostril.

"I'm Detective Lions and this is Detective Calhoun. We're—"

"O-M-G! I thought you guys were never going to show up. I've been on the phone with the insurance company, and like, they keep telling me to file a police report before we can get the glass in the door fixed... And I'm like, *what*? Do you know who we are? We're the Garfield Park Conservatory, one of the biggest conservatories in the world... And then they're like *hold*... I had to wait at least thirty minutes for them just to tell me that we still need to file a report."

"Um... I think you have us mistaken," I say. "We're not here about your insurance complaint. We're detectives investigating the murder across the way."

The young woman pouts. She'd be a bit cuter if she lost the eyebrow hoop. "Oh, *that*. Well, I wasn't around when it went down, so I have nothing to say."

I love when people try to answer cops by repeating what they've seen on television. "And why would you have anything to say?" I ask.

Lions pulls out his notepad and pen. "Because if you were

82

involved in what went down, we'd love to hear what you've got to say."

The young woman slinks down in her seat, lost for words. "I can have my supervisor talk to you if you like."

"Yeah, I think that would be best," Lions smiles.

As quickly as the young woman makes the call, a robust man with a long lumberjack beard comes bouncing through the doors that lead to the conservatory. His hands are covered with floral gardening gloves and his eyes are light green, like the color of water off the shores of a tropical island.

I extend a hand. "Detectives Calhoun and Lions."

He removes his gloves. "Doctor Stephen Phrite." He speaks with a British accent that has just started to take on a hint of the Chicago vernacular.

"We're investigating the murder across the park, and we were wondering if we could check the security tape of the camera you have here in the lobby?"

"We don't have tapes."

"That could pose a problem."

"But we do have digital discs."

"That's great. Could we possibly see the disc?"

"Yes, of course. Right this way."

We follow the doctor through the glass and steel doors and into the conservatory. I stop briefly and take a deep breath. It's probably the cleanest air my lungs have ever had.

"Don't mean to be rude, Doc, but can we pick up the pace?" Lions asks between frantic sneezes.

"Certainly, Detective."

We trek down a winding trail that takes us through a room where light green and radiant, neon pink plants rise up toward the vaulted ceiling. Amongst the plants, a palm tree with various sized coconuts sprouts into the air.

"You see that?" I say to Lions, pointing. "A double coconut tree."

"Yes, the double coconut palm is a rarity," Doctor Phrite says from over his shoulder. "It's one of the largest in the country."

We turn right and our path cuts into another room where violent reds, midnight blues, nightmare purples, and every color of the spectrum collide into a different flower, orchid, or what a renaissance painter might call a masterpiece.

Lions continues to sneeze. We quicken our step and cut across the vast vegetation of the horticulture room. To the right, we come to a secured door where Dr. Phrite has to punch in a combination on a keypad. When the door opens, we're hit with an arctic-cold blast of air.

"Right this way, gentleman."

We walk down a narrow hallway until we come to a door that reads SECURITY. We enter the room and find a slender man by the name of Hank, sitting in front of a monitor. He looks like a former mall guard that moved up the ranks to the cozy position he now holds.

"Hank can help you with whatever you need. Now if you'll excuse me, detectives... My newborn hydrangeas need my attention."

Lions waits until the door closes before turning to Hank. "Is he always this emotional about plants?"

Hank smiles a toothy grin. "More. You should see him during winter. You'd think the apocalypse was upon us." We all chuckle and an image of Doctor Phrite wrapping flowers in scarves crosses my mind. "So how can I help you, gentlemen?" Hanks asks.

"We need you to pull up the recordings of the lobby from the night before last," Lions says.

The man swivels around in his chair and back to his computer screen. He clicks on a few folders, and soon after a video file starts playing on the screen.

"Fast forward to around midnight," I say. Hank runs the cursor across the image feed at the bottom of the video and it speeds up. "What time did we get the call?" I ask Lions.

He opens his notepad and checks his notes. "About 1:15."

"Hank, fast-forward the video to around 12:50 a.m." There's nothing special to see when it comes to a semi-dark empty lobby, but at around 12:56 a.m., we find what we're looking for. Fragments of glass shoot into the frame and then a small chunk of wood from the kiosk flicks up into the air before landing somewhere off camera.

"You see that?" Lions asks.

"Yeah, I saw it."

"Saw what?" Hank wants to know.

We don't have time to explain as we head out the door and double back the way we came. By the time we end up back in the lobby Lions is sneezing his nose off.

"You sure you don't want to wait outside?"

"Ah-ah-ah...Achoo!" he wheezes. "I'm fine."

We round the small black kiosk. The receptionist pretends to be busy on her computer and sinks farther down into her seat with her head lowered. Lions and I drop down on our haunches and examine the desk. About three or four inches off the ground, lodged into the base of the wooden frame, is one of the three missing bullets from our crime scene.

Chapter 19

A six-man crew of forensic technicians works the lobby and the outside of the conservatory while two patrolmen tape off the area, making it a secondary crime scene.

I stand on the sidewalk, just beyond the tape, searching the rafters of the glass roof for more cameras, but there aren't any.

Traffic crawls in both directions on Central Park, so one of the uniforms takes up traffic duty after the initial crime scene is secure.

I turn and look across the park to where half a dozen uniforms are working door-to-doors. It's good to know that the captain is a man of his word. Lions has a bounce in his step as he walks through the grassy park, mumbling something to himself, before he crosses the street. I turn back to watch the forensics team comb through the grass and shrubbery surrounding the conservatory's entrance.

Lions walks up and stands next to me. "Anything?" he asks.

"Nothing yet. How are the door-to-doors going?"

"As we expected. People don't trust cops, especially in this neighborhood. Shit, I had a ten-year-old ride by on his bike yell out *stop snitchin'.* It took everything in me not to snatch his little ass up and throw him in the back of a cruiser."

86

"I hear you."

"Oh, by the way, Bishops sends a big *Fuck You* for the bag-and-tag."

"Yeah, well I can tell 'em where to deposit those bags."

The midday sun beams off the glass shell of the greenhouse while the roar of the El train down the block cuts in between the combustion of cars at our backs.

Lions pops a peppermint into his mouth.

"So you wanna tell me why you were grumbling?" I ask.

"What?"

"When I saw you coming back across the park, you were grumbling. Looks like you were upset about something."

"Oh, yeah, almost forgot. City Hall just put down fifty thousand for any information leading to an arrest."

"Fifty thousand? Wow! They're really looking for heads to roll, huh?"

"Yep, and that's just the beginning. The department has set up phone banks. Number goes live in an hour or so. They're going to run it in the midday news, and guess who gets to take a crack at it?"

"Found something!" one of the technicians yells out.

We duck under the tape and move up the five-step stoop to where the tech is sitting on his knees. He holds up a copper-colored bullet fragment.

"Looks like we've found bullet number two," I say, watching as the tech bags the blunt shard. "So where is the third needle in this haystack?"

"Found something!" another tech yells. He's farther up, near the entrance, to the right of the building. We step up a few more stairs and watch as the tech parts a dark green bush. The ivy growing along the cement wall is covered in blood.

"At least we know where the third bullet went," Lions says.

Chapter 20

The technicians are busy collecting bloody ivy and depositing the samples into glass Petri dishes. The search for more evidence will end in an hour, or at least that's what the head of the team told Doctor Phrite after he came out complaining that his babies were being neglected. On cue, I turn and start down the stairs back to the street. Lions follows.

Reporters and their camera crews begin to cut across the park, each stepping with a quickened pace, as if racing the other in a derby. At this point, word has already spread and motorists are avoiding Central Park like an indicted crack spot.

We both head up the block towards Lake Street. A hundred feet away at the El station, a train rolls in and screeches to a stop. I was sure that Lions and I were thinking the same thing. Since we hadn't found a body behind the bushes, we now had a wounded witness.

"We've gotta find whoever this person is," Lions states, confirming my assumption.

"I know." I slide my hands into my pockets.

"I'm thinking we hit all the hospitals. See if anyone came in with a GSW," he says, as if it's an afterthought.

"The closest hospitals would be what? Mount Sinai and County? I'm betting we're going to come up with a lot of

89

reports."

"What's on your mind, Frank?" Lions says.

"What?"

"We're walking in the opposite direction of our car, which is back at the conservatory." I turn and look down the block. A flock of reporters is setup along the edge of the street and sidewalk. "What's got you wanting to take a stroll?" Lions wants to know.

"That," I point to a traffic light pole at the corner of the block. The roar of the train cracks the air as if it were a whip. Above the dark colored streetlamp, a blue box sits stationary with the CPD five-point star painted on all four sides. Inside the box is a video camera, which is connected to the city's new crime stopper surveillance system.

"Oh *that*," Lions says. "How come we didn't see it last night?"

"Looks like the flashers on top have been knocked out. Wouldn't have seen it a mile away at night." I think about the *stop snitching* kid on his bike possibly riding up and throwing rocks at the camera, trying to disable it.

"I'm thinking you check out the hospital angle and I'll go down to the city's emergency center and see if they can pull the video."

"Sounds good. We can meet back at the office afterwards and work the phone banks. You want me to get one of the unis to give you a lift?"

"Nah, I'll just take the train. The building's not that far from the Ashland station."

I bid my partner good luck and climb the stairs to the station. After passing through the turnstiles, I stand on the wooden platform waiting on the train that heads East into the Loop. The real reason I don't want an escort down to the Emergency

Services Center is because I need time to myself so that I can think. Riding the trains always helps me think.

Now that we know we have a witness, plus possible video footage, I'm beginning to feel pretty good about the case and the direction it's taking. If everything falls into place, the murderers could be in custody before the week is out, and I'll be back on the roster, waiting for my number to be called up.

Chapter 21

U pon arriving at the Emergency Call Center, a polished brown five-story building on the outskirts of downtown, I'm met by a Ryan Newinski, the Director of the Office of Emergency Management and Communications.

On my way in, I update the captain on how we're proceeding with the investigation. He informs me he's going to clear a path straight to Newinski, but what I don't know until this moment is that the man I'm meeting is a bean counter hidden amongst blue-collared workers—born in the perfect image of American management, with his striped silk tie and Ralph Lauren suit jacket. He's a man that my grandfather, father, and uncle would love to hate.

Newinski greets me with an extension of his bony hand. "Detective Calhoun."

I take hold of it, sizing up the tall, skinny man. His hair is cut close. He has the face of a man-child, smooth and hairless. His nose is small, and his teeth are straight, but he has a protruding Adam's apple that makes his neck look like that of a vulture.

"You must really know somebody down at City Hall if you've gotten to me," he says.

"Something like that." I follow him to the elevator and we ride it up in silence.

We get off on a floor that can only be described as mind-blowing. From one end of the room to the next, the main wall is covered with hundreds of screens, filled with streaming images of Chicagoans going about their daily lives.

Newinski likes the awe he sees in my eyes. "Pretty impressive, huh?"

Sitting before the monitors are emergency operators of every possible ethnicity. It's the closest I've ever come to seeing the great melting pot actually work.

Newinski steps over to an Asian female operator and clasps a skeletal hand on the young woman's shoulder. "Christine here will be helping us with today's request." The way he says *request* makes it feel as though she's about to give me a demonstration. "So what is it that you need from us, Detective Calhoun?" I clear my throat and give them the street intersection of the camera that I'm looking for. Christine hits a few keystrokes and a list of cameras pops up on the screen in front of her. "This have anything to do with that officer being killed?" Newinski inquires.

"Maybe, but I won't know until I see what you guys have."

We stand there in silence, watching as Christine runs down her list of cameras before she finds the one I'm looking for. She hits a few more keys and an image of Lake Street from the night before pops up on eight monitors on the wall, out of the hundreds that are available.

The camera's lens is focused on the west side of the desolate street where steel columns hold up the elevated train tracks. They vanish and reappear every ten feet, like specters in the night. McNabb's vehicle isn't visible because it's on the opposite side of the street, facing east, which means that my hopes of catching the murderers in the act are slim to none.

I'm about to have Christine kill the feed when at 1:14 a.m. a car pulls into the frame. It looks like a Crown Victoria, but I'm not entirely sure. The car's windows are tinted and there isn't a license plate on either bumper, but Richardson was right in his description of the fleeing vehicle. It was indeed maroon.

* * *

Before I can push open the swinging doors to the detective's division at the Area Four headquarters, I hear the ringing of telephones. I hesitate, remembering that Lions and I are next up for manning the phone banks.

I enter and find Hughes and Peterson, the last two detectives that make up our six-man division, with phones cradled to their ears and pens moving quickly over notepads. Lions hasn't returned from gathering hospital records. Hopefully he's batting a better average than I am. I take a seat at my desk and massage my temples. For every perceived step that we've taken forward in this investigation we've undoubtedly taken two steps back, with a lack of concrete evidence to tie to a solid suspect.

Hughes is the first to hang up his phone. He takes the pink slip that he's been writing on and punches it down on a pile of other pink slips impaled on a desk nail.

"All right, relief," he says, clasping his meaty hands together. He stands up from his desk at the back of the room and stretches. I can see the rim of his hairy pink stomach sticking out over his belt and pants. "It's all yours," he says to me in passing. His 1985 Mike Ditka mustache looks nastier than the lint in his bellybutton.

I get up from my seat and move down the row of desks to where Hughes sat. Peterson waves and then spins his index finger around the side of his head while rolling his eyes before he forms his appendages into a pistol and blows his own brains out.

As soon as I drop my butt into the seat, the phone rings. I pick it up on the second ring.

"Area Four. Detective's division."

"Is this, um... The Harrison station?" a female voice asks.

"Yes, ma'am. How can I help you?"

"I um... I think my boyfriend might have did the cop and that white woman over in Garfield Park."

I lean forward grabbing a pen and the pink pad. "And what is your name?"

"I thought this was confidential."

"It is, ma'am, but if we don't have a name, how can you claim the reward money?"

She gives me her name, address, and phone number even though I haven't asked for the latter two.

"Now Ms. Robinson, what makes you think your boyfriend committed a homicide?"

"Because he was out all night, and when he came in this morning he didn't want to tell me where he had been. All he kept telling me was that he couldn't say or he'd get in trouble. Then, he went and took a long shower."

"Did he tell you who he'd get in trouble with?"

"No, he just said it was better if I didn't know."

"Is that all he said?"

"Yeah, that's pretty much it."

"Did your boyfriend come home wearing different clothes than those he had left the house wearing? Did you see blood on his clothes?"

"Naw, he came in with the same outfit he was wearing. There

95

was no blood on his clothes, but he did smell like booty sweat."

"I see. We'll look into this, and if indeed your boyfriend did commit the crime, you'll receive the reward. Thanks." I hang up, knowing that if I give her a chance to respond it could turn into a never-ending conversation.

When I look up from the phone, Peterson is gone and Lions is sitting in his place. "Does it sound like a possibility?" he asks.

"Not even." I rip the pink slip off the pad and drop it into the trash. "How'd the tracking of our wit go?"

"Turns out Mount Sinai didn't get any victims of a firearm-related injury last night—but of course County had a few. I'm waiting for them to fax me over their emergency records. How'd the video come out?"

"We got a partial shot, but nothing definitive. All in all, it was a waste of time."

"Well, that's twenty percent of the job. Tracking down crap that leads to more crap."

"I know." I slouch in my seat. "I thought this case was finally beginning to breathe, and that we'd have the assholes by the end of the week."

"You never know, our wit could be sitting in the hospital, waiting for us to find them."

"Yeah, maybe." My phone rings again. I let it ring three times before I pick it up. "Area Four. Detective's division."

"Yeah, like... I know who merked that Black cop and his bitch." The voice is raspy.

"And how do you know that?"

"I was standing out there when it happened."

I look to Lions and then to his phone. "Now?" he mouths.

I shake my head and snatch up the pen and pad. "You were there?" I ask into the receiver.

96

"Yeah, I was there... But before I go telling y'all my business, I need to know what y'all gonna do for me?"

"Excuse me?"

"I need to know what y'all planning to offer a citizen such as myself who has considerable needs and obligations."

"If your information should lead to an arrest and conviction, the city will pay you fifty thousand."

"Yeah, yeah, yeah.... I know all that... But what I'm talking about is like right this minute."

"I can't promise anything until I know what you know."

There's a pause. I can hear the man sucking on his teeth, possibly contemplating how to relate his story without implicating himself. "Aight, I was there, right? And I see this dude—"

"What ethnicity?"

"What?"

"What color was the man?"

"Shit, I'on know... *Black.* But like, yeah, anyway the bitch started screamin' right, and then the dude just started blastin'."

"And where were you when it was all going down?"

"Me? Man, I got low. Shit, you know a bullet ain't got no name on it."

With the phone cradled to his ear, Lions picks up the note pad, scribbles on it, then holds it up for me to read. "What was the color of the car that the female victim drove?" I ask.

"Shit, um... White. Yeah, a white BMW with license plates that say I LOVE THE BROTHAS."

"Thanks, we'll be in touch."

"But you don't even know who I am."

"Yeah, we do. Trust me. Goodbye." I hang up. "Can you believe that?" I ask.

"Told ya," Lions says. "One piece of crap leads to the next."

Lions' phone rings. I snatch up the dozen or so pink slips on the nail and start sifting through them. I have to hand it to Hughes—he has an eye for the details. All of his possible leads are either connected to someone seeing a maroon car fleeing the scene or to a possible witness that overheard the shots at the time of the murder. I slide the notes back onto the nail. The likelihood of this case going nowhere seems to be all we're getting from working the phones.

I look up and see Captain Haggerty coming our way. His eyes look partially glazed over. "How's it going?" he asks once he's within range.

"It's going," I say. "We're waiting on admission records from the Emergency Room at Cook County. We think we might have a possible wit out there somewhere."

The captain checks his watch and yawns. "You guys have been working this case for nearly sixteen hours straight. Go home, get some sleep, and come back in with fresh eyes."

As soon as Lions hangs up his phone, mine starts to ring. I pick it up on the first ring.

"I mean it," the captain says, turning back to his office. "You two get the hell out of here."

"Area Four. Detective's division."

"I saw that cop get killed." The voice is small, an adolescent's, but it's the words of a person who's had some life experiences.

"And where were you?"

Through the receiver, I hear the child swallow hard. "I was standing across the street when it happened."

"What street?" There's a pause and then the voice of a woman in the background breaks through the silence. "How did you get a phone?" The female voice asks. "You're not supposed to be on the phone—you're supposed to be resting!" The line goes dead.

Lions raises an eyebrow. "Another dead end?"

I hunch my shoulders. "I guess so."

"So what do you want to do for dinner?" he asks.

"Not tonight, partner. I'm going home to Gloria and the kids."

"Look at you. You've been tamed. You're a homebody."

"I'd rather be a homebody than to go home to *nobody*."

"Ouch! Such a low blow. But at least I have Junior's Rib Shack to cheer me up."

We head for the door. As we're exiting, I hear the phone ring. I'm about to turn around, but Lions throws his arm around my shoulder. "Let the machine get it. Captain ordered us to get the hell out."

Chapter 22

I stand before the door of Gloria's apartment, which is upstairs from mine, contemplating if I should finally use the key I've been holding onto for the past six months.

One night, while lying in bed, she turns to me and places a silver key in my palm. She says it's in case she or the kids should lose theirs, but I know what she means. My father once told me that a woman will give you her heart in an instant, but her unconditional love is like a layaway plan: you pay a little each time you lie down.

I pocket the key and decide to knock. *One step at a time.*

"Who is it?" Janai's voice squeaks through the solid wooden door.

"It's Frank, Janai."

I can hear the little girl scream to her mother that I'm at the door.

"Get out of the way," I hear Jamal command as the door swings open. He turns away from the door without even a "wassup," or a meeting of our eyes, and returns to the adjoining living room.

"Thanks, Janai," I say to the little girl as I scoop her up into my arms and kick the door closed.

"I got an A on my spelling test," she says.

I try to sound excited. "You did?!"

"Yep." She smiles, showing me a mouthful of precious white jewels.

"Sounds like that deserves a dollar." I hold her up with one arm while fishing around in my pocket for loose change. We move into the living room where we find Jamal lounging on the black sofa watching TV.

"Hey Jamal. How you doing, man?"

His stare doesn't break from the TV. "Aight."

"That's good."

"He mad," Janai says.

"Why's that?" I ask.

"It's none of your business," he growls.

"Because Mama had to pick him up from school today."

"Is that so?"

"Yep, got in trouble because of his uniform."

"I see. Speaking of your mother, where is that beautiful woman at, anyway?"

Janai and I step past Jamal and head down the hall to the kitchen. Just a few weeks ago, we repainted the kitchen the color of mocha chocolate. Gloria is standing to the right of the kitchen's entrance, in front of a black stove. Her hair is pulled back into a ponytail and I can see beads of sweat sliding down the slope of her light skinned neck.

I set Janai down on a chair that matches a small table and a second chair that sits along the far-left wall. I hold a finger up to my lips and Janai slips a hand over her mouth to keep from giggling.

I step across the kitchen on my tiptoes until I'm right behind Gloria. I can hear the grease popping in the pan from whatever she's frying. Stretching out my hands, I form my fingers into

101

claws, then I dig them into Gloria's side and start tickling her.

"Oh, Frank!" she squeals while trying to squirm out of my grasp. Janai explodes with laughter and so do I. *Is this what it feels like to come home to a family?*

I snake my arms around her waist. "What ya cookin', beautiful?"

"You been listening to Fred again, haven't you?" She turns her head to look over her shoulder. If I could take a picture to remember this moment I would. Gloria is beautiful. No, not beautiful—she's *breathtaking*, with catlike eyes that look like they've been plucked out of an Egyptian hieroglyph. Her irises are light brown like an autumn leaf. I gaze over her Coca Cola bottle physique and when she turns to kiss me with her full, naturally light lips, I know I'm a lucky man.

"Ugh, smushie stuff," Janai says, putting her hands over her eyes.

"Janai, go play with your brother," Gloria commands. The little girl slides out of her seat and skips down the hall.

I sniff the seasonings in the air. "What's that you cooking?"

"We're having pork chops and rice." She turns back to cooking, poking out that Magnum Opus of a butt of hers, and bumps me in just the right place. I come alive.

"Don't start nothing you can't handle," I say, backing up and taking Janai's empty seat at the table.

"If I couldn't handle it, you'd know." She gives me a sly smile from over her shoulder.

"Is that right?" I bite my bottom lip.

She turns back to the stove. "So how was your day?" she asks.

When Gloria and I first hooked up, we agreed that, at best I'd discuss my job with minimal attention to the details. It's not that I don't want her to be a part of my life, but my job consists of seeing some evil shit, and I like thinking that she and the kids are my reward for dealing with the depravity I have to face.

"It's been a long day." I sit back in the chair and kick out my feet. "You heard about the officer being killed, right?"

"Yeah, I heard. When I was picking up Jamal from school, I saw a few blue-and-whites with some boys on the hoods of their cars, searching them. Does that have anything to do with it?"

"Yeah, something like that, but that's only the beginning. I knew the officer that was killed and now I'm working his murder investigation."

Gloria turns off the burners. "I'm sorry to hear that, baby." She moves away from the stove and sits down on my lap with her legs dangling over the side of the chair. "Are you okay?"

"I'm fine. But it makes you think, you know? One minute you're here, and the next minute—" I don't want to finish the sentence, realizing I'm about to open up a door with Gloria about my line of work and its level of danger—it's a threshold I'm not yet ready to cross.

Gloria puts her hands around my face and looks into my eyes as though she's looking into my soul. "I'm not going anywhere, and neither are you." She kisses me hard on the lips while pushing her tongue deep into my mouth and dancing it along my gums. If we were the only ones here, I'd have taken her right then and there on the kitchen floor. Our lips separate. "How about you get the table set and I'll bring out the food?" She kisses me once more then stands and turns back to the stove.

I get up from my seat to collect some dishes from the cupboard over the sink and go into the dining room to set the table.

Gloria leads us in blessing the food. We sit at opposite ends of the wooden table while the kids sit across from one another.

"So Janai was telling me you had to leave work and pick up

Jamal from school?" The boy scowls at me.

"Uh-huh, he thought it was fashionable to go to school wearing a Bulls jersey instead of his uniform."

"So what?" Jamal grumbles.

"What you say, boy?" Gloria puts down her utensils. "I asked what did you *say?*"

He's too afraid to meet her gaze. "Nothing, ma'am."

"I pay good money for those uniforms, and I expect you to wear them."

"I hear you, Gloria... But come on, you can't blame the boy. Have you seen those pants? There's nothing comfortable about tight navy blue pants. Might as well send 'em to a Catholic school."

"If I could afford it, I would."

Jamal narrows his eyes at me. My best intentions aren't working out the way I thought they would.

"You'd really take him out of that school? All his friends are there. He's playing on the basketball team. You couldn't take that away from him."

Gloria cuts her eyes at me. "And why couldn't I? He doesn't have any friends, Frank. And he can still play basketball at St. Augustine. Speaking of which, don't you know a priest or two? Maybe you could ask around for me and see what type of scholarship I can get for his tuition."

I don't know what to say. Gloria knows about my time as a Marine chaplain, and the fact that I know one or two clergymen in the Chicago diocese hasn't escaped her memory. "Yeah, I'll see what I can do."

"Always gotta open your mouth," Jamal says under his breath, just loud enough that I can hear him.

"Excuse me, what did you say?" I wasn't about to take shit

104

from a kid.

"Nigga, you heard what I said." He kicks back his chair from the table, allowing it to hit the floor. His eyes burn with a hatred that I've seen before. It's a gaze born in the streets—I've seen the hurt and disenfranchisement in the eyes of other young Black boys, but never from Jamal. This wasn't just contempt for me as a person. It was a distrust and a disgust for me as a cop.

"Sit yo ass down!" Gloria commands.

"Nah, Gloria... Let 'em say what he gotta say."

Jamal's chest is heaving, but his mother's bark has crushed whatever words were ready to escape his mouth. He picks up his chair and sits back down at the table.

"Apologize!" Gloria barks. Jamal stares down at his plate, refusing to look in my direction. "Boy, I said apologize, and I'm not going to ask you a third time."

"Sorry, Mr. Calhoun," Jamal says to his plate.

Gloria stands. "Look that man in his eyes and apologize like a man, Jamal!" The boy looks at me with teary eyes and apologizes again.

"It's all good. I accept your apology." Gloria returns to her seat and we continue with our meal.

* * *

"Who wants ice cream?" Gloria asks.

"Me, me, me!" Janai screams.

I stand up from the table. "Sorry Gloria, but I think I'm done for the night." Jamal and I lock eyes before he gets up from his seat and goes to his room.

"Are you sure, Frank?"

"Yeah, I think I'm just going to head home."

"But what about—" she looks at Janai and cuts her sentence short. She walks me to the door and turns to look into my eyes. "Are you sure you won't stay the night? I'd really like it if you stayed."

"I can't, Gloria. I've got a really early morning and I need to be on top of my game for this case." She nods her head and I kiss her on the lips before exiting.

As I descend the stairs to my apartment, I think about the real reason I decided not to stay. When I looked into Jamal's eyes and saw the contempt he held towards me, I realized my hands had formed into fists under the table—on instinct. I was ready to treat him like any other thug off the street. I need to get my head together. We aren't any closer to catching Richardson and McNabb's murderers than Jamal and I are to forming a bond. I'm afraid of my thoughts and actions because I understand that it won't be long before this case has claws that dig deep into my soul. Next, there will be fangs, and after that, *blood*. Who knows where it goes from here?

Chapter 23

Throngs of women that I loved at various times in my life, all of them wearing black, have gathered inside a semi-dark church. Every other woman lifts a handkerchief to her eyes to dry her tears while those that fail to cry spit to the side as if ridding themselves of a nasty, everlasting taste. Finally, the line begins to move and I can see each weeping woman pass by my open casket before bending over and taking the time to kiss my cold cheek.

I lie there dead to the world, but conscious all the same. "I'm alive!" I scream. "Look at me, I'm alive!" No one hears me because my lips won't move, nor will the rest of my body.

The last to approach my casket is Gloria, wearing a dark veil over her face. I know it's her because of her perfume, a lilac scent called *Whisper*. I realize that if I can smell her perfume, I'm still alive, and all I need is one kiss from her precious lips to make it so. She bends down over the casket and the scent of her body overwhelms my senses. She moves in closer and my fingers begin to come back to life. *Just a little closer, just one kiss.*

She starts to pull back the veil and my toes begin to curl. Inch by inch, the lifting of the veil is somehow bringing me back from the dead.

The veil falls over my face and I lose sight of her. When it's removed, I look up to see her image but instead find the moon-shaped face of Jamal staring down at me, smiling and holding a .32 Smith and Wesson to my left eye.

The cold barrel sucks in the iris of my eyeball, and when he pulls the trigger, my head explodes into a million pieces. The women that once mourned my loss are now celebrating, throwing badges into the air. The metal star-shaped badges clang upon hitting the floor of the church.

A silver star falls into my casket and Jamal smiles again. "That's what you get for opening your mouth." He closes the casket and I'm lowered into the ground.

***

The ringing of my cell phone awakens me. I wrestle around in the darkness looking for it, knocking the digital clock off the nightstand and onto the floor. I finally find my phone and punch the button, answering through a fog of morning breath. "Calhoun."

"Sorry if I woke you, Mr. Calhoun, but I had no one else to call."

It takes me a few seconds before I'm able to place the voice. "How can I help you, Ms. McNabb?"

"Please, call me Kat. I was wondering if you could help me with the recovery of my mother's remains?" She sniffles. I can hear the pain in her voice.

"Sure. Just let me see what time it is."

"It's nine o'clock."

"Okay, how about I meet you down at the coroner's office in an hour?"

"Thank you, Detective."

"No problem." I hang up and place the phone back down on the side table.

I lie in bed, surrounded by darkness. One of the problems with having a windowless bedroom is that I can never gauge the time of day.

I throw back the sheet and slide out of bed. The coldness from the floor sends a shock up my Achilles. I shuffle into the living room where everything is also covered in darkness. After maneuvering past the China cabinet and hardwood dining table, I enter the kitchen where I put on a pot of hot water for tea, then decide to take a quick shower. When I return to my room to get dressed, I see that there's a missed call on my phone from Lions.

"Hey Fred, what's up?"

"Just wanted to let you know that I extended our search on the wit," he says. "We got records from the University of Illinois, as well as Loretta Hospital. Going to try and get through them before lunch."

"I might need a raincheck, partner. I just received a call from Katriona McNabb. She asked if I'd go with her to retrieve her mother's body."

"Is that all you're going to do?" Lions asks sarcastically.

"What are you trying to say?"

"I'm saying that she's a good-looking young woman. Very vulnerable, too."

"And I'm just doing my job, Fred."

"Good. That's what I like to hear. I'll keep you posted on how the search goes."

I hang up. Lions' concern about the motive behind my professional courtesy has me a bit worried, but I decide not to worry about it and ready myself to meet Katriona McNabb.

* * *

109

For the second time in less than forty-eight hours, I find myself standing outside the triangular complex of the coroner's office. Rays of sunshine dance along the concrete sidewalk and I have to stand inside the building's shadow for relief. It's such a beautiful fall day that I feel bad Katriona has to I.D. her mother's body. She should be out with friends, enjoying the brief reprieve from the September gloom.

Without thinking I had put on a black suit and a light-blue collared shirt, along with a black tie. I look more like I'm readying myself for a funeral than a day of work. When I see Katriona stroll up the deserted block wearing faded jeans and a dark blue shawl, with a black tank-top underneath, I instantly regret my choice of clothing.

The smile she forms on her slim face seems harder to create than the day itself. Her eyes are pink and puffy, and I wonder how much strength it must have taken for her to roll out of bed. "Thank you for meeting me here today, Detective Calhoun."

"Think nothing of it." She cracks a small smile, which seems even more difficult than the first. "You sure you're ready to do this?" I ask.

"Truthfully, no. But I know it has to be done." She sighs, then takes a deep breath and exhales. "Okay, let's get it over with," she whispers.

I pull open the door and we enter the lobby. Sitting at the desk is Larry Godfree, the first-shift security guard. Over the years, Larry and I shared cordial hellos and goodbyes before learning that we also shared the same affinity for the Lord.

"Preacha! How ya doing, man?" Larry asks as we approach.

"I'm blessed, Larry. How's your family?"

"We're all doing good. Next week, I'll be married three years, praise the Lord."

"Praise be his name." I sign both our names on the list and we move past Larry to the elevator that will take us down into the tombs.

"Can I ask you something?" Katriona asks as we wait for the elevator.

"Sure, what is it?"

"Why'd that guard call you Preacher?"

I chuckle slightly. Like many in the morgue, Larry comes from the part of the streets that knows me more as Preacher than Detective Calhoun. "Because before I was a detective, I used to be a preacher. And then I became a man of God in the Marines... Or at least I fancied myself as one. Then one day I saw a city destroyed and my faith went with it."

"Oh," she sniffles.

The elevator doors open, and we step inside. We ride down in silence. This is the one part of the job that breaks a cop's heart a little every time they have to do it. I figure that's why Lions didn't object to tackling the hospital records alone. It's better than having to do a viewing in the tombs.

We step off the elevator and walk down a bare white hallway. The viewing hall of the tombs is the only room I've ever been in down here that doesn't have an odor. "You know you don't have to do this today," I say.

She looks straight ahead as she walks. "I know."

She moves closer to me, until our baby fingers brush up against one another. We're less than ten feet away from the viewing window when she grabs my hand and squeezes it. Her breathing starts to quicken, and I attempt to reassure her. "You're absolutely sure you want to do this? I can have them print photos for you."

"No," she says. "I need to see my mother."

She digs her nails into my skin and I allow the sting to push me forward, so that I can help this young woman through the greatest pain in her life. Once in front of the viewing window, I press the intercom and tell the technician on the other side to pull back the curtain.

The blond crown of Katherine McNabb's head is the first thing that comes into sight. Her hair is combed to the side to try and cover up the bullet hole in her head. Her eyes are closed, and she looks like the proverbial Sleeping Beauty.

"Oh!" Katriona's voice gets caught in her throat. She holds my hand tight as she breaks down sobbing. A screeching wail grows in her esophagus before it's released and forms the word *mother*, which awakens a pain in my own heart for the mother I never knew. I want to drop down on my knees and cry with her. I want to scream out so that the world knows of the pain we both share, but instead I bend down and stroke her hair.

"It'll be all right," I whisper. "I'm here for you."

"Will–*sniffle*-you say-*sniffle*-a prayer for my, my—" Her lips are trembling so bad I'm afraid she might be going into shock.

I hold her close to my chest and whisper words that feel almost ancient. "Father God, I ask that you quiet this storm of pain in Kat's heart. We know that there is a divine plan... Of what, we do not know. But we ask that you instill within us an understanding to see past this, and to see how your mercy and love shields us even in our time of need. In Jesus' name, we pray."

"Amen," we both whisper.

We rise from the floor and head back down the hall. My arm is around her shoulder as she clings to my shirt. I can still feel her tears soaking into the fabric.

"Thank you for the prayer," she whimpers. "My mother wasn't a religious person, but she did believe in God."

"Sometimes that's all you need. Just the belief in something greater."

"If that's true, then I believe that you will do all you can to bring my mother's killer to justice."

I look down into her eyes, and at the tears dried in streaks across her glowing cheeks. There are no words I can say, so I nod. We ride the elevator up, and upon exiting, my cell rings. "Calhoun."

"Hey Frank, it's Fred. How long you think you're going to be with the vic's daughter?"

"We're just now finishing. What's up?"

"I found our wit."

"What hospital are you at? I'll head right over."

"No need. We're at the house. I got 'em holed up in one of the interview rooms. We'll be waiting... But hurry up. Brass is already breathing down the captain's neck."

I hang up and look at the heartbroken woman beside me. "I've gotta go. There's a possible break in the case. I'll keep you posted."

Kat's face lights up for a split second and I regret everything I've just said. Lions was right—I'm guaranteeing her a miracle when all I should be guaranteeing is hope.

Chapter 24

W e always refer to the precinct as The House, and like any house in Chicago's twenty-five districts, Area Four is bustling with activity when I arrive.

The booking desk is overcrowded with uniforms busy hauling in a number of repeat offenders for minor drug possession, non-existent weapons charges, or any number of other offenses that will amount to a suspect spending at least 24 hours in a holding cell. It was a tactic the department used routinely to sweep up everyday citizens, no matter the gang affiliation or non-criminality, into a tactical patrol wagon. Based on the size of the line forming at the booking desk, it looks like the patrol officers are pulling in twice as many bangers, hustlers, and addicts as they do during a mayoral election.

Everyone is doing their part to bring heat to the streets. Everyone except Hughes and Michaels, who are throwing a football back and forth across the room when I enter the Detectives' division.

"Ay, Calhoun, think fast!" Hughes says, tossing me the ball.

"Where's Fred?" I ask, tossing the ball back.

"He's in the captain's office."

I cut in between the two men and start making my way down the row of desks towards the captain's office. Bishops is sitting to my left at his desk with his legs propped up. He sneers at me as I pass. I don't have time to pay him any attention—whatever he's about to say can wait.

I knock on the captain's door, wait for a response, then enter. Lions is sitting in one of two armchairs in front of Captain Haggerty, who's rolling his cigar around in his mouth.

"Glad you made it," Lions says, turning and looking up at me. "It'll save me from having to repeat myself." I take a seat and Lions clears his throat. "Our potential witness is Andre Barnes. I say potential, because he says he knows something about Richardson and McNabb's murder... But he's not giving us anything until he hears what the State's Attorney is willing to offer him."

"He got any priors?" the captain asks.

"No, but from the looks of it, he knows how to play the game."

"Has the State's Attorney given any response to how they want to play it?" the captain inquires.

"The A.S.A. is en route right now. I'm thinking we take a run at him and see how hard he really is."

"Okay but go lightly—at least until we know what we're dealing with," the captain cautions.

Lions and I exit the captain's office. We head out the division doors and turn left down a beige-colored hallway that leads to the interrogation rooms.

"How'd that thing go with the McNabb kid?" Lions asks.

"Like a perfect shit storm. So the hospital records paid off?"

"What?"

"The wit. You tracked him down through the hospital records, right?"

"Nah, that was a dead end. Turns out Gore and his narc buddies came through... Delivered Barnes right to our doorstep.

I got him in box three. Just been waiting on you."

"Was the wit injured as we had suspected?" I ask.

"Not from what I could see."

"But what about the blood?"

"What about it? Right now, it's a variable in a complex equation."

As we come to a stop in front of the door to Interrogation Room Three, Lions places his hand on the doorknob and unlocks it. "You got your game face on?" he asks with the utmost seriousness. I look at him with an expression that lets him know he doesn't need to ask. "Okay, then let's go do the work of men," he says. He pushes open the door and we enter. A sour scent fills the room.

Barnes is a sickly 130-pound, light-skinned man with large, deep-set eyes. His lips look rough and chapped and are pink like the color of a gumball. He lifts his head up off the steel table and stretches.

"Man, how long this shit gone take? I got things to do," he says, looking me over before turning his attention to Lions.

"This is my partner, Detective Calhoun," Lions tells him. "He'll be helping with the questioning as we try to get to the bottom of your story."

"Man, I ain't saying shit to nobody unless I hear from the State's lawyer."

Lions pulls out a chair and sits. I decide to stand before circling around the table like a hungry shark.

"I hear you," Lions says to Barnes. "But we can't be wasting the State's Attorney's time if what you tell us isn't true. You gotta give us something if you want something in return."

Barnes licks his lips. "Aight, bet. Whatcha wanna know?"

Lions shoots me a glance, then leans in over the table and

says to Barnes, "You originally told Narcotic Detectives Gore and Ramirez that you possessed information about the double homicide that occurred yesterday morning at around 1:00 a.m. in the West Garfield Park neighborhood. Is this true?"

"You mean about that cop and that white woman who got merked? Yeah," Barnes smirks. "I might know a little som-som' about that."

"What's a little *something-something*?" I ask, folding my arms over my chest as I lean my back against the wall.

Barnes looks up at me, then back to Lions. "Ah yo, you got any gum?" Lions opens up a fresh pack of spearmint and slides a stick across the table. Barnes unwraps the gum with his calloused fingers and pops it into his mouth. "So, yeah, I heard what happened in the park, right? But at first, I ain't really pay it no mind. Then, I thought about it some more and it clicked."

"Hold up, hold up... Go back," I demand.

"Back where?" Barnes chews the gum like it's the best thing he's ever had.

"To the beginning," I say. "Start with how you heard about the murders."

"Damn, really?" Barnes looks to Lions for confirmation.

Lions nods. "Really."

Barnes snorts. He smacks the gum in his mouth at least three times and then leans back in his seat with one arm dangling over the back of the chair. "Shit, I'on know when I really heard about that cop. Probably like some time yesterday afternoon. But you know how it is on the streets—cop gets killed and some people be celebrating that shit like it's 9/11."

"We get it. Word travels fast," I say, pulling out a chair and taking a seat. "So if you heard about the murders mid-afternoon, what makes you think you know who did it?"

Barnes wags his index finger and smiles, showing his yellowed teeth. "I knew you was going to ask that. See, I got a call from a chick I know named Yolanda. She said one of her ex-boyfriends had just hit a lick on some soft-ass nigga and his white chick. She scooped me up and then we rode around getting blowed. The next afternoon when I heard about the murders, I put two and two together and got four. And there you have it."

"There you have it, Fred." I clap my hands together. "Just like that."

"What? You think I'm lying?" Barnes accuses. "Is that what you callin' me: a liar? On King Neal, I ain't sayin' nothin' else till I hear what that state lawyer gotta say." The fact that Barnes is trying to use the name of the Traveling Vice Lord's founder as proof of his credibility doesn't have either of us convinced. For all we know, he was one of the shooters.

"My partner isn't calling you a liar," Lions tells him. "We just need to corroborate your story with this Yolanda lady."

"You willing to take a polygraph test?" I ask.

"A poly what?"

"A lie detector test," Lions says, reassuringly.

"What for? I ain't do shit."

"If you didn't do anything, then you should have nothing to worry about," I reply, trying to read the young man.

"I knew some shit like this might happen."

"Like what?" I ask.

"Like *this*. A nigga try and help y'all out and y'all turn the tables on a nigga—make it look like he the one guilty of doing some shit. Man, fuck y'all." Barnes spits the gum out onto the table. "I'on need this shit. I want a lawyer."

I push back from the table and hop to my feet. Before my chair can hit the floor, Captain Haggerty sticks his head into the room.

"Detectives, a minute."

Barnes smiles as if we've been caught in an act of tomfoolery by a disciplining parent. I smile back at him. "Don't worry. This will only take a second, and then I'll get back to you."

As we exit the room, I catch a glimpse of Barnes out of the corner of my eye. The smile is gone from his face, and he's biting his nails.

* * *

Assistant State's Attorney Dennis Perlenski is staring at Barnes through the two-way glass when we enter the observation room. He's wearing a three-hundred-dollar, ash gray Hugo Boss suit. His blond hair looks as manicured as his nails. He's a shoo-in for State's Attorney one day, but if he has any ambition of being mayor, or any other politician for that matter, then he'll have to retire the expensive suits for a bargain warehouse brand. And he'll have to get his hands dirty, which, at this point, I'm not too sure he can. "Detectives," Perlenski says, continuing to stare at Barnes. He lost my vote the minute he didn't offer to shake my hand. "What does this possible witness want from the State Attorney's office?"

"We're not really sure," Lions answers. "Right now, he's claiming to know a young woman named Yolanda that might know an individual that could be connected to Officer Richardson's homicide."

"And what do you think of his story?"

"I don't really know what to think," Lions says. "He was brought in by narcs as a CI, but until we run down his story, we have no way of knowing if he's telling the truth."

"And you, Detective?" Perlenski asks, talking to me.

I turn and look at Barnes through the two-way mirror. The young man looks like a chameleon or a gecko. He continues to bite his nails, spitting the scraps onto the table where his discarded gum sits in a pool of saliva. "I think he's playing us. He might be one of the shooters."

"Shooters?" Perlenski questions.

Captain Haggerty butts in. "Detectives Lions and Calhoun have a theory that there might be two shooters."

"I see." Perlenski adjusts his tie. "Is there any evidence to suggest that there were two shooters?"

"We've got two different firearms used in the murders," I say.

"But nothing conclusive to point to two shooters?"

"No."

"Then let's assume that we have one shooter, and that this young man might be the key to us catching him. Can we do that?"

"Yes, we can do that," Captain Haggerty says, speaking for all of us.

"Good. Now that we're all on the same page, let's go see what Mr. Barnes has to say."

When Lions, Perlenski and I reenter the interrogation room, I realize that the sourness I mistook earlier as human musk is more likely to be cheap marijuana treated with an insecticide. The stench is coming from Barnes' clothing.

"Who's this?" he asks.

"I'm Assistant State's Attorney Perlenski. I hear you've been wanting to talk to me."

"Yeah, I have," Barnes says matter-of-factly.

"Then start talking."

Lions and I fall back and allow Perlenski to take the lead. This is his show now.

"So, um... Yeah, as I was telling these officers..." Barnes starts off.

"You mean detectives," Perlenski corrects.

"Yeah, as I was telling these *detectives*... I might know who did that double murder over by the conservatory."

"Before we continue, I need for you to sit up straight."

"What?"

"We're about to conduct serious business, which means I need you to sit up straight and act like it," Perlenski demands.

Barnes does as he's asked. It's possibly the first time he's ever done something against his own will. I imagine he'll beat himself up over it later, because he did it for a white man, without hesitation.

"Now what is this information that you possess?"

"I know a chick that knows a guy who did the murders. Before I go telling you who, I need a few reassurances."

"I'm listening."

"I just need to know that I'm not going to be arrested for this murder."

"Did you commit it?"

"Naw, man, I mean as an accomplice... You know, after the fact."

"And why would you be an accomplice after the fact?"

"Because I was riding around with the nigga. Like I was telling the detectives, I didn't even know he had done it until I thought about it later on."

"If what you say is true, I'm sure you'll be free from prosecution."

"Cool."

"Was that all?"

"What?"

"You said you wanted assurances—meaning more than one."

"Oh, yeah. If what I'm tellin' y'all is the truth, I'm still able to get that fifty stacks, right?"

Perlenski puts his hands on the edge of the table and leans in, so that he's staring right into Barnes' eyes. "You have the assurance of the States Attorney's office that if your cooperation leads to the arrest of the shooter of Officer Richardson and Katherine McNabb, you will receive the reward. But let me assure you that if you should fail a gunshot residue test and be found to be a shooter or an accomplice in this matter, I will prosecute you to the fullest extent of the law. Do you understand?"

"Cool. Let's shake on it," Barnes says with a smile. "After all, we're doing business, right?"

Chapter 25

Half an hour later, Lions and I are racing down Hamlin Avenue on our way to Yolanda Eddy's home. Barnes told us that he and Eddy had met up around 2:00 pm before they picked up her ex-boyfriend. "Some dude," he had said, but couldn't recall his name. All he could remember was a bulldog tattoo on the guy's left arm.

Perlenski cut a deal with a backdoor clause in case Barnes turns out to be one of the shooters. Any real hustler who has done time in an interrogation room would have lawyered up, because a lawyer would have never allowed Barnes to enter into such an agreement, even if he was innocent. It tells me a lot about Barnes' street cred, and his cred as a confidential informant.

"Fred, something's not adding up," I say from the passenger's seat.

"And what's that?" He turns on the sirens to the Crown Vic, so we can blow through a red light at West End Boulevard.

"The fact that we found blood at the conservatory, but no body. Or a third bullet."

"I hear ya, but let me play devil's advocate for a minute. Maybe the person who took that bullet was homeless. They could be anywhere in the city. Besides, we've got two witnesses that can finger our shooter, which means they trump any other hypotheticals."

"For now. But what happens if that hypothetical turns up as a body, then what?"

"We simply tack it on to the shooter, close the case, and move on to the next one."

We hang a right at Franklin, then a left onto Central Park. On the right side of the street, the Conservatory starts to come into view. Lions makes a right just before a viaduct that separates the neighborhood. We follow it around a bend until we come to a narrow side street. He pulls over and throws the car into park.

Through the windshield, I see two squad cars with their lights flashing as they barrel down the small street in the opposite direction.

Lions and I hop out of the car and head towards the Senior Citizen Building. It's a twelve-story monolith that resembles the ancient project towers that once littered some of Chicago's most notorious neighborhoods.

"Cover the back of the building!" Lions barks to the uniforms.

We move through the foyer and into the lobby that's guarded by a female security guard. We flash our badges and continue on to the elevator, which smells like urine and VapoRub. We step out of the elevator and onto the eighth floor. We make our way down the brightly lit hallway until we reach Apartment 807. Lions knocks and we wait for a response.

"Who is it?" an elderly-sounding woman asks, her voice barely audible through the door.

"Police, ma'am."

The door opens slightly. Standing in the doorway is a frail brown woman with gray hair, wearing an orange nightgown.

"Yes, how can I help you?"

"Ma'am," Lions says. "We're looking for a woman named

124

Yolanda Eddy."

The old woman sighs as though she's feared this day for quite some time. "You want her, there she is." She throws open the door and steps aside, allowing a full view of our second witness, asleep on a loveseat with her legs dangling over one of the armrests.

* * *

Yolanda Eddy stares down into the paper cup of her lukewarm coffee, fighting back the headache she's mentioned for the tenth time while we sit across from her inside an interrogation room. She's young, possibly twenty at the most, with long straightened black hair. It took her a whole ten minutes to wake up and get ready before she decided to voluntarily accompany us down to The House.

"So how do you know Andre Barnes?" I ask, waiting for her to lift her eyes from the coffee cup.

"I told you I know Dre from around the way. He just one of my buddies."

"You mean fuck buddy? Or, what's that you young people call it—a dip?"

Yolanda narrows her pretty brown eyes at me. If it wasn't for the sneer on her face, I would have thought she was as sweet as her namesake. "Naw," she says. "Dre ain't my dip. We just cool like that."

"We see," Lions says. "So you two are just friends, that's all?"

A small smirk appears on her face. "Yeah, just friends."

"So let me ask you something," I interject. "Last night, did you and your ex-boyfriend pick up Andre and you all go... How'd he put it? Oh yeah, *hittin' the blocks*?"

"Yeah, something like that."

"What's your ex-boyfriend's name?" Lions asks.

"Why?" she responds snidely.

"Because we believe that he might be connected to an investigation we're conducting."

"What investigation?"

"We'll ask the questions," I say.

She rolls her eyes at me. "Whateva, nigga."

Lions stretches his hands across the table. "How about you run us through last night... Right around the time that you picked up Andre."

Yolanda smiles. "I picked Dre up around two and then we drove to get some sacks."

"You mean marijuana?" I question.

"Yeah, we grabbed a couple of sacks and stopped over on Roosevelt and Homan to grab a cocktail from Rothschild's. Then we got up with Marquis."

"Is Marquis your ex-boyfriend?" Lions inquires.

"Yeah."

"What's his last name?"

"I'on know."

"Wait, wait..." I interrupt. "How long did you date this Marquis?"

"For a few months," she says without emotion. "Why?"

"And you don't know his last name?"

"Nope. Why I wanna know his last name?" She stares at me, waiting for an answer, as if we're playing a round of Jeopardy.

"Let's just move on," Lions says. "So, you pick up Marquis and then what?"

"After we picked up Marquis, we just hit a few blocks, getting rock star wasted."

"Getting what?" I ask.

"You know... Rock star wasted... Like the Gucci Mane song."

"Right," Lions agrees, pulling her back into the questioning. "What did you all talk about as you rode around?"

"I'on know... Stuff."

"What kind of stuff?"

"You know... Like what gang was into it with who... When the new Jordans was coming out... You know, hood shit."

"At any time did you all talk about the lick that Marquis had hit?"

She takes a second to think about it. "Oh, yeah, Marquis kept talking about some sweet lick he had hit on some soft ass nigga. Said he caught him slippin' over in the park."

"You mean Garfield Park?"

"Duh. What other park is there?"

"All right, you sit tight for a few minutes. Detective Calhoun and I are going to step outside."

"Cool. Do y'all," she says nonchalantly. "But this time don't forget the aspirin."

* * *

"Do you believe her?" I ask Perlenski upon entering the observation room.

Captain Haggerty is busy watching Yolanda Eddy through the glass, as she picks at an old scar on her leg.

"Sounds like hers and Barnes' stories sync up," Perlenski says. "That's good enough for me."

"They do, but we still need to check 'em out," I say.

"And who are you going to ask? The liquor store owner?" Perlenski jokes.

"That's a starter. We can also question Yolanda's grand-mother."

"Detective, please. Like some liquor store owner is going to remember seeing those two. I bet he can't differentiate them from any of his other customers."

"But we need to check out their stories."

"No, Detective—what you need to do is get back in that room and find out where this Marquis fellow resides, so you can bring *him* in for questioning."

"With all due respect I think we're forgetting—"

"Detective Calhoun," Captain Haggerty cuts me off. "Get back in there and get the information the ASA needs. We can tie up the loose ends later."

I look at the captain and then at Lions. *Am I the only one still not playing team ball?* "Fine." I swing open the door.

Halfway out, I hear Perlenski speak to Captain Haggerty, "I think your detective is forgetting the pressure we're under to close this case with a conviction."

"I wouldn't say that," Captain Haggerty retorts. "He's just used to doing things by the book."

Chapter 26

We're riding deep.

Five cars with four officers in each vehicle, plus we've got a paddy wagon trailing. Lions is at the wheel and I'm literally riding shotgun. Gore and Ramirez are in back—since they came up with the informants, we thought it was only right that they ride along for the bust. We're all wearing jeans and T-shirts covered by black Kevlar vests. Our suspect, Marquis Jackson, is considered armed and dangerous, and the department isn't taking any chances on losing another officer.

We speed down Homan Avenue heading north with our lights flashing and sirens silent. Cars pull to the side of the road as we run through intersections and blow red lights as if we're on a racetrack. My palms are sweaty with nervous excitement. Our suspect lives less than a mile away from the crime scene.

I bring up the picture of Marquis Jackson on the com-link inside the car. He's a caramel-complexioned young man with a short fade haircut. He has eyes the color of walnuts and a smile that reminds me of a newborn baby.

"That's our boy?" Ramirez asks from the backseat.

"Yeah, that's him."

"His priors read like a stick-up kid's handbook."

Below the picture of Jackson is a list of unlawful accomplish-

129

ments: robbery, robbery with a weapon, assault, possession, possession with intent to distribute. The list goes on, but we don't need it to tell us what kind of man we're after. Once a lowlife asshole graduates to taking lives, he or she becomes public enemy number one, especially if that life was an officer of the law.

As the car speeds past Washington Boulevard, I steal a look in the rearview and watch as half of the CPD caravan breaks a hard right and starts heading east.

We turn right onto Karloff, a residential street lined with two-flat buildings and brown public row houses. Small children are running up and down the street, throwing rocks and laughing without a care in the world. A group of young men and women are standing out in front of a wrought-iron gated community of row houses when both divisions of cars come speeding up the street in either direction.

Lions hits the brakes, throws the car into park, and we all jump out with weapons in hand. The teens that are leaning on the gate throw up their hands. We move past them and into the small, dirt-filled courtyard. The remaining twenty officers create a secure perimeter in case the residents of the row houses decide that our arrest of the suspect goes against their street code of justice.

We follow the concrete pathway down to the third row-house on the left, then climb the ten concrete stairs and pound on the door to the apartment of Marquis Jackson.

"Police! Open up!" Lions yells. We don't get an answer, so we call the officer with the battering ram up from the rear and Lions gives the order. "Hit it!"

The officer takes one good swing with the ram and the aluminum door flies off its hinges. We storm into the apartment, yelling out as we go. The first room we enter is a combination living and dining room that cuts into a small hallway leading to two bedrooms. The door to the bedroom on the right is the first to open. We raise our guns just as an elderly woman comes stepping out.

She shrieks and then the door to the bedroom on the left opens. "Grandma, what's wrong?" Marquis Jackson asks as he stares down the barrels of our guns.

Just as quickly as he opened his bedroom door, he goes to close it, but Lions barrels down the hall, throwing his shoulder into the door.

"Wait, wait!" the old woman pleads as I brush past her.

I give the plywood door a hard kick and it flies open, knocking Marquis Jackson on his ass. He lifts himself up from the floor and quickly turns, sprinting across the small room for the window.

I jump over Lions, who's fallen into the open doorway. "Police!" I yell as I lunge for the suspect. We collide and go tumbling out the window. Even though we're on the first floor, my heart gets caught in my throat as the world turns upside down. Our bodies hit a dry section of grass that separates the building from the parking lot. I feel like a wrestler being body-slammed on a rock-hard mat.

The suspect is the first to get up. *A hustler's intuition is to always keep moving.* I grab his foot and he goes down chin-first into the dirt.

"Ahhh, fuck!" he screams. He bounces right back up, but this time it's into the sights of twenty pieces of cold black steel.

"Aight," he says, holding up his arms. He slowly gets down on his knees.

I stand up and whip out a pair of cuffs. "Come here, you piece of shit." I throw my knee into his back and press him down to the ground as I wrap the cuffs around his hands extra tight.

"What I do?" he wants to know. "What I do?!"

"You know what you did," I say, standing him up.

The whirling red and blue lights cut across our faces as I walk him over to the awaiting paddy wagon.

"He didn't do a thing," the elderly woman pleads, somehow breaking past the perimeter of officers. "You got the wrong man!" Her face is covered with tears and the few wrinkles that she has look to be deep cuts in the soul of her life. Lions plays intercept while trying to explain what we're doing, but the old woman is persistent as she continues to push towards me.

I lead her grandson across the asphalt parking lot to the back of the open transport. Before I push him in, I turn him around and pat him down. His eyes are filled with so much hate that he could blast my head off with that killer stare.

I read him his rights. "You're under arrest on suspicion of double homicide." As soon as I say the words, I wish I could take them back, or that I'd at least had the forethought to wait, because a high-pitch scream cuts me in two. Startled, I turn and find the elderly woman sobbing heavily in Lions' arms, as if our intrusion into her life is also the comforting embrace that her battered soul now needs.

Chapter 27

"I t's not your fault," Lions says, opening the driver's side door.

I sigh before scanning all the Black faces that stare back at us, filled with hatred. "Yeah, I know."

"If he hadn't done what he did, his grandmother wouldn't have a need to be crying," Gore says from behind me, putting a hand on my shoulder.

"I'm just tired of seeing families broken up over stupid shit like this."

We pile into the car. Lions throws it into reverse, and we wait until the wagon pulls out of the parking lot before we follow it down the street. The box-shaped truck hooks a left onto Kedzie just as Lions turns right and heads to the precinct.

"And where do they think they're going? The House is in the opposite direction," I say.

"They're taking the long way," Ramirez responds from the back. "Gotta make sure he gets the scenic route before he shows up to the district." I realize he means the driver of the wagon is going to roll over every speed bump without slowing down and hit every turn as sharp as he can, so that whoever is in the back will be thrown around like a Cabbage Patch doll.

"That asshole should be thankful that's all he's getting," Gore says emphatically. "Back in the day we would've pulled out the phone books." I don't agree with the phone book method of beating the accused, but when you're part of the Blue Religion, you learn to share your opinions sparingly. "By the way," Gore says, "I heard the department isn't going to bury Richardson in uniform."

I look up into the rearview and catch his eyes. "Where'd you hear that?"

"A guy I know works in West's office. Says the city isn't too sure it wants to foot the bill for a big funeral after finding out that Richardson's brother is Prince Paul."

"That's bull!" I hit the dash with my fist. "What the hell does that have to do with anything?"

"It's all politics," Lions says, turning into the precinct's garage. "Everybody's walking on eggshells."

"Yeah, except for us. We crush all the eggshells and don't even get to eat the omelet. When do we get to worry about the politics?" I ask.

"I'll tell you when..." Gore says. "When you stop giving a fuck about the job and focus more on the money you make." We exit the car laughing and enter the building.

* * *

Captain Haggerty and Perlenski are standing there waiting when Lions and I enter the division office.

"So where is he?" Perlenski questions.

"Where's who?" Lions asks.

"Marquis Jackson, our suspect."

"Oh, he's en route," I say, blowing past him to my desk.

"En route?" Perlenski asks. "What the hell does that mean?"

"It means he's being transported to the station."

Perlenski stomps down the row of desks after me. "By whom?"

"Does it really matter?" I pull open my drawer and place my gun inside.

"Yes, it matters. If something should happen to the suspect it could jeopardize the whole case and I won't have you—"

"Me? Don't talk to *me* about jeopardizing this case. I'm trying to solve it!" Perlenski is silent. The captain isn't going to back him up this time. "Now if you'll excuse me, we have a suspect to interrogate." I bump his shoulder as I brush past him.

"I'll be observing, detectives," Perlenski says. "I'm sure I don't have to say it, but be mindful of the fruit of the poisonous tree!"

Lions and I don't say a word as we exit the squad room. Perlenski's warning about obtaining a confession by violating a suspect's rights is past due. Once the upper brass unleashes the beasts of burden, the fruit of the poisonous tree is a mere afterthought compared to the actions of the officers out on the streets.

Chapter 28

"I ain't do nothin'!" Marquis Jackson states defiantly after we enter the interrogation room. He has a red lump on his forehead and a matching knot on his upper left cheek—clearly results from the scenic route inside the wagon.

"Noted," Lions says. "We just want to ask you some questions."

"Man, I'on know nothin'."

"How do you know that when we haven't even asked you any questions?" I ask while dropping down into a seat.

"Those too tight?" Lions nods at the cuffs. "I think we can take 'em off. Whatcha think, Frank?"

"Hmm..." I hunch my shoulders.

Lions rounds the table and unfastens the cuffs. Jackson stares at us with a mean expression while rubbing his bruised wrists. "What the fuck y'all want with me?"

"We'll ask the questions," I respond. "And watch the language. I'm sure your grandmother raised you better than that."

Jackson looks down at the table, then licks his lips and snorts before looking up at me. "Aight, whatcha want?"

Lions leans in over the table. "Let's start with the most obvious question: where were you early this morning, around 1:00 a.m.?"

"I was at home."

"Anybody see you at home?" I ask.

"My grandma."

"Nah, not her," I quickly say. "She might, you know..."

I wink my eye and Jackson's nostrils flare. "What you tryin' to say... My grandma is a liar?"

"Nah," Lions says. "He's not saying that, are you, Frank? He's just saying that she was probably asleep around that time." I fold my arms over my chest and smile without a word. "Did you go out before one or after?" Lions asks him.

"Yeah."

"Yeah, what?"

"I went out about one-thirty."

"And how long do you think you were out?"

"Probably a few hours."

"And what were you doing out so late?"

"Chillin'."

"At one in the morning?"

"Yeah, so what? It ain't like I got a curfew or anything. I'm a grown man." The way he says *grown man* has all the conviction of a boy trying his best to act like one.

"So you went out chillin'? Can anyone besides your grandma back up this story?" I ask.

Jackson screws up his face and slashes his thumb across his right nostril as if he were cleaning up blow. "Yeah, this chick I know named Yolanda—she slid down on me last night."

"By 'slid down on you,' you mean she picked you up?" I question.

"Yeah she scooped me and we went ridin'."

"Around what time did she pick you up?"

"Shit, I'on know... Probably close to one."

"You said a few seconds ago that you went out at one-thirty, and now it's one. Which time is it?"

"I'on know, man. I wasn't really paying attention to the time."

"Why is that?"

"I just told you I'on know." I stare at Jackson for a full minute before he breaks eye contact.

"Let's take a step back," Lions suggests. "You said you went out at about one-something with a woman named Yolanda. What's her last name?"

"I'on know."

"You let a woman pick you up at one-something in the morning and you don't know her last name?"

Jackson hunches his shoulders. "I was just fuckin' on her—it's not like I was tryin' to marry the bitch."

"I bet that would have been something to see," I say.

Jackson narrows his eyes at me. "What's that supposed to mean?"

"It's nothing," Lions says. "Now let's continue on. So, after you got up with Yolanda, where did the two of you go?"

Jackson leans back in his chair. "Just ridin'... You know, kickin' the bo-bo."

"I understand, but let's pretend that I don't. Where did you go riding to?"

"Well, we started out going to the circle, but the cops had it on lock. So, we rode down on the FO end on Pulaski & Jackson and grabbed a few sacks. Then we parked and blew a little."

"So after purchasing marijuana from a member of the Four Corner Hustlers, where did you go to smoke it?"

"Um... I think we just stayed on Jackson somewhere."

"You think? Or you know?" I interrupt.

Lions doesn't break character as he moves on to the next question. "And after you and this Yolanda chick finished smoking, then what happened?"

"After blowing about two sacks, I was trying to get her to jump down, but she said she needed a little bit more before she could start suckin' dick. At that point, I was like *'shit I ain't got no mo' money.'* She said she knew a sweet ass nigga we could drink and smoke off of—then we could just get rid of him and do what we wanted to do later."

Lions rubs his chin as though he's deep in thought. I move into place and take up the questioning. "So you're telling us that you and this Yolanda woman picked up a third passenger who could supply you both with all the weed and drinks you wanted to consume?"

"Shit, I couldn't believe it... But as they say the proof is in the puddin'." Jackson smiles, showing yellow, tar-stained teeth. A feeling of accomplishment displays across his face at the notion of getting over on another man's hard-earned dime.

"Where'd you pick up this third passenger?"

"Somewhere on Sixteenth Street near Independence, I think."

"You got a name for this him?"

"He told it to me, but I was so blowed I forgot."

"What time did you pick up this unnamed male?"

"Couldn't even tell you, but it had to be before two."

"And why is that?"

"Because Rothschild's Liquor Store stops servin' at two."

"So after you and Yolanda pick up this guy, you all swing by Rothschild's, grab some drinks, and then where did you go?"

"We just drove around getting slapped."

"Slapped, huh?" He smiles and it takes everything in me not to hit him. "You do know that drinking and driving is illegal and that you could have possibly killed someone?"

"It's only illegal if you get caught."

Under the table, Lions puts his hand on my arm. "Let me get this correct," Lions says. "You rode around for the remainder of the night, drinking and smoking weed. Am I right?"

"Yep, that's about it."

"But what happened to you and this Yolanda woman consummating your agreement?"

"What can I say? Sometimes, things don't work out the way you plan 'em."

"Isn't that the truth." Lions says. "I once had a nice-looking woman tell me that she wanted to sleep with me and my sister. But like you said, some things just don't work out."

Jackson's eyes come alive. "Damn, she must have been a *super* freak!"

"Yeah, she was *some kind* of freak. So tell me this, Marquis: if you were intending to sleep with Yolanda, how'd you end up missing your shot?"

"Truth is I got too deep into the leaves. Last thing I remember is waking up on my grandma's couch with the Maury show playing on the TV."

"Now I understand." Lions smiles reassuringly. "We're going to check out your story and see if we can track down this Yolanda woman. If everything pans out, we'll kick you loose within the hour."

Jackson nods his head. "Cool. Ay, yo, detective... Can I get a phone call also? I need to make sure my grandma is cool."

"Sure," I say. "I'll try and get someone to take you to a phone as soon as possible."

We rise from the table and exit the room.

Perlenski is waiting just outside the door. "Nice job, detectives.

Anyone mind telling me what that was in there?"

"It's called an interview," Lions states matter-of-factly.

"I know it was an interview, but what was all that about a woman wanting to sleep with you and your sister?"

Lions looks at me. "What?" he says. "It's a true story. I had to give him something he could relate to, so that he'd start to trust me."

"Let's try and keep personal stories to a minimum," Perlenski scolds him. "I don't need something like that coming back to haunt us when we take this to trial."

"Something like what? We're just doing a basic bait-and-switch."

"You don't need to explain that to me, Detective Lions."

"Good, because I would have thought you'd appreciate the work real detectives do."

"I appreciate the work, but that doesn't mean I condone entrapment."

Lions raises his voice. "Entrapment?!"

I grab him by the arm. "Stay focused on the mission at hand, partner."

"Okay, Perlenski," Lions says. "We'll play it your way: one hundred percent by the book. But if this case falls through, it's on you—not us."

"I can live with that, Detectives. Now when can I expect round two?"

* * *

The only way to go at a suspect like Marquis Jackson is to go in as Bad Cop and Worse Cop. The fact that Jackson is a seasoned hustler when it comes to interrogations makes the hour that we took in between questioning seem like a walk in the park.

As soon as we open the door, he yells, "What the fuck happened to my phone call?"

"Lines got disconnected," I say.

"Yeah, I was expecting something like that to happen. Same ol' shit. Y'all cops don't change."

"And neither do dumbasses like you. But you knew that, didn't you?"

"Whatever, nigga."

I walk over to Jackson, bend down, and get right in his face. "What did you call me?"

"Look, man, how about we just kill all this good cop/bad cop bullshit and get right to it?"

"You hear this, Fred? He thinks we're trying to play him."

"Well, he's dead wrong," Lions says, pulling out his chair. "If anything, he better get serious before we fuck him up."

"You hear that?" I whisper into his ear. "My partner wants to fuck you up."

"Shit, I ain't scared. Let him bring it, but I already know how y'all gone play it."

I walk around the table and take my seat. "Tell us about last night."

"I already told you what happened."

"Well, tell us again," Lions demands. "And this time, tell us the truth."

"I did tell you the truth."

"Really?" I question. "Then, how come we don't believe you?"

"Believe what you want. Why do I care what you believe?"

"Because we believe you had something to do with a Chicago police officer being killed. And we don't like cop killers."

"Bullshit!! I'on know what y'all talkin' 'bout. Y'all ain't

pinnin' that shit on me!"

"Tell us why you did it," Lions demands. "Was it for money? Drugs? Why?"

"I ain't do shit." Jackson opens his arms wide as if offering a hug. "I told you I was just driving around."

"Driving around getting high and killing police officers," I say.

Jackson pushes his seat back from the table and stands. "Man, fuck y'all!"

"Sit the fuck down!!" Lions commands.

"Fuck y'all. Y'all ain't puttin' this shit on me."

"I said sit the fuck down, now!" Lions stands up with his chest puffed out and his face fixed with the menacing glare of a junkyard dog. Jackson reluctantly sits.

"So you ready to run us through that story of yours again?" I ask.

"Look, like I told you... I went out around one-something with this chick named Yolanda. We went and grabbed a few sacks and picked up one of her buddies. If you don't believe me, you can track down Yolanda. I know where she stayin' at. She'll back up my story."

"You sure?" Lions asks as he sits back in his chair and studies Jackson.

"Hell yeah, I'm sure."

I lean back in my chair. "Before we go about doing that, how about we start at the point before you went out. Where were you between 12:00 a.m. and 1:00 a.m.?"

"I told you I was at home."

"By yourself?"

"Naw, my grandma was there, too."

"Right, right, I forgot about your grandma. She was asleep

around this time, correct?"

"Probably. So what?"

"Was there anyone else in the home?" Lions questions.

"Naw."

"Did you leave the house during that time?" I ask.

"No, I was home all night."

Lions sneers. "Well, that can't be true. You just said you left around one."

"You know what I meant."

"No, I don't know what you meant."

"I was home until about one-something. Then I stepped out with a friend."

"And you're sure you didn't leave the house before that time?" I ask.

"Yes."

"You didn't have a smoke or go get some smokes? Did you cop some weed or something else?"

"No, I was in the house until I went out."

"With his Yolanda woman?" Lions chuckles.

"You think I'm lying, don't you?"

Lions is getting annoyed. Playing his part just right. "I think you're not telling us the full truth."

"Marquis, did anyone see you and this woman together?" I ask, already knowing the answer.

"Maybe, but nobody that I know. But like I said, Yolanda can vouch for me if y'all would just listen and stop tryin' to pin this shit on me."

"You mean, Yolanda Eddy that resides in the 3700 block of South Franklin?" I ask.

"Yeah, that's her—wait... You mean to tell me y'all had this bitch's name all this time and y'all still tryin' to put this shit on me? Did y'all at least talk to her?"

"Yeah, we talked to her. And some things just aren't adding up."

"Like what?"

"How about you tell us about this lick you hit."

"What lick? Oh, you must mean that sweet ass nigga we picked up."

I look at Lions. "Naw, he's talking about that other lick you came up on last night."

"What other lick?"

"The one that you told Yolanda you came up on."

"What the hell y'all talkin' 'bout?"

"Don't even try to play us, Marquis. Yolanda already told us the reason she picked you up was because you had hit a sweet lick."

"What? That bitch lyin', yo!"

"Yeah, well... She's not the only one singing that tune. Your mysterious third passenger, a man named Andre Barnes, said, and I quote: *'I hit a sweet lick on a nigga and his white chick over in the park.'*"

Jackson's face goes blank. I can barely register the disbelief in his eyes, and just as fast as it appeared, it's gone. The animal instinct to survive is now alive in his pupils. "That bitch *and* that nigga is a liar!!" He hops up from his seat. "Get that bitch in here and tell her to say it in front of my face!"

"Sit down!" Lions yells.

"I ain't sittin' nowhere. You sit down." Jackson is pacing back and forth. "Y'all ain't pinnin' this shit on me."

"I said sit down," Lions rises from his chair.

"Come make me, you bitch ass pig!"

Before I can get to my feet, Lions is moving around the table.

145

He grabs Jackson by his shirt and throws him up against the wall. "Listen to me, you punk piece of shit—when we're done convicting you of these murders, we're going to make sure you share a cell down in Statesville with an evil motherfucker who'll buttfuck you until the day they bring back the death penalty, just so we can strap you down and run a needle through you!"

I grab Lions' hands and pry them free from Jackson's shirt, then push Jackson back towards his seat.

"Yeah, come on, hit me!" Jackson demands, still standing. "This is harassment. I'm going to sue this whole fuckin' city!"

Once I'm sure Lions is back in his seat, I turn to Jackson.

"Suing the department should be the last thing on your mind. He's just the beginning of a whole line of cops that want to break a foot off in your ass. Now sit down and let's see if we can't get to the bottom of this." Jackson doesn't say a word, wiping down his shirt and retaking his seat. The room is silent, but I wait until we all have cooler heads before continuing the questioning. "Do you own a maroon car?"

"Yeah, why?"

"Because a maroon car was seen leaving the scene of the crime."

"Hold up. You tryin' to say that it was my car?"

"Was it?"

"Nah, couldn't have been mine."

"And why's that?"

"My car is in the shop."

"In the shop, huh? When did you take it in? Today?"

"It's been in there for at least a week. That's why that trick Yolanda had to pick me up."

"So what you're saying is that Yolanda is lying?"

"Yeah, that bitch lyin'."

"Then let me ask you this: why lie? Unless she and Barnes had a hand in helping you out, and they're trying to save themselves?"

"That could be. Who knows?"

I smile. "So you're saying they were your accomplices?"

"What? Naw, I ain't sayin' that. I'm just sayin' that who knows why they lied. Why don't you ask them?"

"Maybe we will."

"Yeah, you do that."

Lions and I stand up from our seats. "While we're gone you might want to ask yourself what happens if you go down for this all by yourself?"

We leave Jackson in the room contemplating his future and the possibility of facing a death sentence. Out in the hall, Perlenski is leaning up against a wall cleaning his nails. "I thought we were playing it by the book, detectives?" he says, without looking up.

"We did play it by the book," Lions says. "But you don't get results by not leaning on a perp like Marquis Jackson. If we had done this straight up, he'd skate right out of here."

"Ay, Calhoun," Peterson yells from down the hall. "You got a call on line three. Says it's important."

I leave Lions and Perlenski in the hall and head for my desk inside the division office. Peterson is busy at his computer typing up a BOLO report when I pass.

I snatch up the receiver. "Calhoun."

"Frank? It's Gloria." Her voice is high-pitched.

"What's wrong?"

"Some cop pulled Jamal over after school. Ripped apart his book bag and slapped him around."

Unleashing the hounds always has its consequences. "Did Jamal tell him that I was cop?"

Her voice begins to break. I can only imagine her cradling the phone to her mouth as her bottom lip trembles uncontrollably. "Yeah—that's when the cop told him to shut his little nigger mouth." She starts crying. "He—he hit my baby, Frank."

"It'll be okay, Gloria. Just call the police and—"

"What!?"

"Right, right... Look, I'll handle it when I get home, but I can't right now. I gotta go."

"Okay." The pain in her voice sounds bittersweet.

"I'm so sorry, Gloria," I say, not sure why I'm apologizing. When she doesn't respond, I know it's because, as a cop, I'm as much to blame for her son being harassed as any one of my brothers and sisters in the Blue Religion.

* * *

Twenty minutes pass and we are right back at it: going for the kill shot, trying to acquire a confession. When I look into Jackson's eyes, I can tell that he has put the pieces of the interrogation together. He's resolute in that he's innocent, and he's sticking by it.

"Where'd you stash the gun?" Lions starts questioning.

"I'm telling you——you got the wrong man."

"Evidence says differently. From our angle, it looks like we got two witnesses that can place you at the crime scene... Plus, we got your maroon car. And oh, before I forget, no alibi to back up anything you've said."

"Man, that shit don't mean nothin'."

"It means a lot when you pair it with your previous armed robbery convictions." Jackson goes quiet. If we don't keep him talking, we're going to lose the possibility of a confession.

148

"Marquis, how about you help us help you," I say. Still no answer. "Just tell us where you dumped the weapon and we'll put in a good word with the State's Attorney's office. See if we can't possibly work out a deal for you. I'm trying to help you while I can before officers find the gun in the heating duct of your grandma's apartment or somewhere else. Once they recover the weapon, I can't help you anymore."

Jackson lifts his gaze up from the table and looks at me. He snorts. "I want a lawyer."

I shoot a look at Lions. Our time is running out. "Okay, we'll get you a lawyer, but how about we—"

"I said, I want a damn lawyer--now!"

Lions stands up from the table. "I'll get him his fuckin' lawyer," he grumbles before leaving the room.

I wait until the door is closed before I go right back at Jackson. "While we wait on your lawyer how about we talk about why you did it?"

"I told you I—"

"I know... *You didn't do it.* Maybe it was an accident. Maybe you didn't mean for it to happen. I can understand that. You saw a sweet lick and maybe you thought, this is going to be easy... Just walk up on 'em, pull out the piece and say, 'Give me everything you got.' Maybe the bitch started screaming and you got nervous... The gun goes off, you're like 'Oh shit,' and before you know it, you've done the unthinkable. It was an accident, and no one can fault you if that's what it was."

"It's not like that—you got it all wrong."

"Then what's it like, Marquis?"

"I told you I was at home. Then I went and chilled with that lying cunt and that bitch ass nigga. But y'all ain't trying to hear that, so fuck you."

149

The door opens and Lions steps back into the room, carrying a brown legal-size folder. "Called for a lawyer. They're sending one down as fast as they can." He takes a seat. "Let me ask you something... What gives you the right to take another person's life?"

Jackson looks surprised. "What?"

"You heard me, you piece of shit." Lions opens the folder and removes headshots of Richardson and McNabb from when they were alive. "What gives you the right to destroy two innocent lives—not to mention the countless family members whose lives you've damaged with your reckless actions?"

"Man, fuck you, you ain't puttin' this on me."

Lions holds up the photos. "They were two loving people, struggling to make it in this world like the rest of us, but you couldn't see that. All you saw was an opportunity to get paid. Now look at what getting paid has done." He drops the photos onto the table and removes two crime scene photos from the file. He holds them up so that Jackson can see their bloody bodies. "Look at them!!" he yells when Jackson diverts his eyes. "Look at what your careless actions have done."

"I told you I didn't do it!"

"Yeah, you did. And you want to know how I know you did it? Because not once have I seen a grain of sympathy in your eyes for their deaths."

"Man, you don't know what you're talkin' 'bout. Sympathy... Why should I have sympathy for someone I don't even know, huh? Why should I give a damn about people like that when all they've ever done was look the other way when they saw me coming? I can't even walk down the damn street without one of you crooked ass cops throwing me to the ground and jingling my balls. Fuck sympathy! Fuck them and fuck you!"

Jackson wasn't the first, nor would he be the last of society's forgotten souls to cry foul over the disparaging conditions of being born poor. He was just the latest. Any weight we had towards garnering a confession was losing steam. If Jackson didn't have sympathy for a total stranger, I was betting he only harbored such feelings for one other soul.

"Is that what your grandma taught you?" I ask. "Did she teach you to say, 'Fuck the world,' or was that something you learned from the streets?"

"You don't know me, man."

"Yeah I do. I used to be you. You think that no one loves you, and you have to go around acting hard and being hard, because that's what the streets think you should be. But if you took a second to think about it, you'd realize that someone does care about you: your grandma."

"Don't try and play me with that 'been there, done that' bullshit."

"It ain't bull—but if that's how you feel, that's how you feel. But you can't deny that I'm right about your grandma. Why else would she try and fight through a squad of armed policemen for your innocence? Because she loves you. What do you think is going to happen when she finds out you've broken one of the ten commandments, and taken not one, but two lives?"

Jackson looks down at the floor and then back up at me, staring into my eyes. "I've done a lot of things, Lord knows I have, but I ain't killed no one. You hear me? I ain't killed no one, but if y'all pin this on me, y'all gonna be breaking her heart, not mine. And if she should die from that heartbreak, I put it on everything I love: I'ma take a life or two then."

I sit back in my seat. Jackson is holding strong to his convictions. His grandma has taught him well.

A knock comes at the door and Captain Haggerty sticks his head in. "Detectives, outside."

We slide out of our seats and step out into the hall, where the captain is rolling his cigar around in his mouth. "You're out," he says.

"What do you mean we're out?" I ask. "We're close to breaking him."

"Not anymore. He asked for a lawyer."

"Yeah I know."

"You get 'em one?"

I look to Lions. "We're working on it," he says.

"I'd advise you to work harder, because your time's up here."

"Captain, what's going on?" I ask.

"Jackson's grandma has kicked up a media shitstorm, and we're right in the eye of it."

He turns and we all start walking down the hall. "The media or a suspect's family has never stopped us from conducting an interrogation before," Lions says.

"That was before we had a possible riot on our hands."

We move through the wide doors of the division office and down the row of desks into the captain's office. He goes over to the blinds and raises them. Below, we see Jackson's grand-mother along with two other gentlemen in suits. Flanking either side of them are photographers and video cameras. Standing behind them, in front of the precinct's glass wall, is a raging crowd, shouting, "Free Marquis Jackson! Free Marquis Jackson! Free Marquis Jackson!"

Chapter 29

"**I** want him free now!" Mrs. Lula Jackson demands. Her thin eyebrows are furrowed, and her small nose is crinkled at the bridge. The hate in her eyes says all I need to know about how she feels about the institution of law enforcement. She's probably never known a good cop.

We're sitting in a small conference room. On one side of the table sits Mrs. Jackson, Alderman Franklin Hayes of the 26th Ward, and Reverend Timothy Rawls from the Rock of Gibraltar Church and President of the Gospel Ministers Against Injustice.

"We can't release him," Captain Haggerty says from the other side of the table where Lions, Perlenski and I sit.

"And why not?" Rawls wants to know. He's a big man, over six feet tall, with wide shoulders and strong arms that bulge under his suit jacket. He's the color of a dark cherry lost at the bottom of the basket.

"Because Mr. Jackson is being held for questioning in a double homicide," the captain states.

"My baby didn't do anything," Mrs. Jackson says, pointing a finger at the captain. "You damn devils are always framing Black folks!"

"Calm down, Sister Jackson. We'll get 'em free." Rawls turns back to look at us. "This department, and Area Four in particular, has been terrorizing this community for far too long. Your officers forced their way into this elderly woman's home, scaring her half to death while pointing guns in her face."

"We were serving an arrest warrant," Lions says.

"And yet Marquis hasn't been officially charged, has he?" Rawls narrows his eyes at Lions. "I didn't think so."

Perlenski jumps into the fray by clearing his throat. "Mr. Jackson hasn't been officially charged yet because the State's Attorney's office is reviewing the evidence, as well as the detectives' interrogation, to see if an arrest is warranted."

"Warranted for what? For being Black? For living near the crime scene?!"

"Excuse me, Mr. Rawls, but are you insinuating that the State's Attorney's office is being racially biased towards its questioning of suspects? Let me remind you that the slain officer was African-American."

"And let me remind you, Mr. Perlenski, that this department still has a certain white officer on duty while a Black mother mourns the loss of her young son, shot dead by one of your very own. Maybe this latest travesty, which resulted in the loss of an officer's life, is but a direct contention to the lawlessness that this department has bred."

"Are you condoning the murder of police officers, Reverend?"

"Gentlemen, gentlemen," Alderman Hayes pleads, showing a mouth full of off-white teeth. "I'm sure Reverend Rawls is not saying that murdering cops is okay. I believe what the good pastor is trying to say is that these two incidents may be linked. And, if so... We may have a larger problem on our hands." A larger problem means riots. Something the city doesn't need, especially since the presidential election is just around the corner, and one of Chicago's very own is on the top of the ticket.

Mrs. Jackson brings us back to the real topic at hand. "All I want is my grandson freed."

"It's not that simple," the captain says.

"And why not? Suspects are always questioned and released on Perry Mason. Why can't y'all release my baby?"

Perlenski adjusts his tie. "Because there are procedures in place that we must follow. As of now, we have the right to hold Mr. Jackson for an allotted forty-eight hours in connection with this investigation. If we determine that he is not a suspect, we'll release him... But that's only if we clear him off our suspect list."

"And what about his right to an attorney?" Rawls barks.

"We've notified the public defender's office. They're sending someone over."

"Can we at least talk to him and make sure he's all right?" Rawls asks.

"No, I'm afraid not. To do so would interfere with the detectives' investigation."

"How do we know you're not using Burge's *tactics* to beat a confession out of him?" Reverend Rawls contends.

John Burge, the former police superintendent from the 80's, was under indictment for torturing suspects in order to garner confessions. A local paper equated him to being worse than a waterboarding CIA agent with an Al-Qaida member—one more dark cloud the department has to live under.

Captain Haggerty folds his hands in front of him. "I can assure you, Reverend Rawls, that my detectives and this department do not, and have never, practiced these so-called terror tactics."

"I wish I could believe you, Captain... But tell that to the two dozen or so men who've been wrongly imprisoned for over half their lives."

Captain Haggerty taps his fingers on the table. His meaty digits are turning red. "Fair enough, Reverend Rawls. But we will do our job to the best of our ability, and we will bring justice to this community."

"Good to know, Captain. But I'm not here for this department's justice. I'm here for Sister Jackson and for the wrongful imprisonment of her grandson Marquis Jackson. An imprisonment, I might add, that has rallied this community more than any justice this department can deliver."

"Speaking of enthralled communities, how does the department plan to defuse the crowd protesting outside this building?" Alderman Hayes wants to know.

"Well, we were hoping you and Reverend Rawls could disperse the crowd before things get out of hand," the captain states.

"Oh no I can't," Hayes says. "Those are my constituents out there and they are angry—which means that I must also be angry. I am simply here to show my support for Mrs. Jackson and her plight. Until Mr. Jackson has been proven guilty, I must believe that he is innocent."

Captain Haggerty stands up from his seat and we all follow suit. He places his palms down on the table. His knuckles turn white from the pressure of his weight. At this moment, we're a united front—whatever the captain decides, we'll go along with it, even if that means going down with the ship.

"Okay, Reverend Rawls," he says. "What say you? I already know what protocol dictates, but if you want this to explode into something it's not, that's your decision. But know that we're holding Marquis Jackson for the full forty-eight hours, whether you and everyone else out there like it or not."

* * *

156

The spectrum of black faces that stares back at us is living proof of the racial disparity that traces its roots back to slaveowners who fathered fair-skinned children, and the Black mothers who later gave birth to their dark-skinned counterparts.

A good two-thirds of the crowd is made up of women of all shapes and sizes. The group, numbering somewhere around a hundred, is unmoving as they hang on every word that Reverend Rawls speaks. He stands before the makeshift congregation and the TV cameras with his back to the glass wall and doors of the building. Lions and I stand just inside the lobby, watching the events unfold.

"What was all that about officers shooting kids?" Lions asks.

"He was talking about Richter's partner. The guy gunned down a kid while off duty."

"Damn, they're going to hang him for that."

"Maybe. Right now he's babysitting a desk, waiting for DOPS to give him a sign as to how they're going to swing the axe."

"I'm glad I'm not in his position."

"Have you looked around? It isn't looking too good on this side of the tracks either."

"Detectives," Perlenski calls us away from the window. "Based on your preliminary interview and subsequent interrogation, do you think Mr. Jackson is good for the double homicide?"

"That's hard to say," Lions replies.

"There's still a lot of police work that needs to be done," I add.

"I understand that detectives. But what I'm asking is, do you think you would have gotten a confession if you hadn't been interrupted?"

"Maybe," Lions says. "We went hard on him, but he held strong. I think Frank might have been getting somewhere with the grandma angle, but as you saw, we didn't really have time to push the issue and see what might have developed."

"I understand. What are your thoughts on the two statements given by the witnesses?"

"At best, they're just statements," I say. "I don't know if we can call them witnesses just yet."

Perlenski nods. "But Barnes' and Eddy's statements did lead us to Jackson, and we do know that his car is maroon, right?"

"Where's this going, Perlenski?" I ask.

He smiles. "Just trying to process the evidentiary chain is all. Did the suspect give any clue as to what he may have done with the guns?"

"None. For all we know, they could be floating down a sewer drain or at the bottom of the Garfield Park Lagoon," Lions states.

"Have we drained the lagoon?"

"No, but if Jackson did do it, I doubt he'd be stupid enough to drop the guns less than a hundred feet from the crime scene."

Perlenski taps his index finger against the side of his head. "You'd be surprised how many criminals I've prosecuted for doing stupid things."

"I understand that, but Jackson isn't a spring chicken. The only way we're going to get that gun is if he gives it to us—or if whoever is holding it gives it to us."

"So you really think there might be more than one shooter?"

"It's a possibility we're not ruling out," says Lions.

"Didn't I read in Jackson's file that he used to run with a stick-up crew?" Perlenski inquires.

"Yeah... About two years ago. The leader of the crew is doing a dime up in Milwaukee. It doesn't look like Marquis has been involved with anyone from his old world."

"Detective Calhoun, if there is one thing I've learned as a

prosecutor, it's that old habits die hard. Maybe Mr. Jackson has moved beyond being a follower and is now a leader of his own crew."

"That's a possibility," I say. "But it'll take good police work to determine if that's true."

"I understand. Let me just say that you detectives have done a great job today. Now if you will follow me, let's try to quiet this crowd and this cocky minister before he puts the department in the crosshairs of whatever agenda he's pushing." We follow Perlenski past the lobby door and outside to the awaiting crowd. Some people boo before Reverend Rawls quiets the storm.

Perlenski runs a hand through his fluffy light brown hair and adjusts his tie once more. He stares past the faces of the protesters and clears his throat as we stand on either side of him. "Citizens of Chicago... On behalf of the State's Attorney's office of Illinois, I am here tonight to inform you that Marquis Jackson, a suspect in the double homicide that occurred earlier this week in the West Garfield Park neighborhood, in which a Chicago police officer was killed, will be formally charged with the murders of Officer Tavares Richardson and Katherine McNabb."

Chapter 30

I can barely contain myself until we're away from prying eyes. Once we're upstairs and outside the detectives' division, I grab Perlenski by the collar of his tailored shirt and slam him up against the wall. "What the hell do you think you're doing?!" I yell.

"My job, Detective."

Lions tries to pull us apart, but I'm not letting go. "I thought your job was to prosecute, not throw our case under the bus!"

Perlenski smiles. "Your case is *my* case. Always has been. I made a call based on the evidence we have in our possession."

"Evidence? Everything we have is circumstantial at best."

"I beg to differ, Detective Calhoun. I believe our evidence is quite solid. Plus, with two witnesses on the stand, a conviction won't be hard to come by for the life of a slain officer."

Perlenski smiles again and Lions has to grab both of my hands to keep me from hitting him. "Remember, Frank," Lions reminds me, "you just got reinstated on the force. You don't want to lose your shield over something like this." I release Perlenski and take a step back. Lions is right, even though the bile that boils in my stomach says differently. "Our witnesses' testimony is hearsay at this point," he says to Perlenski.

"Maybe," Perlenski says. "But I'm sure by trial, their testimony will be strong against the defense."

"What are you implying?" I ask.

"I'm not implying anything. I'm just stating the fact that normally, given time, a witness' recollections will become stronger."

"That's bull and you know it!" Lions scoffs. "I wasn't going to say anything, but Frank's right. You pulled the trigger on our case too soon."

Perlenski rolls his eyes. "Listen to yourselves. You still think this is about *you*."

"Why don't you enlighten us as to what this is about then?" I demand.

He wipes his hands together as if brushing off dirt. "This is about justice for Officer Richardson and Katherine McNabb."

"No it isn't," I say, looking him dead in the eyes. "This is about politics. This is about you trying to make a play off the headlines—why else would you move so quickly to charge Marquis Jackson? Because you know, like those protesters out there, that once he enters a courtroom with a police officer's and a white woman's death hanging over his head, it's going to be an uphill battle to convince a jury he's innocent."

"Those are assumptions, Detective Calhoun. Now, I suggest we put this little altercation behind us and move forward with trying to locate the murder weapons. I have faith that if given enough time, which you now have, you'll be able to determine the whereabouts of said weapons from Mr. Jackson."

"If you want to put him away so bad, how about you interrogate him your damn self?"

I start for the fire exit. If I have to look at Perlenski one more second, one of us is going down those stairs.

"Detective, you get back here and do your job! You work for

me!"

"We used to work together to bring down criminals," I say over my shoulder. "Now I can't tell the difference."

* * *

The porch light is on, but every window in my building is as dark as the night I inhabit. It's ten o'clock and the working-class men and women of my neighborhood are just about settling in for the night's news.

I fumble around in my pocket for my keys. The first one I come across is for Gloria's place. "Dammit," I say aloud, remembering she called me earlier about Jamal's run-in with an officer. I really don't feel like hearing about Jamal's problems. I have my own problems—besides, why should I care? The little brat probably deserved a little smacking around. But then I feel ashamed of myself for even thinking that way. I have to help him, because even the smallest injustice is an injustice, no matter the situation.

I flip Gloria's key to the back of the ring and open up the door to my own place. I'll handle Jamal's problem tomorrow. I go into the kitchen and grab a bottle of Goose Island root beer from the fridge. *It's days like this that I wish I was a drinker.*

I head back to the living room and plop down on the worn brown leather couch and turn on the old Zenith floor model that's been in my life since I can remember. The tube slowly warms before a picture finally appears. I flip it to a local news station. The top story is about Marquis Jackson being charged for murder. I flip to two other stations that are both running the same story. Marquis Jackson is guilty—at least in the forum of public opinion.

I click off the TV and sit alone in the dark, sipping root beer and thinking about Marquis Jackson's claim of innocence. I don't know if he is, but there's something about his plea that's developed a knot in my stomach. And that knot won't allow me to stop thinking about him.

I take another sip and savor the dark, sweet liquid. Normally, I don't give a suspect a second thought unless I'm trying to crack 'em in an interrogation, and even then, my mind is always more focused on the individual pieces of the puzzle, rather than the bigger picture.

My cell rings. "Calhoun."

"Hi, Detective."

"Kat? Hi, you alright?"

"Yes... I... I just wanted to call to say thank you. I saw the news. You kept your promise."

"No, Kat... I just did my job."

"That may be, but knowing that you've done your job will help me sleep tonight."

"That's good to hear. I really do hope you have a great night's sleep, Kat."

"Yeah, me too. Oh, before I forget... I printed out a copy of my mom's client list. Do you still need it?"

"The way it's looking, we probably won't. But keep it around at least for your own records." There's a moment of silence. "Are you sure you're okay, Kat?"

"Yeah, it's... It's just that you're the first person I've talked to since things turned bad."

"It's going to take some time before you start to heal, but things will get better."

"I know." Her voice cracks. "I just really miss her."

"I know you do. Are you okay to be alone?"

"Yeah, I'm fine. Thank you, Frank... For talking to me."
"It's nothing. Have a good night, Kat."
"You, too. Good night."

Chapter 31

Marquis Jackson's arraignment is the main attraction in Chicago's media circus. There are reporters scattered all around the Cook County Courthouse, circling like buzzards. Perlenski is busy working a group of reporters when Lions and I pass him and enter the building.

"And to think that could be our future Mayor," I say.

"The day that happens, I move to Green Bay and become a Cheesehead," Lions quips.

After passing through the metal detectors, we take the elevators up to the courtrooms. Sitting outside the door to Courtroom Number Five is Reverend Rawls, comforting Mrs. Jackson as the old woman cries into a handkerchief. When he sees us, he nods hello. Lions and I return the gesture and enter the courtroom.

The small room is empty, save for a tall bailiff who stands to the side of the door. We flash our badges and take seats in the back row. The wooden pews carry the odor of lemon-scented Pledge and menthol mothballs.

"Fred, let me ask you something. How do you feel about all this, man?"

"I don't feel anything about it," Lions says. "We did our job and now it's up to the prosecution to do theirs."

"Yeah, I get that. But don't you feel like something is miss-

165

ing?"

"Like I said--we did our jobs. I don't feel anything and don't care to feel anything, but it sounds like you do. What's on your mind?"

"It's nothing, really. I just keep feeling like this case isn't a hundred percent cleared."

"Now, *that* I can't argue with... But the powers that be want this case put to bed. And they're getting what they want."

"Even if that means putting away an innocent man?"

Lions turns and looks me up and down. "Innocent? Have you seen Jackson's rap sheet? Plus, *we* don't know if he's guilty or innocent. That's not our job. That's for a jury to decide."

"I guess you're right."

The door to the courtroom opens and Katriona McNabb walks into the room followed by Perlenski, then Reverend Rawls, Mrs. Jackson, and Marquis' public defender, a pasty white man with dark curly hair and a thick blubbery face.

"Detectives," Perlenski says in passing.

A minute later Marquis Jackson enters the courtroom through a bolted door at the opposite end. He's wearing a white collared shirt, and black slacks. His wounds have been cleaned up, but the purple bruises still look fresh.

Mrs. Jackson reaches out a frail hand as though she's going to wipe away his injuries, but before Marquis can reach her, she breaks down into her handkerchief. Rawls throws an arm around the old woman and then looks over his shoulder, cutting us both down with his accusatory gaze.

A sheriff's deputy leads Jackson to the table where his lawyer sits sifting through papers, trying to look busy.

The last person to enter the courtroom is Prince Paul, sporting a white T-shirt and baggy jeans. His tattoos of devils with pitchforks, and the six-pointed Star of David are visible for all to see. He sits two rows up from us.

I get up and slide into the pew behind him. "What are you doing here, Paul?" I whisper.

He looks forward, never turning around. "Seeing the face of the nigga that killed my brother."

"I hope you're not thinking of doing something stupid."

"Like what? Pulling a pistol and shooting him?"

"Yeah, something like that."

"And how am I supposed to get a gun in here? You're thinking too hard, Frank. This isn't the movies."

"You're right, this is real life... Remember that."

I get up and move back to my seat. Lions leans over to me and says, "I'm waiting for him to give me a reason this time around."

"Well, I sent the message. Loud and clear."

Judge Larkin enters and everyone rises from their seats. She's in her late fifties, and her hair is the color of salt and pepper. She puts on a pair of thin-framed glasses, bangs the gavel and brings the court into session. "This case is the State of Illinois versus Marquis Jackson, in two counts of first-degree murder. How does the defendant plead?"

"Mr. Simon Crown for the defense, Your Honor. My client pleads not guilty."

"Very well, Mr. Crown. The court recognizes the defendant's plea." Judge Larkin opens the docket and reads through the file. "Mr. Jackson, the state is charging you with two counts of first-degree murder in connection with the homicides of Officer Tavares Richardson and Katherine McNabb. Do you understand these charges?"

Marquis stands up. "Yes ma'am."

Judge Larkin looks to Perlenski. "Does the prosecution have anything to add before I decide on bail?"

"Yes, Your Honor... The state requests that bail be denied to the defendant."

Crown looks up from his paperwork. "Based on what?"

Perlenski comes out of the box gunning for Marquis' life, giving Crown a taste of what to expect going forward and during trial. "Based on the fact that the defendant has a history of aggravated assaults and robbery with a deadly weapon. Not to mention, a police officer has lost his life. It would be a heinous act against this court if a cop killer were to—"

"Enough, Counselor—save your arguments for trial. This court is well-aware of its duties and honor." Judge Larkin removes her glasses. "Will the defendant please stand." Crown and Marquis do as she asks. "Mr. Jackson, in light of the Prosecution's protest, this court has decided to deny you bail. The defendant shall be held in the Cook County Jail to await trial on—"

"What? Y'all gone deny me bail?" Marquis yells.

"Mr. Jackson, please refrain from speaking out. Counsel, I'd advise you to get your client under control."

Crown reaches for Marquis' arm, but he snatches it away. "How y'all gone set me up like this? I'm innocent, dammit! Innocent!"

Mrs. Jackson starts to weep. Katriona McNabb closes her eyes and puts her hands over her ears as she shakes her head.

Marquis Jackson kicks his chair to the floor. "I'm innocent!!" he screams.

Judge Larkin pounds her gavel as if she can hush the young man's savage screams. "Bailiff, get this man out of my court!"

The two officers of the court grab hold of Marquis Jackson and tackle him to the floor. "I'm innocent!" he keeps screaming as they pick him up by his bound hands and legs and carry him back through the bolted door from which he came.

Judge Larkin pounds her gavel to silence the room. She hasn't even broken a sweat. "This court will take a brief recess." Everyone stands.

The first to leave are Mrs. Jackson, Reverend Rawls, and Simon Crown.

"I guess the real world catches up with us all," Prince Paul says with a smile as he passes.

Perlenski walks past us without saying a word as he fixes his tie and hair for the cameras. The last person to leave is Katriona McNabb. Her face is flushed and wet with tears, but she manages to nod at us and exits out the door.

"Kinda reminds you of something, don't it, Frank?" Arnie Ratcliff says from behind me, leaning in the doorway of the courtroom.

"Yeah, what would that be, Arnie?"

"Don't tell me you don't know, Frank."

"No, Arnie, I don't know. How about you give me a clue?"

"I'll do you one better, Frank. Think about it. Doesn't Jackson's plea sound just like your old man when he was first arraigned on murder charges?" Ratcliff exits the room.

He's right. Not only did Jackson's appeal for innocence sound like my father's, but it was my father's voice that I heard in that interrogation room, and all the way into today's arraignment. And even though I wanted my father to be innocent, I knew that he was guilty. I can't say the same about Marquis Jackson and the two murders hanging over his head.

Chapter 32

Simon Crown's office is located inside the courthouse on the third floor of a large room that has been converted into eight cubicles. His is the farthest away from the door at the end of a tiny aisle.

"Mister Crown," I say as we approach the opening of his cubicle.

The pasty man has just taken a bite out of a Snickers bar. He chews with his mouth open as he waves us into the cluttered space that's covered with the manila folders of case files. Lions decides to stand on the outside of the cubicle while I stand at its entrance.

"What can I do for you, detectives?" he asks, still chewing.

"I couldn't help but notice that you played the Jackson case by the numbers," I say.

"Yeah, so what? How else was I supposed to play it?"

"I don't really know, but I thought you'd fight a little harder for your client's bail."

"Are you trying to tell me my client's innocent, Detective?"

"We're not saying that," Lions says. "I think what Detective Calhoun is trying to say is that we want to make sure this case is handled with as much professionalism as possible."

Crown chuckles. "You want to talk to me about professionalism when my client has bruises on his face?"

"Bruises that we didn't put on him," I add.

"Maybe not with *your* hands—but somebody in your department did."

"Anyways," Lions says. "We were more concerned for your client's grandmother than your client."

"When did the Chicago Police Department start giving a damn about the family members of accused cop killers?"

"I think we've said enough, Frank," Lions says to me. "Let's go."

We turn to leave. "If you two want to help me with any of the other two dozen cases I've got, I'm sure my clients would be very happy." Crown laughs at our backs.

I quickly turn around. "Let me ask you something, Mr. Crown. Have you checked out your client's car?"

"What car?"

That's all I needed to know.

* * *

"Well, we tried," Lions says. "But you gotta know that was crazy, Frank. We're detectives. And right now our job is to get the murder book in shape for the prosecution to have for trial."

"Thanks for backing me up, Fred. I just needed to know that Jackson had a lawyer who was really gonna fight for him."

"Don't mention it. Let's just get back to the office and get this over with."

I want to tell Lions that I feel like we haven't done our jobs one hundred percent, but his sense of justice doesn't extend past the State's Attorney's official charge of a suspect. Our job is now to prepare as much ammunition as possible for the prosecution in order to secure a guilty verdict when the case goes to trial. It's as simple as that.

"Tell you what, Fred" I say. "I need to take care of something for Gloria. After I finish, I'll meet you back at the office."

"Sure, Frank, it's not like we don't have other cases to work. Just don't be too long. I don't want to have to lie to the captain if I can help it."

"I promise. I just gotta get this one thing done and then I'll be straight."

Chapter 33

Marquis Jackson spits at my feet through the bars of his 8 x 10 holding cell when he sees me enter the small adjacent room.

"I ain't talkin' to you. Ay, guard, where's my lawyer?" he asks the sentry standing just outside the entrance.

"He's busy sucking down Snickers bars while you're scarfing down choke sandwiches," I say. Lunchtime in Cook County Jail usually consists of four, inch-thick slices of bologna in between thin slices of bread, which requires the eater to choke down the sandwich if he or she doesn't chew it carefully.

"Man, what the hell you want? Y'all already jammed me up on this bullshit murder charge. I'm tellin' you now--I ain't confessing."

"I just want to know what happened to your car."

"It broke down—that's what happened to it."

"What mechanic did you take it to?"

"Why?"

"Because I want to know."

Jackson snorts. "I took it over to an alley mechanic in K-Town named Phil Good."

"Like F-E-E-L?"

"Nah, like the name... You know, like King Philip and shit."

"And does this alley mechanic have an address?"

"Somewhere on Gladys in the 4400 block. He operates out of a garage."

"You said his name was Phil Good, right?"

"Yeah, man, but it's not like it fuckin' matters. He ain't no legit Pep Boys muthafucka, so who gone believe him, right?"

"I guess we'll just have to wait and see."

* * *

It doesn't take me long to track down Phil Good. His shop is a gray garage in the middle of a garbage-covered, rat-infested alleyway. He's standing just outside it, arguing with a young Black male who looks to be about seventeen.

"Nigga, didn't I tell you I wanted the TV's to be connected to the radio system *and* the laptop. Damn, what's hard to understand about that?" the young hustler asks, pointing to a 1982 Grand Marquis with spinning rims.

"And I'm telling you if I hook it up like you want, you're going to kill your radio and possibly blow out the TV's. Your whole system needs rewiring." Phil Good is a tall thin man, maybe a hundred and sixty pounds. He's darker than the motor oil he changes. His ragged jeans have so many stains from the daily grind of fixing cars, they look like freshly tarred asphalt.

"Nigga, I'on need no rewiring bullshit. Just give me back the money for installing the TV's."

"That money gone," Phil Good says, wiping his nose with the back of his hand.

"Gone? Nigga, you betta pay up my money." I push myself off the telephone pole I've been leaning against, deciding it's time to intervene. "Nigga, what you want?" the young hustler asks as I approach. I flash my badge. "Okay, so what?" he hunches his shoulders. I pull back the flap of my blazer and show my gun. "Aight, I'll get back at you later, Phil Good." The hustler jumps into his car and takes off down the alley.

"You didn't have to do that," Phil Good says, turning and walking into his garage.

Lining one wall of the dingy garage are toolboxes stacked upon one another, which I can only imagine must be filled with ratchets, pliers, grips, screwdrivers, and Allen wrenches. A pair of rimless tires sits against another wall. On the floor are two hydraulic jacks and hanging from the low ceiling is a workman's light. "I could have handled that myself." He pulls an oily rag from his back pocket.

"It didn't look like that to me. If I hadn't intervened, he probably would have killed you with one of your own tools."

"Man, y'all cops think y'all know everything." He looks up from his rag with bloodshot eyes and I realize he's high on something. "That boy was just talk."

"Yeah, well... You never know."

"Trust me, I know *hard*, and he ain't it. So whatcha want this time?"

"Excuse me?"

"Look, man, time is money... What can I do for you?"

"I'm looking for a car."

"Well, that I could assume. What kind of car?"

"A maroon Chevy, possibly."

"You mean that boy Marquis' car?"

"Yeah."

"Look, I plan to get rid of it today. But as you just saw, I've been a little busy."

"And why would you want to get rid of it?"

"Because y'all told me to."

"Who told you to?"

"Come on, man... Don't try and play me like a fool. Y'all—" He pauses as if he's trying to recall something, and then he slowly starts to tip over. I'm not sure if he's about to pass out or what, but he's leaning forward at about a forty-five-degree angle now. Lost in a heroin trance, or a "dope lean," as they call it on the streets.

"Phil Good!" I say loudly.

He comes out of his trance, rubbing his nose hard. "Y-y-yeah, man..."

"Who told you to get rid of Marquis' car?"

"You did, man."

"What do you mean I did? I just met you."

"You know what I mean... Cops, man."

He starts nodding off again. I grab him by the arms and shake him. "Cops? Did a cop tell you to get rid of Marquis' car?"

"Yeah, man... Damn, you didn't have to shake a nigga like that."

"What did these cops look like?"

"Shit, I'on know. Big and white. They came down here throwin' shit everywhere, tellin' me to get rid of it by today. But as you can see..." He smiles. His eyes are redder than chili peppers. "I've been busy."

"You still got the car, right?"

"Yeah man, I still got it."

"Where?"

"Right over there." He points across the way to another garage.

"Over there?" I point to the red garage. "You sure?"

"Yeah, man, I'm sure."

I pull my pistol from its holster. I'm not sure what to expect. The alley is covered by the shadow of a cloud. I feel as if I've stepped out of Phil Good's garage into the beginning of a nightmare. A few articles of trash blow past my feet as I approach the red garage.

I turn to get a quick look at Phil Good. He's leaning half-way down to the ground, rocking back and forth, somehow defying gravity's pull. I turn back to the garage and bend down to look for a handle, but there isn't one. I feel along the edges of the vinyl door, looking for space between the door and the concrete but none exists. Surprisingly, the door slowly starts to rise, creaking as it goes.

I raise my sidearm while crouching. From behind me, I hear Phil Good laugh. "Pussy," he blurts out.

I follow the rising door with my pistol until it curves and locks itself in place under the apex of the roof. Parked in one of the two spaces is a car, but the darkness from within the garage conceals it.

"Phil, you close this garage door on me while I'm in here and I'm going to shoot you." When I look back to see if my threat has registered, I find him still leaning, with a long line of drool spilling from his mouth to the ground.

I turn my attention back to the garage. Attached to my keys is a Maglite, which I click on before venturing inside.

The smell of antifreeze clings to the grease-spotted concrete and wooden walls. I sweep the light over the body of the maroon car, filling in the contours of its slick curves. It's a sedan, just like the one in the video feed from the traffic light. I shine the light into the driver's side window. There's a thick layer of dust on the dash. This car hasn't been moved in quite some time.

I cast the beam of light down on the insignia of the car. It reads

Buick, which means that this car is a Regal. Right color, wrong model. I kill the light and step out of the garage. Phil Good is still leaning. "Ay, wake up!"

He snaps to attention as if there's a scorpion in his pants. "You done lookin'?" he asks, closing the automatic door on the garage.

I pull a twenty out of my wallet and wave it in front of his face. "You see this?" His eyes follow the bill back and forth like a metronome. "I need for you to keep this car a secret."

"Shit," he snorts. "First, you want me to get rid of it and now you want me to keep it a secret? Who am I gonna tell--the rats?"

He reaches for the bill, but I pull it back. "Just make sure you don't get rid of it, understand?"

"Yeah, I understand." He snatches the bill, inhaling the funk off the dirty money.

I leave him inside his garage to wallow in his own filth. The fact that Marquis Jackson was telling the truth about his car has me wondering what else he may have been telling the truth about.

Chapter 34

I park across the street from Rothschild's Liquors on Roosevelt & Homan. Traffic is moving at a steady pace. Before I can exit the car my cell rings. "Calhoun."

"Frank, have you looked into our problem?"

"Um... Not yet, Gloria. I've been kinda busy."

"Busy, huh? I know Jamal isn't your child, but I'd like for you to at least try and give a damn about his safety."

"It's not like that, Gloria—this case has just been taking up a lot of my time."

"I understand that, Frank. But my kids' safety is my top priority."

"I know, Gloria. I care about their safety, too. Look, I promise I'll look into it, okay?"

"Okay, Frank." She hangs up without saying goodbye. I understand her concerns, but I'm sure Jamal will live.

I get out of the car and cross the street. The small parking lot of the liquor store is occupied by a few winos and a teenage boy selling nickel bags of marijuana. He freezes when he sees me coming, his eyes wide like a fawn's. I step past him and pull open the door to the store.

Some thirty feet in is an octagon-shaped counter with tempered glass, extending up from the countertop to the ceiling.

To the right is a line of four people waiting to play the state lottery. To the left, three customers wait in another line to make purchases. Behind the bullet-proof glass are shelves filled with cigarette cartons, hard liquor, over-the-counter drugs, contraceptives, and various small household items.

I move towards the front of the line.

"What ya think this is? The aide line?" a female customer asks.

I quickly flash my shield, killing any more argument from the small crowd.

The man at the register is of Middle Eastern descent. He smiles, showing a smoker's crude brown and yellow teeth. His hair is dark and oily, but his beard is streaked with gray.

"How can I help you, Officer?"

I look up at the camera behind him that's aimed down at the register. "I need to see your security tapes."

"Sure, sure," he smiles. He yells something in Arabic to the man at the lottery machine.

I move out of line and wait about a minute before a skinny man comes strolling out of the back wearing an Armani T-shirt and tight dark jeans. "I'm Eddie. You wanted to see me, Officer?" He rubs his hands together, ready to make a deal.

"I'm Detective Calhoun," I flash the badge once more. "I need to take a look at your surveillance tapes, Eddie."

"Sure, sure, my friend. Right this way."

We start walking towards a glass door that separates the two halves of the counter.

"Nothing went down in the hood last night, did it?" Eddie asks. I almost laugh. I didn't realize he was from "the hood."

"No, nothing went down," I say. "I'm just checking up on something that happened a few days ago."

180

Eddie stops in his tracks. "No good. Tapes no good."

"What do you mean they're no good?"

"If nothing pops off inside the store, then we tape over the tapes from the night before. If you're looking for something from a few days ago, then it's already gone."

"I see. Thanks for your time, Eddie."

"No problem, Detective. Ay, you want something to drink? Some juice, Gatorade, or something?"

"Nah, I'm good. Thanks." Outside, the kid who had been pushing weed has moved on down to the corner. My cell rings again. This time it's Lions. "Hey, Fred. What's up?"

"We got 'em."

"Who?"

"Marquis Jackson, that's who. We recovered a .32."

"Don't tell me they found it at his grandma's house."

"Nah, a block over. Some garbage men found it."

The discovery of a weapon cancels out the fact that Marquis' car is sitting in Phil Good's garage. Even if the car hasn't been driven, the weapon is impossible to overlook. "Has ballistics matched the bullet to the gun?" I ask.

"Yeah, it's the same gun that killed Officer Richardson. The techs didn't get any prints, but now that we've got a gun to put on the table, we can run back at Jackson and see if we can get that confession."

"Sounds good to me, partner. I'm gonna grab some lunch and then I'll head in." I hang up. Deep down, I want to believe that Marquis Jackson is innocent—but maybe that's because I want my father to be innocent too. But wanting and knowing are two different things, and I have a job to do that has nothing to do with what I want.

I cross the intersection and get in my car. I look across the way to the Rothschild's parking lot where two drunks argue over the last can of a six-pack. I start the ignition before stealing one last look at them. By this time, Eddie has come out of the store and is trying to defuse the situation.

Wait, how'd he know?

I kill the engine, get out of the car and start back across the street. "Ay, yo, Eddie. Come here for a second." I wave him over. The squirrely looking man walks with a street hustler's swag. "Tell me something, Eddie. How'd you know a fight was about to break out in the parking lot?"

He smiles. "I got cameras out here. Gotta have 'em in case somebody gets jacked or merked, you know what I'm sayin'?" Eddie uses street lingo like a politician uses promises.

"I bet a lot of stuff jumps off in this parking lot, huh?"

"Man, you don't know the half of it. Almost every night there be girls out here giving blowjobs while the dude's friend is in here buying them alcohol. That kid Andre moves more weed than a monk moves prayer beads."

I have to hand it to Eddie. The man is walking propaganda for BET. "Tell me you don't erase those tapes, Eddie?"

He smiles. "Never."

* * *

The back of Rothschild's is like a small warehouse. Eddie and I are standing inside a reinforced concrete room that houses a desk, a thirteen-inch TV/VCR combo, and a three-drawer file cabinet. Outside the office, covering much of the building's space, are pillars of boxes filled with various products.

Eddie opens the file cabinet. All three of the drawers are filled with videotapes. He scans them with his index finger until he finds the one that corresponds with the night of the murders. He pops the tape into the bay on the TV and it starts running. There's a pause and then an image of the parking lot appears on the screen along with the time of 9:00 p.m.

"Fast forward it to about midnight." The reels of the tape run their course. An image of young boys foot dancing plays across the screen. "Fast forward it to about 1:00 a.m." Eddie does as I ask. At about 1:15, a white car pulls into the parking lot. It's one of three cars.

Eddie points out that the Lincoln Navigator with the twenty-five-inch rims is his vehicle. "Nice, huh? I'm killin' these boys out here," he says.

The doors to the white car open and a woman and a man step out. "Pause it there." The frame goes still, and the couple is frozen under the parking lot's lights.

The woman is wearing a faux fur-lined jacket along with dark jeans. Her hair is curled. Her companion sports a blue track jacket with baggy blue jeans and white gym shoes. The two look like newfound lovers, and even if they aren't, I can still tell that it's Yolanda Eddy and Marquis Jackson.

Chapter 35

A ndre Barnes' mother tells me I'll find him down on Lake & Washtenaw, possibly peddling CDs or small vials of cologne. When I find him, he's moving adult DVDs outside of Red's, a small Polish sausage and burger joint that has some of the best food outside of Maxwell Street.

I park half a block up from the establishment. I don't want Barnes to see me coming until I'm already up on him. "So is this like a full-time profession?" I ask.

Barnes is a bit startled. "Oh hey, Detective. What's good? You lookin' for a little entertainment? I got white-on-Black, Asian-on-Black, phat asses and small titties... You name it, I got it."

"Nah, Barnes... I just came by to ask you some follow-up questions."

"Follow-up questions? I already told y'all everything I know." Some guy exits the restaurant. "Yo, yo, homie. I got that *Freaks at Night* video." The man quickly turns with money in hand but takes one look at me and turns back for his car. "Man, how long you gone be here? I'm losing money with you around."

"Like I said—I got some questions to ask."

"Aight, ask 'em and let's get this over with." He puts a leg up against the exterior wall of the structure and leans back.

"You told me and Detective Lions that Yolanda Eddy and Marquis Jackson picked you up at around 1:30 a.m. Am I right?"

He snorts. "Yeah, that's what I said."

"You also stated that Marquis Jackson said he hit a lick. Am I correct?"

"Man, if you know what I said, why you asking me?"

"Because what you said isn't matching up with the facts."

"Facts? What facts?"

"Come on, Barnes. Don't act stupid."

"I ain't actin' stupid. What facts you talkin' 'bout?"

"The fact that you lied."

"Lied? I ain't lied 'bout nothin'."

"Oh yeah? Well, can you tell me why the surveillance cameras at Rothschild's show Yolanda and Marquis on the property at around 1:30 a.m.?"

"Okay, so what?" He hunches his shoulders. "Maybe I got the time wrong."

"Yeah, you got it wrong all right... *Dead wrong*. But that's not all."

Barnes pushes himself off the wall. His eyes dart from left to right.

"Whatchoo mean that's not all?"

I sneer. "You almost had us."

"Man, what are you talkin' 'bout?"

"I'm talking about the fact that you said it was Yolanda and Marquis who picked you up that night, but that couldn't be."

"And why not?"

"Because Marquis' car was in an alley mechanic's garage the night of the murders."

"I was, um...um..."

"What? Lying through your damn teeth?"

"Man, you don't understand."

"Don't understand what? That you're a lying piece of shit?"

"I had to. I didn't have a choice."

"You didn't have a choice? What does that mean?"

"I was just doing as I was told."

I shove Barnes against the wall. "What do mean, as you were told?" Barnes looks down at his feet. I shove him a bit harder against the wall. "Who told you to lie?"

He hits me with a right hook and takes off running. A line of X-rated DVD's trails him. I give chase as we head south on Washtenaw and into a residential neighborhood. Barnes moves with the agility and speed of a field mouse being hunted by an owl. He cuts in between parked cars, zigzagging as he goes. My legs burn and my throat is dry, but I'm not ready to give up yet.

Barnes cuts into a slant, heading for a line of two-story apartment buildings. I continue to pursue as I slide over the hood of a car. By the time my feet hit the asphalt, I'm drawing my weapon, but Barnes has disappeared down a gangway.

This is bad. I'm not sure if he's carrying, and there's no way for me to really know. "Barnes!" I yell as I approach the entrance to the gangway. "Don't make this harder than it has to be." The entryway smells like piss. It's enveloped in darkness and it's probably twenty feet to the other end, where light clings to the exit's silhouette.

I enter the gangway with my gun drawn but pointed down. There's no telling where Barnes is hiding. I walk cautiously, keeping my eyes trained on the exit ahead of me. My heart pumps double-time even though I've slowed my breathing. Small rocks and pieces of broken glass crunch under my heels. A shadow darts past the exit. I duck down and raise my gun. Somewhere beyond the abyss of the gangway, I can hear two squirrels squeaking while playing in a nearby tree. Then comes the sound of a dog barking.

Shit. I lower my gun and run towards the light. Barnes' shadow blurs past the exit once more. When I come out into the light of day, I turn to my left and follow the direction in which Barnes' shadow has gone. I watch as he goes up and over a chain-link fence, landing on the other side, where a Doberman immediately gives chase.

I run to the edge of the fence, trying to decide if I should jump it too, but that would mean shooting the dog. Instead, I watch Barnes sprint the length of the small, dirt-filled yard. He hops the other side of the fence like a jackrabbit and keeps on going, not even stopping to see if I'm still in pursuit.

Chapter 36

Pico's Tacos is filled with lawyers in solid-colored suits, pouring over briefs and consuming burritos and tacos. Pico, the owner, is standing at the ancient cash register near the door, ringing up a group of Sheriff's deputies.

I move past him and the deputies to find Crown sitting at a small square table, with nothing but a dark accordion briefcase for a lunchtime companion. He's just finished pouring salsa over a meaty torta when he looks up and sees me coming. He sighs, cleaning his pudgy fingers with a paper-thin napkin. "What is it now, Detective Calhoun?"

"Just wanted to discuss a few things with you--off the record." Crown narrows his eyes, sizing me up. "Can I sit?" I ask. He nods. I set his briefcase on the floor and take a seat.

"Why 'off the record,' Detective Calhoun? Are you about to tell me that your department framed my client?" He says it so nonchalantly that I believe if I say yes, he'll jump out of his seat and start dancing.

"No. We didn't set your client up, but I have made some significant discoveries that might help him get free--if he has a lawyer who will argue his case with some conviction."

Crown leans forward in his seat. "Are you trying to imply that I don't do my best to represent my clients, detective?"

"I'm not implying anything, Counselor. I'm just stating that your client is going to need a fighter in his corner, because as I'm sure you're aware, the whole city is against him."

Crown is silent. Weighing my words on his own personal scales of justice. "What do you have?"

"As you know, before Officer Richardson died, he reported a maroon car leaving the scene. Your client owns a maroon car, but what you might not know is that a traffic camera caught the fleeing vehicle. From what I've seen, it looks like a Chevy. Now if you were to go over to the 4400 block of West Gladys and ask around for an alley mechanic by the name of Phil Good, you'd find your client's car hidden in a garage. And if you check the DMV's records, you'll discover that your client's car is registered as a Buick."

Crown sits back in his seat, nodding his head. He's putting the pieces of the puzzle together. "How'd you come up with the traffic video? I don't remember seeing that in the discovery file."

"It was left off the evidentiary chain since we figured it didn't add anything to the case that we didn't already know."

Crown pushes his meal to the side and pulls out a small pen and pad and starts writing. I stand up. "Anything else you can give me?" he asks.

"No. That's it." I keep the discovery of the Rothschild's video to myself, at least for now. I want to have another shot at Barnes to find out why he lied, because the revelation of that tape bars his statement from the investigation.

"Detective Calhoun," Crown calls after me as I turn to leave. "Why help my client?"

I stare into the lawyer's eyes. "Because I couldn't help my father."

Chapter 37

"The prodigal son returns!" Lions says from behind his computer screen. "Took you long enough. Where'd you have to go, clear across the city?"

"Not that far, but nowhere near walking distance." I plop down in my chair, which squeaks under my weight. "How goes the murder book?"

Lions sneers. "It's coming along. Already filled out the preliminary reports from the ME, and now that we got one of the murder weapons, I'm finishing up a chain-of-evidence on the discovery."

"Sounds like you've got everything tied up on this side of the case."

"Yeah, I guess so. Just waiting for Perlenski to sign off on it and then it's all his." Lions returns to typing. I'm not sure if Crown is going to use the information I gave him, but I can't tell Lions that I just shot a huge hole in our case. If the captain finds out what I've done, I'll be nursing a desk. Maybe even worse. I get up from my seat.

"And where do you think you're going?" Lions asks. "We've still got at least twelve other cases that need working."

"Yeah, I know. I'm just going to chat with the captain for a sec."

"Be careful. I hear he's been on the phone with Rawls and his gang of ministers pretty much all day."

I stroll down the aisle past the empty desks of the other four detectives that make up our division.

I knock on the captain's door and wait for permission to enter. "Come in!" he yells. The small office is stuffy. Captain Haggerty sits behind his desk spinning a quarter on its side. "Detective, what can I do for you?"

"Just thought I'd drop in and talk to you about the developments of the case."

"I hear the recovered weapon is a match for the one that killed Officer Richardson."

"Yes, sir—at least that's the way it's looking."

"Is there something on your mind, Frank?"

"Kinda, sir. I was just curious to know if the department and the city had made a decision about Officer Richardson's funeral arrangements."

Captain Haggerty stops spinning the quarter. "Right now, it's still up in the air. But I'm sure in a day or two... Once the heat on Jackson's arrest has had time to simmer and set in, word will come as to how the department will handle it."

"Thank you, sir."

"Frank, why'd you ask?"

"Going off something I heard, but it's nothing."

"You know, word in this department can spread like wildfire. What did you hear?"

"It's really nothing, Captain. I just overhead some unis say the city wasn't going to bury Richardson in uniform because his brother is Prince Paul. They don't want the bad publicity to tarnish the badge."

Captain Haggerty stares at me. "Frank, I give you my word

that I will personally fight to see that Officer Richardson is not only buried in uniform, but that he is presented with colors and given the same consideration as any other fallen officer."

"Thank you, Captain."

He dismisses me with a nod. I'm confident that the captain will hold true to his word, but it isn't about one man's word—it's about the actions of several men, politicians, mainly. And one can never tell where the line will be drawn between a man's word and his politics.

Chapter 38

It's around seven at night when I arrive back at Gloria's apartment. I decide to finally use the keys she's given me. When I enter her apartment, I find the place quiet. I expected to find Jamal sitting on the couch watching TV or playing video games, but it's not to be. "Anyone home?" I call out.

"I'm in the kitchen," Gloria responds.

The apartment smells like stale corn chips, which is unusual because Gloria always keeps a vibrant fragrance of fruity concoctions whirling about in the air.

I step into the kitchen. "Where's everybody at?" I pause, watching the cigarette in Gloria's hand burn slowly. She's sitting at the kitchen table with tears running down her golden cheeks. "What's wrong?" I look around the small room, but nothing's out of place.

She takes a drag off the cig and turns to look at me with puffy red eyes. I've never known Gloria to smoke, but the way she holds that cigarette without an ash falling from her hand tells me she's had years of experience. "What do you want?" she snarls.

"Baby, what's wrong? Where are the kids?"

"Why do you care?"

193

The question damn near bites my head off. "What do you mean why do I care?" I start to move towards her.

"The kids are gone, Frank."

My heart belly flops into the pit of my stomach. "What do you mean they're gone?" I turn around and head back towards their rooms.

"I sent them away!"

I turn back to face Gloria. "Why?"

"Because we need to talk. Because Jamal was attacked again by the same cop!" My mouth falls open. I don't know what to say. Gloria flicks the ashes onto the floor. They flutter downwards like fallen angels. She takes another drag and releases a puff of smoke from her nostrils. She's ready to do battle. "I thought you said you were going to handle it, Frank?"

"I-I-I was, but this case..."

"Damn the case, Frank!" She drops the cig onto the floor and stomps it out. "Do you know Jamal was afraid to go to school today—to even go outside and play with his friends? My baby peed his pants in the car, because he heard a siren. A fucking siren!" Gloria stands up and meets me halfway in the short hallway. "Do you know how that makes me feel? I'm his damn mother and I can't even protect him."

"Gloria, listen... I'm sorry Jamal had to endure such pain, but I promise I'll look—"

"No, Frank. I'm done waiting for you to look into this. And I'm done waiting for you to realize that I'm part of a package deal... That we're a family."

"It's... It's not like that, Gloria. It's just—"

She throws up a hand. "I know, Frank... Your job is the one thing that keeps you going in this world. But at some point, you're going to have to realize that your job is not your life."

"I know it isn't my life, Gloria."

"Really? Then tell that to my son."

I'm silent. There's nothing I can I say to her that she doesn't already know. She's the first person I've let into my life since my father's incarceration two years ago. Even before we started dating, she stuck her neck out for me and risked being arrested. But now, when she needs me the most, I can't even come to her aid. I grab hold of her hands and begin massaging them. "Gloria," I whisper. "How can I make this right?"

She shakes her head. "You can't, Frank. Not this time."

Being this close to Gloria, I want to hug her. I can smell her perfume beneath the layer of cigarette smoke. "So where does this leave us?" I ask.

Gloria drops her head. "I don't know."

I lift her chin with my finger and stare down into her brown eyes. "How about we take some time apart and you think about it?"

She shakes her head no, but mouths the word, "Okay."

I kiss her on the forehead and turn to leave. She and the kids are my only family besides my Uncle Skeet, and I'm losing them to the job just as fast as I'm losing this case to the streets.

Chapter 39

I lie awake, wondering what could've driven an officer of the law to single out Jamal for harassment. He isn't a hustler or a gangbanger, which are usually one and the same in this city.

Now that Jackson is officially charged with double homicide, the leash on officers, and their aggression, is slowly being tightened by the upper brass. The city can't risk a stack of lawsuits, plus the Department of Professional Standards is already dealing with Richter's case. If another Black kid goes down at the hands of police officers, heads at City Hall and across the board will have to roll. Whoever is tormenting Jamal hasn't given the consequences of their actions any thought.

Outside, the howl of sirens reminds me that the criminals in this city never sleep, which is probably why I never do either. I wonder if Gloria is sitting awake, smoking cigarette after cigarette, trying to figure out a solution to her problem. I can envision her light velvet lips pushed together pouting, as she exhales a long swirl of smoke. Her eyes are low, but I can imagine the tears. Her hand is steady while her fingers balance the lit menthol with an acrobatic finesse.

She's hurting like I was when I had to arrest my father for murder, but for very different reasons. Her heart and mind are at war, which means she loves me—but I'm not sure if I love her. At least not in the way she wants me to. I think she came to that realization the moment she lit that cigarette to ease her troubled mind.

Chapter 40

"Where are they?" Perlenski shouts as he throws open
the doors to the detectives' division.

Michaels is sitting at his desk with his legs up
working a Sudoku. "Where's who?"

"Lions and Calhoun."

"We're right here, Perlenski. What can we do for you?" Lions
inquires.

Perlenski's face is flushed red. His tie is loose, and his navy-
blue jacket is open, revealing a light blue shirt with thin red
pinstripes. "You detectives fucked me!" he says.

"What the hell are you talking about?"

"You know what I'm talking about, Detective Lions! You and
your partner screwed me out of my prosecution of Marquis
Jackson."

"What the hell are you talking about?" I say, playing up the
part.

"I'm talking about the fact that Marquis Jackson is free,
walking the streets."

"How the hell did that happen?" Lions wants to know.

"Because you didn't do your job."

Lions stands up from his seat at his desk. "Hold the fuck up,
Prosecutor. Don't come rolling up in our house, telling us we

didn't do our jobs. If anything, *you* didn't do yours."

"I'm going to have your badges!"

"If you want my badge," Lions says, defiant, "come and take it, you piece of—"

"Ay, what the hell is going on?!" We all turn to find Captain Haggerty standing in the doorway with a cup of Dunkin' Donuts coffee in one hand, and a box of munchkins in the other. "Detectives, Prosecutor... In my office——now!"

* * *

"What has everyone so heated?" the captain asks as he takes a seat behind his desk.

"Your detectives are the problem, Captain Haggerty. Their elementary investigation has led to our prime suspect being freed."

"I understand your frustration, Counselor... But if we're going to continue this conversation, I'm going to need you to show my detectives a little respect."

Perlenski breaks out his politician's smile. "Of course, Captain. Please forgive me, detectives."

The captain pops a munchkin into his mouth and takes a sip of coffee. "Now that that's settled, how about you give us the rundown on how Jackson was freed?"

"Well, it's pretty simple. Jackson's lawyer tracked down his vehicle, which is a different model from the car reported in the case files. And to complicate things even more, he uncovered video from a traffic camera that shows that his client wasn't at the scene of the crime. Now if your detectives had done their job..."

"We did our job," I say. "If you recall, we told you not to

charge him, but you did anyway."

"Enough!" Captain Haggerty commands. "Both sides dropped the ball, now let's move on. We still have a cop killer out on the streets. So how do you want to play this, Prosecutor?"

"I still think Jackson is our man. I'm going to need your detectives to bring in the witnesses for re-questioning."

"But we have their statements," Lions says.

"Exactly. They put Jackson at the crime scene at the time of the shootings. I want to nail down their statements and make sure there aren't any holes this time."

"If you had just done that in the first place..." Lions mumbles.

"What was that, Detective?"

"Nothing, Captain."

"Good. Then I'd advise you and Detective Calhoun to carry out the prosecutor's request immediately."

* * *

"The nerve of that prick," Lions says as we wait at the elevators. "Like it's our fault Jackson slipped through the cracks. I'm telling you this job just gets better every day."

"I hear you, partner. So where do you think we should start first?"

The elevator doors open and we step inside. "Let's grab Yolanda Eddy and then we'll grab Barnes. If things go right, we can hand over the murder book with their statements to Perlenski and consider this case closed."

We ride the elevator down to the lobby and take the small walkway over to the connecting garage. As we head out, two uniforms are hauling in J-Rock, one of Prince Paul's boys. He sneers at me as they push him beyond the doors.

"Was that who I think it was?" Lions asks.

"Yep, they always find a way for us to get 'em."

We hop into a reserved Caprice and Lions starts the engine. "Let me ask you something, Frank." He stares straight ahead with the engine idling between our silence. "You didn't fuck us on this case, did you?"

"Why would I do that?"

"I'm just asking. You know—-to cover my ass. Besides, you had to know I'd ask, seeing as how you had to run errands yesterday, and now we're back out on the pond, fishing for wits."

"It wasn't me. You heard Perlenski. I guess the legal aide actually got off his fat ass and started doing his job."

"Yeah, I guess he did. If you can't count on a public defender to help you get a conviction, who can you count on?"

Lions reverses the car and pulls out of the garage. I want to tell him the truth, but the less he knows right now, the better—especially if this thing blows back on me, and Marquis Jackson is indeed involved in the slayings.

Even though the tape from Rothschild's clears him from being one of the shooters, it doesn't clear him as an accessory after the fact. The only ones that can do that are the real shooters: Yolanda Eddy and Andre Barnes.

* * *

Yolanda's grandmother opens the door after only two knocks.

Lions dips his head as though he's tipping a hat. "Sorry to bother you, ma'am. We need to speak to your granddaughter again."

"She ain't here. Tore out last night all frantic like... Ain't seen her since. Forgot to even play my lottery before she left."

"You have any idea where she could have gone?" I ask.

"Naw, she ran out after that dirty punk she's been seeing."

"Is his name Andre Barnes?"

"Hell if I know. All I know is that he wears his pants down past his ass, walking like he got shit in his drawers."

"Thank you for your time." We turn and leave.

"You think she hitched up with Barnes?" Lions asks.

"Probably. Sounds like she might've heard about Jackson getting free."

"Well, we better find 'em before we get another case file added to the heap."

* * *

We're back on the streets headed to Barnes' apartment. Lions cuts across Central Park, heading south.

"If Yolanda left all of a sudden, I don't think Barnes is stupid enough to just be sitting at home, waiting for something to pop off," I say.

"I see what you're thinking," Lions says, "but we gotta start somewhere."

"Word on the street is that Barnes slings DVDs and CDs over on Washtenaw & Lake down at Red's Hot Link's stand. We should probably swing by there first. A good hustler never stops hustling."

Lions agrees and makes a U-turn. "So what's on your mind, Frank?"

"What are you talking about?"

"Come on, man... Is it Gloria? I can see it in your eyes and read it all over your face."

I turn to look out the window, then back to Lions. "Yeah, it's

Gloria. We had a fight last night."

"At least you can look forward to the make-up sex."

"Not this time. We just might be done."

"Nah, she's probably just mad at you. Give her a little space and then go crawling back."

"I don't think that's going to work. I let her down."

"Whoa, whoa, whoa, hold up... Are you telling me you cheated? Oh man, you sly dog! I knew the spirit of a player was in you somewhere. Now we can really hang, like boys."

"I didn't cheat on her, Fred. I let her down by not protecting her kids."

"Man, I've seen you with those kids. You'd give your life for them."

"I would. But lately my head's been so far into this case, I neglected to follow up on Gloria's complaints about a uniform harassing Jamal."

"What? A blue-and-white is harassing her kid? Dumb fucks. Did the kid tell 'em who you were?"

"Yeah. And apparently it didn't mean a thing."

"See, it's cops like that who make it harder for the other cops to go in and build relationships with the community."

"I know."

"So what ya gonna do?"

"I don't really know yet. Gloria said she handled it, but I got a feeling her way may not be enough. Either way, I don't need to be thinking about this right now. We've got a case to solve."

"You sure?"

"Yeah, I'm sure. Gotta keep my head in the game, especially out here on these streets."

We pull into the busted-up parking lot of Red's. The little yellow shack is an eye sore in need of a coat of paint. Standing along the chipped-up wall is a trio of junkies. Their dealer is a skinny waste of time who walks off when he sees us pull in. Barnes isn't anywhere in sight, but we hop out anyway. One of the junkies, a light-skinned woman with dirty dreads, starts sashaying towards us. "Looks like your kind of woman, Fred."

"Yeah, cheap and dirty. Just how I like 'em."

The woman cracks a slight smile. "Officers."

"It's *detectives*," Lions says.

The woman has green eyes, and I can see the fading beauty in her freckled face. She wears a shade of light brown lipstick that makes her lips pop even under these cold conditions. She's probably broken many hearts on her road to substance abuse. "You two looking for a little trouble?" Her speech is perfect, or what some would call *talking white*.

"No, but you might be," Lions brushes past her.

The other two junkies, both men and dark like burned charcoal, keep their eyes to the ground as we pass them and enter Red's. The aroma of Polish sausages being grilled over an open flame and the alluring smell of caramelized onions dominates the small space. Behind tempered glass, a man and two women work effortlessly preparing food. There are two young hustlers in the corner waiting on their meals. They eye us and the room suddenly goes quiet.

"Ay, either of you see the DVD dude around?" I ask. They divert their eyes.

"My partner asked you a question," Lions says.

One of the men hunches his shoulders. "Which DVD man?"

"The one with the porn DVDs."

"Nah," says the other male. "He ain't been around today."

We exit the small restaurant. "Adult DVDs?" Lions looks puzzled.

"Yeah, that's what Barnes is peddling."

"Looks like we're going to be doing a lot of running around. If we're lucky, maybe only eight percent of the people we run down today won't bullshit us."

"We can only hope." We walk back to the car, then slide into our seats. Lions starts backing the car out. The green-eyed junkie is still leaning against the chipped wall. She looks like a lost lamb amongst wolves. "Stop the car," I say. "I've got an idea."

"Well, let's hear it."

"Just park. I'll explain over lunch."

* * *

Almost an hour has passed since Lemon, the green-eyed junkie, took the job of tracking down Barnes. "You think she's gonna come back with something?" Lions asks before he bites into his Italian beef sandwich. The juice from the sweet Giardiniera peppers splatters onto the steering wheel.

"Oh yeah, she's coming back. But with what? Your guess is as good as mine."

"What made you think to use her, anyway?"

"Simple rule of the streets: use what the streets give you." I take a sip of Sprite and bite into my Polish.

We both chew silently. Lions is the first to swallow. "I get the whole streets thing," he says, "but what makes you think she'll have any success finding Barnes? You know as well as I do that crackheads are unreliable."

"That may be true for some." I take a long gulp of Sprite. "But in my experience, crackheads can also be some of the best go-getters around. A good crackhead could find sunken treasure.

Plus, you saw her eyes when I offered her money. She'll come back... But again, who can say what she'll bring us."

Lions shakes his head, laughing. "You keep surprising me, Frank."

"Good. That means you won't get tired of me."

"Now you're starting to sound like my sister."

"Oh, come on... I thought we were *boys*?"

Tap, tap, tap. I look over at my window and find Lemon standing in front of it as if she's a ghost that's just appeared. I roll down the window. "Whatcha got for us, Lemon?"

"I found him." She smiles, rubbing her hands together.

"Where?"

"Money talks." I reach into my pocket and pull out two twenty-dollar bills. "Come on, sugar," she says. "You gotta come better than that." She snorts back a line of snot from her runny nose.

"It's forty. That's what we agreed upon."

"I know, but I walked pretty far to get this information. The way I see it, you two must really want this guy or you wouldn't have come to me."

"Forty, Lemon—that's my final offer. *Or* my partner can run you in for solicitation."

Lions narrows his eyes and smiles. Lemon looks to her left, then to her right, before she bends down to the window. "All right, forty it is." She snatches the money, a bill in each hand. "The guy you're looking for is holding out at an apartment on Washington & Pulaski, above a chicken shack or something like that."

"Thanks, Lemon. Now get yourself something to eat."

"Yeah, I will," she says.

We wrap up our food and pull out of Red's parking lot, heading west on Lake Street. "Good call with Lemon," Lions says.

"Let's just hope her info is accurate, and we find Barnes and Eddy together. Who knows... Possibly even with their pants down."

Lions forms a crooked smile on the edges of his lips as he hits the accelerator. We shoot down Lake Street, past the beams of the elevated trains that sprout up out of the asphalt as if mapping our destination to Barnes' safehouse.

Chapter 41

G reater Sunshine Baptist Church is a poor man's dream
turned into a subpar reality. The exterior of the two-
story brick building is whitewashed with the word
SUNSHINE painted in large yellow block letters at the top of
it. On the opposite corner is a liquor store where a group of teens
are hanging out in front.

I slide out of the car and wait until Lions has departed down the
street before crossing. As I make my way up the street, I glance
up at the windows to the apartment over Sunshine Baptist and
see that the ocean-blue curtains are pulled closed. Nearing the
outer doorway, I unclip my holster. Better safe than sorry. I
gently turn the knob on the glass door, but it's locked. *Dammit.*
I call Lions on his cell. "You in place?" I ask.

"Yeah, I'm ready."

"It looks like you're going to be playing point. The outside
door is locked. I'll wait down here, and when he comes running
my way, I'll grab him."

"Sounds good. Be ready." We hang up.

If we play this right, Barnes and Eddy will attempt to flee once
they hear Lions' knock. Before they know what's going down,
they'll run right into my hands. I stand back from the glass door
and wait.

Over at the liquor store two amateur comedians start riding one another. The first individual is a heavyset man with thick dark cheeks and small beady eyes. He takes a deep breath. "Yo momma so fat, that when she went to the beach, a whale swam up and sang, *'We are family... Even though ya fatter than me!'*"

The crowd bellows with laughter. The second individual, short and skinny like a stalk of sugar cane, retaliates. "Yo momma so fat, that Dora can't even explore her!"

The crowd continues to roar with laughter, but it's not long before my attention is distracted by a loud banging sound coming from inside the building. I look up at the glass door and see Barnes and Eddy coming down the stairs, just like we planned. I lock eyes with Barnes, and for a split second, he shows no emotion. Then he raises a pistol and takes two shots at me. The glass door shatters as I hit the ground. I can feel the wind rip as the bullets whiz over my head. The crowd of teens hits the pavement, ducking behind cars for cover.

By the time I remove my pistol and take aim at the stairs, Barnes and Eddy are gone. I roll to my right, taking cover on the side of the door panel. "Barnes, this is Detective Calhoun!" I yell into the vacant stairway. There's no answer. I take a quick peek around the corner of the doorway to confirm that the stairway is empty. The shattered glass crunches under my shoes as I step through the opening in the doorframe and into the stairwell.

I climb the stairs cautiously, two at a time. There's no sign of movement coming from within the building, save for the creaking of the stairs under my own weight. Even though Barnes has taken two shots at me, I'm more concerned for Lions because he made first contact. I don't know if he's dead or alive.

The front door to the apartment is slightly open. The smell of Chinese takeout and burned gunpowder worms its way out of the opening. I push at the door, keeping my gun raised as I slowly enter the apartment.

To my right is a hallway that leads past a bathroom and farther down into a kitchen area. I can see that the back door is ajar, but there's no sign of Lions. "Barnes, it doesn't have to be this way," I call out.

"Don't come in here!" he yells from a bedroom to my left.

"Fred, you in there?"

"Yeah, I'm here. He's holding Yolanda at gunpoint."

I maneuver around a beat-up couch and take a position ten feet away from the bedroom door so that I can get a clear view of the room. Lions is on his knees with his gun raised. In the farthest corner of the room, Barnes stands with a forearm wrapped tightly around Yolanda Eddy's neck and a gun to her head. I keep my gun trained on him as I walk slowly towards the room's entrance.

"You okay, Fred?" I tap him on the shoulder as I enter the room, which smells like sweat and sex. On the floor is a single mattress with disheveled blankets and empty condom wrappers.

"I told you not to come in here," Barnes says, his firing hand trembling.

"You did... But I also said that we didn't have to do it like this, and I meant it."

Barnes darts his eyes from one side of the room to the other, as if he knows a secret way out. "Y'all don't understand," he says.

"I think we do. You lied about Marquis. It's as simple as that."

"You don't know shit."

"Please, baby," Yolanda Eddy pleads. "Don't kill me."

"Just put the gun down, Barnes... And we can talk about this."

"Talk about what? I'm a dead man walkin'." He presses the

barrel into Eddy's skull.

"You're not dead yet." I holster my gun. Lions keeps his pistol trained on Barnes.

"Shit, I let y'all take me in and I'm dead no matter what."

"Not over this. We can chalk this up as a mistake—can't we, Fred?"

"Sure, it's just a little misunderstanding in my book."

"See? Let's put down the gun and talk this out." I take a step closer.

Barnes tightens his grip around the gun. "Y'all just couldn't let shit ride the way it was going. All y'all had to do was charge Marquis and things would have been good. But naw, y'all had to keep diggin'."

"We're sorry about that, but we were just doing our jobs. If we hadn't, the prosecutor would have."

"Bullshit! That straight-laced muthafucka was looking for any nigga to throw under the bus! His job was done the moment he walked into that interrogation room."

"*Please*, baby! Don't do this, *please*," Yolanda Eddy pleads again, her voice breaking.

"Listen to her, Barnes. You don't want to do this. Think about your family. What's going to happen to them when they find out you're dead?"

Barnes' eyes start to water. I can't tell if I'm getting through to him or if he's just scared of dying. "Look," he says. "How about we cut a deal?"

"What kind of deal?"

"You get that prosecutor down here, and if he gives me a get out of jail free card—"

"You mean immunity?"

"Yeah, that shit... Then I'll tell y'all who told me to lie on

211

Marquis."

"It doesn't work that way. We can't possibly give you another potential hostage."

He drills the barrel of the gun into Eddy's head. "I'll kill this bitch! Get him down here--now!!"

"You won't kill her," Lions says coolly.

"What?" Barnes looks directly at Lions. "I'll blow this bitch's brains out right now."

"No, you won't," Lions states with no inflection in his voice.

"You think I'm playing?"

"No, but I think you're afraid," Lions continues. "The minute you pull that trigger, I'll blow your brains all over that wall."

Barnes presses the barrel of the gun harder into Eddy's skull. She squeaks like a scared mouse.

"He means it, Barnes," I say, not really comprehending the words coming out of my own mouth.

Barnes looks at the gun in Lions' hand, then over at me. "Fuck it—we all go!"

Lions cocks the hammer of his gun.

"You hear that? That's going to be the last thing you hear," I reassure Barnes. "And the bullet in that gun is going to be the last thing you feel. No more weed, no more drinks, no more pussy... Nothing."

Barnes bites his bottom lip, then looks around the room for another way out. He stares at Lions' gun, focusing on the barrel. Lost in the thought of one single shot equaling life or death. He looks at me with a tear rolling down his cheek and unwraps his arm from around Yolanda Eddy's neck, setting her free.

I quickly shoot past her and disarm Barnes, then throw him to the floor and wrap his hands behind his back so I can cuff him. "I told you we didn't have to do it this way."

"Yeah, maybe," he mumbles. "But it doesn't matter any-more."

I stand him up and march him out into the living room where Lions is waiting with a weeping Yolanda Eddy. "Let's get 'em back to the station, and then we can figure out what they know," he says.

"Sounds good to me." I push Barnes towards the door of the apartment, then steer him down the stairs, with him still in front of me. Lions and Eddy follow. With the glass from the front door to the building blown out, I can hear cars swishing by.

When we reach the bottom of the staircase, I grab Barnes by the cuffs. "One foot at a time." I look down at the broken door. "If I even *think* you're trying to run, I'm going to shoot you in the leg." I don't mean it, but I have to give him an incentive not to run.

Barnes doesn't say a word. He steps one foot over the broken partition in the doorway and then the next. Two shots ring out. Barnes falls back in through the door as I hear a car pull off down the road. I try to reach for my weapon, but it's no good because I'm shouldering Barnes' weight. I slump down to the floor with him in my arms, my hands completely covered in blood. Somewhere at the top of the stairs, Yolanda Eddy screams. Barnes' eyes are wide open, and he's looking up at me as if to say: *Why do I have to die?* But all I can do is hold him as his life slips out of my hands.

Chapter 42

I'm sitting on the curb, staring down at my bloody hands when the first car to arrive on the scene pulls up. It's Lieutenant Gore. Behind him an ambulance screeches to a halt. Two EMTs jump out and rush past me towards the entrance of the apartment building where Barnes' body is laid out. Lions is busy taking witnesses' statements and trying to secure the scene.

"You alright?" Gore asks me.

"Not my blood."

"That's good. What about the shooter?"

"Gone with the wind. Didn't even have time to draw my piece before the vic fell."

"We got a DOA!" one of the EMTs yells from the recess of the hall.

Three squad cars pull up, followed by Captain Haggerty. "Whatta we got people?" he asks, scanning the scene. "You all right, Frank?"

I stand. "Yeah, I'm good, Captain."

"Is that who I think it is?" he nods towards the open doorway.

"It's our wit, Andre Barnes."

He removes his cigar stub from his jacket pocket and places it in his mouth. "Run me through it, step by step."

"We got word from a CI that Barnes was shacking up in the apartment behind us with our other witness, Yolanda Eddy. I took the front and Lions worked the rear. Upon Detective Lions' announcing himself, shots were fired. I responded by trying to enter the front of the building. That's when Barnes saw me while attempting to flee and pulled a weapon, firing twice. I did not return fire, but pursued the offender up the stairs and into the apartment where I found him holding Eddy as a hostage. After Lions and I talked Barnes down, I took him into custody. Upon exiting the premises, shots were fired from a moving vehicle and Barnes was struck in the chest."

"Did you get a make on the vehicle?"

"No, sir. All I heard was two shots and then Barnes went down. By the time I got to my feet, the vehicle was long gone."

"I understand. Get yourself cleaned up and call it a day."

"If it's all the same, Captain, I'd like to continue working the investigation. There's a lot of people to question and I wouldn't want to leave my partner in a bind."

Captain Haggerty rolls the cigar around in his mouth. "Okay... But get cleaned up and report back to the house."

"Yes, sir."

* * *

The captain has a uniform drive me home. As I turn the key in the lock to my apartment, I think about Gloria and what she said about us being a family. I haven't had a family in a very long time. I nearly lost my life less than an hour ago and there's no one I can tell—maybe my Uncle Skeet, but not anyone like Gloria.

My apartment feels damp and cold as I head for the bathroom.

215

I peel off my blood-soaked shirt and toss it into the trash. Specks of crimson line my undershirt as if it were a tattoo over my heart.

I run water in the sink and wait until it's half full before I thrust my hands into it. The water instantly turns red, as if I'm washing away my sins, but in my world it's never that easy. Barnes' blood is just one more reminder that I was baptized in a sinner's world.

I turn out the light and go to my room where I quickly change out of my pants, throwing on a pair of black slacks, along with a freshly pressed shirt. I button it up and head for the door.

Outside, the patrolman is still waiting. I start down the stairs but then stop. I flip open my cell and dial Gloria's number. The phone rings for a few seconds before going to voicemail. I kill the call and bound down the stairs and into the cruiser. I hate being right. I don't have anyone like Gloria... At least not anymore.

Chapter 43

The Detective's division is working like a well-oiled machine. Michaels and Bishops are manning the phone lines while Simpson and Daniels take witnesses' statements from the teens at the scene of Barnes' murder that they could convince to come in.

Lions has just come out of the captain's office when he sees me enter. "Shit's hitting the fan," he says.

"What's going on?"

"Word just hit the airwaves that Prince Paul was Richardson's brother. Media's already calling Barnes' murder a gangland slaying."

"Well that's stupid."

"And why is that?" Lions says. "Who knows what Prince Paul is thinking and doing out here on these streets? He had no qualms about drawing on us in a restaurant full of cops, so I'm sure he'd have no problem ordering Barnes' murder."

"True, but I don't see why Paul would have Barnes killed when he's a witness to his brother's murder."

"Why not? You heard what Barnes said about him having to lie. Maybe it's Paul that put him up to it—maybe it was Paul that whacked his own brother... You ever think about that?" Lions moves past me towards the division doors. What he's saying makes sense, but a part of me doesn't want to hear or even think that Paul could kill his own brother. Lions is halfway out the division doors before he turns and looks back at me. "Are you coming or what?"

We head down the hall to the interrogation rooms. I follow, unsure of what to say. I can easily argue that I've seen Paul shed tears over his brother's death. Hell, I even thought I felt his pain in some way. But the realization of what I thought I saw and what I really felt was just a direct response to me losing my own brother. Even now, there are times when I think my father could never have committed such a heinous crime—but in the end, I have to accept the possibility that Paul could have killed his own brother, just like my father did mine.

"I'm thinking we just run a routine good cop, bad cop on Eddy," Lions states. "She might look tough, but I bet that gun to the head was a wakeup call."

He turns the doorknob and we enter the interrogation room. Yolanda Eddy is still shaking after the ordeal. Her eyes are red and puffy. "Can I like get another cup of coffee?" she asks, even though it's clear to both of us that she hasn't finished the one she's holding in her trembling hands.

"Sure you can," I say.

She takes a sip, then slowly lowers her cup. "Whatchoo want, murderin' pig?" Her eyes might suggest that I'm a murderer, but her turned-up lip and evil stare are more an expression of disgust at the sight of me than fear.

"We just got some questions to ask you," Lions replies. We both take seats. Lions rests his hands on top of hers. "We know it's been a long, stressful day, and we'll try to get through the questioning as fast as possible." *Great, I was going to be the bad cop no matter what.*

Eddy pulls back her hands and folds them in her lap. She looks almost like a lost child. She sniffles. "So what y'all wanna know?"

Lions withdraws his hands. "Well, first we want to know if you have any idea why Barnes would pull a gun on us?"

She sits there, staring at the table. I can tell she's reliving the moment with the gun to her head. She hunches her shoulders. "I don't know why my baby did it, but he was scared."

"Scared of whom?" I ask.

She cuts her eyes at me. "I'on know. Maybe you."

Lions brings her attention back to him. "You said that Barnes was scared. Was it because Marquis Jackson made bail?"

"Naw. Why would he be scared of Marquis? Marquis can catch a bullet like anybody else can. All I know is that when Dre came to pick me up, he said we had to lay low for a while until everything blew over."

"By blowing over, you mean this thing with Marquis Jackson?"

"I'on know. I guess."

"Let me ask you something," I interrupt. "Did Marquis ever tell you he hit a lick or did Barnes put you up to it?"

"Yeah... I mean, naw—look, y'all got my statement. Y'all know what I said."

Lions sits back in his seat and folds his arms, allowing me to take the lead. "Yeah, we got your statement. But I also got a video of you and Marquis entering Rothschild's Liquor Store fifteen minutes after the murders occurred, which means either you and Barnes did the hit and now you're trying to pin it on Marquis... Or all three of you were involved—which one is it?" Out of the corner of my eye I see Lions looking at me with his mouth partially open, his arms still folded.

Eddy narrows her eyes, shakes her head, and smiles slightly.

She drops her head, then lifts her knees up to her chin. "It wasn't supposed to be like this," she whispers.

"Like what?" I ask. She's silent. "*Like what?!*"

She jumps in her seat. "Dre said all we had to do was come in and give statements. That everything would be cool, and we'd get paid."

"Paid for what?"

"You know, telling y'all what y'all needed to hear about Marquis... So y'all would think he was the shooter."

"So you're telling us that you and Barnes lied?" She starts crying, but I'm not about to show her pity. After all--I'm the bad cop. "Why did you and Barnes lie?" She continues crying. "Answer me! Why would you lie?!"

"I-I-I don't know. Dre said he got into a little trouble, and if we did this thing he'd be good, and we'd get paid in the process. He said we weren't going to hurt nobody, so I said okay."

I hit the table with the palm of my hand. "You weren't going to *hurt* anybody? You were going to take away a man's freedom, possibly send him to the death chamber, and you weren't going to hurt anybody? What world do you live in, sugar?"

Lions gets up from his seat and exits the room. Eddy is dropping tears into a bucket, but fuck it. My words cut hard just like I wanted them to. I slide back from the table, leaving her to think about what she's done. Out in the hall, I see Lions heading for the restroom and I follow.

Chapter 44

"**S**o it *was* you that fucked us," Lions says to my reflection as he washes his hands.

"I didn't fuck us, Fred."

"Damn right you did! Don't stand there and lie to me like you didn't."

"Okay, I won't... But I didn't fuck our case. I just couldn't see an innocent man going down for something he didn't do."

Lions turns to face me. "Who the hell do you think you are?" He points at me. "Your high standards for justice just killed this case. You don't know that Jackson isn't our shooter."

"Yes I do, Fred. I've seen the tape at Rothschild's. It couldn't have been him. He's been telling the truth from the start."

"Truth? You know how many assholes come through here telling the truth? Our job is to get at the truth, but not to define it. That's for a jury to do."

"Listen, Fred, it's the right thing—"

"Don't try and feed me that 'right thing' BS, Frank. By withholding evidence, you've put both our careers on the line."

"But that's why I didn't want to tell you, because the less you knew, the better."

Lions gets up in my face. "Better for who? For you? So now you can sleep without having your father's deeds hanging over your head? Let me tell you something, Frank. We're a team, a two-man team... Which means you watch my back and I watch yours. But the minute you forget to respect the rules of this fraternal order, is the minute they bury you under a desk with a shitload of paperwork, until you either give up and leave, or hit your thirty. And I don't plan on retiring anytime soon. You remember that."

Lions pushes past me and exits the restroom. He's right and I know it. The Blue Religion doesn't allow for secrecy between officers, especially when those secrets free a potential cop killer.

Chapter 45

When I exit the restroom, I find a uniform leading Yolanda Eddy down the hall to lockup. Lions is leaning in the doorway of the interrogation room with his arms crossed. "She's done for," he says, "but they just brought Jackson in. Time to see if all your crusading was in vain."

We walk down to the next interrogation room and enter. Marquis Jackson is sitting cuffed to a railing on the side of a small square table. "Man, how many times we gone play this game?" he asks.

"You hear that, Frank? He thinks we're playing games." I smile. This is all Lions' play. "Let me tell you something Marquis... We're not playing a game. And if you think it's a game, you're going to be in a world of hurt."

"Man, whatever," he fans Lions off. "Where's my lawyer?"

"I'm sure he's on his way. But for now, how about we talk about why you killed Andre Barnes?"

"Who?"

"The man you said lied on you."

Jackson sits up in his seat. "Hold up, you telling me dude is dead?"

"Don't try and play dumb. You know he's dead and I wanna

know why you did it!"

"Me? Shit..." Jackson slouches back in his seat. "Like I told y'all the first time, I didn't kill no cop, and I didn't kill dude either."

"You hear him, Frank? He expects us to believe him."

"Believe what you want, Detective."

"So tell us where you were around four this afternoon."

"At home. Trying to stay out of trouble."

"Can anyone back up your story and give you an alibi? Oh, let me guess--your grandmother, right?"

"Yeah, my grandmother. And my damn lawyer, which you'll be talking to about harassing me."

Lions leans over the table and drops his index finger down on the surface. "You know what's wrong with you assholes having lawyers? You always think you can say what you want without repercussions, but you can't."

"It's America. I got freedom of speech."

"Wrong. This here is Lions Country, and the only right you have is to be a dumbass, cop-killing maggot."

"Man, I ain't gotta listen to this. Where's my lawyer?"

"You're going to listen, and you know why? Because we recovered a .32 in a trash can a block over from your home. That's right... *A block over*."

Jackson tenses up and diverts his eyes away from Lions. "So what? Doesn't mean it's mine."

Lions clasps his hands together. "So what are you saying? That somehow a gun connected to a murdered police officer just happens to be in your hood, out of all the other neighborhoods in the city?" He chuckles. "I can't wait to let a jury hear this. You're guaranteed to get the needle."

Jackson stares at Lions with pure hatred. I'm sure that if he wasn't cuffed to the wall, he'd go right at Lions, even with me sitting here.

Lions rises from his seat. "We still got Eddy's testimony and now we got a gun. Plus, when a jury hears about Barnes' death, just hours after your release, they're going to put two and two together and see right through you. And then it'll be too late. But if you start talking to me now, I may be able to save you from that hot shot."

Jackson looks down at the table. He starts biting his bottom lip and tapping his feet. He looks up at us, shaking his head with tears in his eyes. "How many times I gotta tell y'all, man? I didn't kill no cop, and I damn sure didn't kill dude. Why y'all tryin' to pin this on me? What did I do to you?"

"We're trying to get at the truth," Lions says.

I've been studying Jackson since we walked into the room. He's telling us the truth about murdering Richardson, but he isn't off the hook for Barnes' murder, and the way that Lions is going at him, he's liable to break and give us just about anything we want.

"Lord why? Why me?" Jackson cries into his interlocked hands as he rocks back and forth in his seat. "I didn't mean to do it."

Lions and I both look at each other. It looks as if Jackson is breaking sooner than I thought. Lions retakes his seat. "You didn't mean to do what?" Jackson continues rocking, holding his head down and praying. "You didn't mean to do what?" Lions asks again.

Jackson doesn't answer him but keeps on whispering. "I'm sorry, I'm sorry. Please Lord, let me get out of this. I'm sorry."

I lean over the table. "Marquis, son, look at me when I'm talking to you," I say in my calmest voice. He does as I ask, raising his red watery eyes to meet mine. "What are you sorry about?"

He sniffles as if he were a small child and wipes his face clean. "Because of what I did earlier today."

"And what was that?"

"I... I—" His voice gets caught in his throat.

"It's okay... Just take your time and let it come out."

"I stole money from my grandma earlier, to go buy some weed, and now God is seeing that I'm punished for it."

"Is that all you're sorry for?" I ask.

"I don't know what I was thinking stealing from my grandma. After all she's done for me, I turn around and steal from her. I'm a fool, yo."

Lions gets up from the table. "This is bullshit," he whispers as he exits the room.

"We'll be right back," I say, getting up from my seat and heading for the door.

Outside the interrogation room, I find Lions pacing the hall. "He's playing us," he says. "That asshole is playing us."

"I don't know. I thought he sounded pretty genuine."

"What? Come on, Frank. Don't tell me you bought that whole sappy story about him stealing from his grandma. You've seen his rap sheet—you know what he's capable of."

"We're all capable of murder, Fred. But I'm not reading him for Barnes."

"Just because he might have told us the truth about where he was when Richardson was killed, doesn't mean he didn't do it."

"I'm not saying he did or didn't. All I'm saying is that I don't see him being a murderer."

"Maybe that's the problem, Frank. You're not looking at this case with your eyes wide open."

The double-doors down the hall part open. We turn to see Crown and Captain Haggerty making their way towards us. "Is my client free to go, detectives?" Crown asks with a confident, snarky grin. "Because I'd hate for there to be more protests in front of this precinct."

"Yeah, he's free to go." Lions steps into the interrogation room with Crown following.

Captain Haggerty pulls me to the side. "Word just came down that DOPS will be holding a special review of the Barnes shooting at 10:00 a.m. down at HQ. Your attendance is required, so get your story together. Understand?"

"Yes, sir."

Crown and Jackson exit the interrogation room. The plump lawyer has a meaty hand on his client's shoulder, steering him like a priest directing a sinner to a confessional. Jackson keeps his eyes glued to the floor, more in shame than anything else.

Crown stops and looks at Captain Haggerty. "If your detectives continue to harass my client, I'll have no choice but to direct him to a civil lawyer and then this department could be facing a massive lawsuit." Captain Haggerty doesn't say a word, but words are never needed when *lawsuit* is thrown around. Crown and Jackson head for the double doors.

"There goes our last chance at getting a confession out of that asshole," Lions says, coming out of the interrogation room. We watch the two men disappear.

"Oh, before I forget," the captain says. "Those hospital records from Cook County just came in—I left them on your desk, Fred. Also, there's a DOPS meeting at 10:00 am down at HQ. See that you're there."

"A DOPS meeting, already?" Lions questions.

"The department already has one high profile OIS, so DOPS

wants to make sure they send the right message— —that we're not killing innocent citizens, no matter what some may think." The captain steps away and starts down the hall.

"I guess we should start in on those hospital records, huh?" I say to Lions.

"I'm done, but you have fun," he says. "Maybe you can put another hole in our case and help it bleed out some more."

Lions walks off, leaving me to wonder if we'll still be partners tomorrow. He's the second person to walk out on me this week, and I'm starting to realize it's not this case that's destroying my relationships. It's my lack of faith in those around me to do what needs to be done.

Chapter 46

The September night is brisk when I finally arrive home. I stop just before the open gate and stare up at Gloria's apartment. Jamal is standing in the front window, staring down at me. We lock eyes for a minute. If I could take away all his hurt and mistrust, I would. But I don't know where to begin.

He turns away from the window and the lights go out. Seeing Jamal reminds me that Gloria and I haven't spoken in two whole days. I'm a fool for allowing this case to take up so much of my time, and now I'm paying the price.

I climb the stairs to my apartment and enter. It's somber and lonely. There isn't a home-cooked meal waiting for me, as I've become accustomed to, and my stomach growls in protest. I make my way to the kitchen and flick on the light. The dish tray is empty. I haven't used a plate, pot, or pan in almost a month.

I yank open the freezer. It's empty except for a microwavable lasagna I stashed away long ago. I consider going down to Roy's Rib Shack, but then I might run into Lions, and right now we both need our space. Frozen lasagna it is.

* * *

After a quick shower I retrieve the lasagna from the microwave along with a bottle of root beer from the fridge, then head for the dining room table.

The long, polished oak table was my father's, and before him, my mother's. It's one of the rare items that I possess of hers. Sitting here with only my belches to keep me company, I regret not bringing the hospital records home. It would have at least given me something to do.

A loud rumble comes from overhead. I can tell by the sound of their feet that it's Jamal chasing after Janai, probably over something she said or did to him. I witnessed him chasing after her many times, while she ran for the protective cover of her mother's scolding stare. In the end, it was just playful antics between siblings.

I flip open my cell and dial Gloria's number. The phone barely rings before I hang up. I think about complaining about the ruckus, but I know Gloria will see right through it, especially since I've never complained in the two years they've been living above me.

I set the phone down, reach for it, then stop and contemplate calling, before going through the motions all over again. It's killing me not talking to Gloria, not sharing pieces of my world with her, so that I can be redeemed in her eyes and washed clean from the death and blood that stains my life. A family and a home-cooked meal were my rewards, and now I've lost them both, because I put the job before them.

The phone rings and I quickly pick it up. "Hello? Gloria?"

"Um... No, Detective Calhoun. It's Katriona McNabb."

"Oh, sorry Kat. What can I do for you?"

"I... You know what? It's probably crazy—I'm sorry I called."

"It's okay, what's on your mind?"

"I just feel like... I need to talk to someone. I've got so much going on, I feel like I'm losing it."

"I understand."

"I just—" She starts crying. "How can they let him free? You promised me."

"How about I come by and pick up those records? Then maybe we can grab a cup of coffee and talk."

"Sure... Thank you, Detective Calhoun."

"No problem. I'll see you soon."

I hang up and think long and hard again about calling Gloria but decide not to. Two days isn't all that long. Besides, Katriona McNabb is in distress, which means that the job is calling.

Chapter 47

Katriona McNabb stands in the doorway of her condo with a glass of white wine in her hand. She's wearing a beige cashmere sweater and a pair of dark skinny jeans. Her strawberry-blond hair is pulled back and tied into a ponytail. "Detective, please come in. I hope you don't mind, but I decided I needed something stronger than coffee."

"To each their own." I step into the loft. The lights are turned down low to allow the city's magnificent skyline to shine true through the large bay window.

"Isn't it beautiful?" Kat says. "Seeing all that manmade beauty really can put things into perspective, you know?" She downs her glass of wine and turns back to look out the bay window with her arms crossed over her chest. "Can I offer you a drink, Detective Calhoun?"

"You can call me Frank. And yeah, I'll take a glass of wine."

She turns away from the window and walks over to the open kitchen. "All I have is white... Is that okay?"

"That'll be fine."

I step over to the bay window and stare at the jutting skyscrapers, watching the yellow and white lights from the buildings illuminate the city like fireflies on a midsummer's night.

"Here you go," she says, handing me a glass. We stand there

232

for a few seconds, admiring our great city, lost in the knowledge that far away from those glitzing lights there's another side to this city, a murderous side where everything is cold and dark. "I don't know if I can live here anymore," she says, breaking the silence.

"Yeah, it'd probably be best if you got a new place. Living here and knowing that you and your mother shared this space could be very hard."

"I don't mean just this place—I mean this city."

I don't know what to say to that.

Katriona brings the glass to her lips and sips her wine. "I mean, what type of city just lets a murderer walk free?" She turns away from the window and sits down on the black leather couch.

I take a sip and follow. "You have to understand the way the law works, Kat. We can't go around locking people up and putting them away without any evidence."

"But you had evidence, or you wouldn't have brought him in, right?"

I take another sip of the wine. It's bittersweet. "We didn't have evidence—what we had was probable cause to question the suspect." I take a seat on the couch. "Just because we questioned the suspect doesn't mean he's guilty."

"But that State's Attorney went on the news and said he was charging that man with the murders."

"I know, but Perlenski jumped the gun. I shouldn't be telling you this but—"

"But what?" She looks at me with those doe-like eyes of hers and I can't help but tell her the truth. After all, it's my fault for instilling a sense of justification in the justice system without allowing for the possibility that there could be a failure.

233

"The man we thought was responsible for your mother's murder is actually innocent."

"What? No... That can't be." Her mouth is open, and her eyes begin to fill with tears.

"I'm afraid so. We have proof that he couldn't have committed the murders."

"But if it wasn't him, why'd you arrest him?"

"Because we thought we had the right guy, but it turns out we didn't."

Tears stream down her pink cheeks. "That means my mother's murderer is still out there."

It was more a confirmation than a question, but I answer anyway. "Yes." She breaks down into long sobs. I was once on the receiving end of similar bad news, and I know that there are no words that can comfort her. I set our glasses down on the coffee table and scoot over to wrap my arms around her. If I can't say anything to ease her troubles, I can at least let her know that I'm here for her when it feels like no one else is.

She clutches me tightly and cries out her soul onto my shoulder. "Why? Why'd you take my mother, God? Why?" I want to tell her that I've been asking that very same question about my own mother since I can remember. We're two faces of the same coin. She grips me tighter and sobs into my chest. "I'm sorry," she says.

"There's nothing to be sorry about. I totally understand. I lost my mother, too."

She pulls back a few inches and looks into eyes. Maybe she sees her reflection in my irises. "You do understand, don't you?" She leans in and kisses me. Her lips are warm against mine. She digs her nails into my back as she leans forward, pushing me back against the sofa. Our tongues entangle and she exhales a carnal sigh as she diverts her lips from mine and onto my neck. I run my fingers up her curved spine and undo her bra with a flick. She moans and leans deeper into me, taking in my scent. "Fuck me," she whispers into my ear. Her warm breath massages the side of my neck. She sits up, straddling me while removing her sweater and bra. Her nipples are small and pink, but her breasts are more than two handfuls. She grabs my face and we lock lips once more. She stabs her tongue into my mouth, probing me, and all I can do is sit back and enjoy it. Then she unbuttons my shirt and slides her tongue down my bare chest, taking the time to lick and kiss it as she goes further down. "Mm... I need this," she says through clenched teeth, while grabbing at my belt buckle.

My manhood is bursting to be let out. I close my eyes, waiting for her mouth to take me in. It would be beautiful, just as it always was when Gloria... Suddenly I open my eyes and stare at the ceiling. *What am I doing?* I sit up.

"What's wrong?" she asks, still unzipping my pants.

"I can't do this."

"Sure you can. Just let me show you what I can do."

I grab her hands before she has a chance to undo my belt. "No, it wouldn't be right."

She looks up at me with those doe-like eyes and I know I have to get the hell out of here. "It's her, isn't it? Gloria? The name of the woman that you said over the phone when I called?"

I release her hands. "Yes, it's her."

"I understand." She stands up with her breasts bouncing. I start to re-button my shirt. "I guess I should give you the files, so you can get out of here, huh?"

"That would probably be best."

She turns and walks back to the kitchen, where she grabs a

manilla folder off the counter. "Here you go," she says, walking back over to me, her breasts bouncing with every step. "All of my mother's old clients." I take the file and smile. I want her to know that I'll still be there for her, but I'm not sure what to say. "I'll be okay, Frank," she says, reading my mind. "But you're right, you know? It wouldn't have been good to sleep with a cop, especially one who makes his living off murders."

Chapter 48

An hour later I'm sitting in the Golden Nugget diner, still contemplating Katriona's words. Was her slight aimed at me, or the entire justice system? I honestly don't know. But now I feel like I owe it to her to give this case my all. If it goes on the books as unsolved, I can live with that—but I can't live with the fact that I gave my word to find her mother's killer, and all I've done up to this point is put an innocent man in jail.

The waitress, Karen, whose name I gleaned from her name tag, is making the rounds with a fresh pot of coffee. We make eye-contact, and she loops her brown bangs behind her ear and smiles at me. I've had enough woman trouble for the night, but I can't shake the fact that I want Gloria in my life more than I thought I did.

"Working late, Detective?" Karen asks as she saunters over to my booth.

"What?"

She eyes the manila folder on the table with Katherine McNabb's real estate records in it. "You working a late case?" She fills up my cup.

"How'd you know I was a detective?"

"Cops are my regulars. Usually blue-and-whites, but I can

spot you guys a mile away."

I lean back in my seat. "Oh, yeah? How's that?"

"Because you guys are always looking for two things: some-one who looks like trouble, and a way out. I bet you've got at least three customers in here on your radar, and about four different ways to make it out of here alive, if a firefight happens to break out."

I smile. "I guess you do know cops." She smiles back and loops her bangs behind her ears again. I can tell she has a thing for cops but I'm not biting. "Thanks for the observation, Karen. I'll do my best not to look so suspicious."

"No problem, Detective. Hope you solve your case. If you need anything, let me know." She switches her hips on down the aisle and back up to the long counter. I start to wonder how many of my brothers in blue have taken Karen up on her offer but decide it's not worth the effort.

I open the manilla folder and start combing through the stack of papers. The first three clients are individuals that have purchased condos in the trendy Wicker Park neighborhood. The next few leaflets show mixed-income families that have purchased or rented homes in the now gentrified neighborhood of the infamous Cabrini Green housing projects.

Since McNabb was an independent realtor, she wasn't be-holden to a single neighborhood. Her client list reads like a smorgasbord of middle-class and low-income families. I flip through a few more pieces of paper before I find her client 'list' for Garfield Park, which consists of exactly one client: G&D Housing. The records show that the company owns a few rental properties. At the end of the dozen or so addresses there's one with an asterisk next to it, which happens to fall right in the middle of my crime scene.

I drop a five down on the table and head for the door. Karen is standing at the counter, going through her receipts and calculating her tips.

"You done for the night, Detective?" she asks, smiling and licking her lips.

I know she wants me to stop and give her a nice pick-up line or drop my number down on one of the receipts, but I push forward, opening the door. "I'll be done when I'm dead," I say over my shoulder.

Chapter 49

The Garfield Park neighborhood where McNabb and Richardson were killed is quiet. Remnants of yellow and red crime scene tape caught on the end of a chain link fence blow in the harsh, cold wind. It's a simple reminder to any residents that venture outside that death is just around the corner.

I park at the end of the C-shaped block where the street curves into Central Park Avenue. Since the murders, the city has ensured residents that all the neighborhood's streetlights will now be working. I can even see that the blinking blue light of the crime stopper camera at the corner of Lake Street has been repaired.

As I walk up the block, I check the paper with the address on it. A small, two-story house that's been boarded up sits in between two four-story apartment buildings. The chain link fence around the dilapidated building has been torn down and all that remains erect are its rusting poles. Weeds sprout up through a busted walkway and two rats the size of raccoons leap from the growing foliage and into an adjacent bush as I pass.

Over the paint-chipped door of the two-story building is a sign that reads CARLUCCI DEVELOPMENT, followed by a phone number.

I expected to at least find that the property belonged to G&D Housing since they had been McNabb's most prominent client. Maybe I'm barking up the wrong tree, but I have to exhaust all possibilities.

I turn and start walking back up the broken walkway. The bitter cold licks at my face, so I turn up the collar of my jacket to shield me. The thing about living in this city is that you never expect it to be quiet, but tonight it's like a ghost town. The wind blows litter across the dried brown grass. I walk up the block to where Richardson fell, in front of a red two-story wooden frame home. The blood-soaked dandelions have been trampled, and there is a brown outline where still more of Richardson's blood has dried.

I put my hands in my pockets and stand there for a while, staring at the bloodstain as if it's my first time seeing it. All this time, I've tried to think of Richardson as nothing but another victim, but I can't escape the fact that I brought him into the Blue Religion. And yet, I didn't keep an eye on him. If I had he might still be alive.

"Don't beat yourself up over this case, Frank."

I look up and see Arnie Ratcliff walking towards me. A cigarette dangles from his lips as he shields it with his hand and lights it. "Now you're stalking *me*, Arnie?"

"You're not that popular anymore, Frank. Just doing some follow-up questions with a few residents, seeing if anyone wants to talk."

"Any luck?"

"Everyone is as quiet as Catholics on Sunday." He blows out a cloud of smoke and wrinkles his pointy nose. It's the first time I've ever seen Arnie smoke. "That's really something, huh?" He nods at the dried puddle of blood. "Man loses his life over nothing, but still seems to leave his mark."

"Yeah, it's something," I whisper.

"I heard about the shooting today. It's good to see you're all right, Frank. It would've been a shame to have to..." He lets his words trail off.

"A shame to have to what, Arnie?"

"It's nothing... I mean... Forget I said anything."

"Just say whatever you were going to say."

He takes a drag off his cigarette, exhales and looks down at the blood. "It's a good thing you came out on top. You know, I'd hate to have to tell Joe that you were gone."

"Joe, huh? You call my father by his first name now?"

He takes another drag. "Yeah, that's what I call him. You know we've been writing this book together... We don't have a title yet, but we're working on it. Anyway, your old man talks a lot about you. If you want, I'd be happy to let you read a few chapters."

"Don't try and play me. Not right now—not here. What do you *really* want?"

He takes one last drag and stomps out the cigarette. "No catch, really. I just thought you might want to read what your father has been writing. A lot of it has to do with your half-brother."

"I already know the ending to *that* story. Blue's dead, and my father is in jail for his murder. Pretty simple if you ask me."

"Yeah, I guess it is." We stand there in silence for a few seconds as if we've lost our place in the world. "So I hear that you had to kick loose Marquis Jackson... Mind telling me why? Did you guys arrest the wrong person?"

I smile and shake my head. Arnie Ratcliff will always be Arnie Ratcliff, a reporter in mind, body, and soul. "No comment," I say. "But you can quote me on this..."

"Oh yeah, what's that?"

"I won't rest until I bring the killer to justice."

Chapter 50

It's close to 1:00 a.m. by the time I get home. The night has grown colder, and sleet has just begun to fall. I pause at the gate and look up at Gloria's apartment. All the lights are off, and I can only imagine lying in bed with her warm body next to mine.

I flip open my cell and think about calling her, but I know that giving her space is just as important. Plus, I need to sort out my own feelings. I'm not sure if I love her, or just the thought of being loved.

I trod up the stairs and enter my home. I might not know how I feel about Gloria, but I know I'm crazy about her kids. Once I'm done with DOPS, I'm going to handle Jamal's problem once and for all.

Chapter 51

Hurdy's Soul Food is located on Roosevelt Road & Cicero Avenue, right down the street from the Bare Assets strip club. Late at night the place is a rest stop for hustlers, pimps and whores—but during the day, it's a pitstop for truckers and working-class men.

I've come to Hurdy's at 9:30 in the morning to catch Reverend Rawls and a few other ministers having their daily prayer breakfast. The restaurant is laid out with no conventional wisdom in mind. On one side of the nearly thousand square foot space brown booths are aligned against a wall. Next to the booths there's a row of white square tables and steel chairs, then another row of booths. In between all the seating there's just enough space for the waitresses to maneuver. The other side of the establishment is full of small wooden tables and chairs.

There are three waitresses working. They look like old school nurses with their all-white, one-piece uniforms and white triangular hats. The place reeks of fried bacon and collard greens cooked with soft pork.

Reverend Rawls sits at a table with two other men that I know from my time as a missionary. All three men are dressed in solid-colored pressed suits, with off-color ties.

"Morning Frank," Reverend Rawls says, greeting me with his

trademark smile.

"Morning Reverend. Ministers. Can I take a seat?"

"Sure you can, brother. Have you come to fellowship with us this morning?"

"Something like that," I say, taking a seat.

To my right sits Minister Ozay Rudolph, a tall skinny man with dark, oily skin. Across from him sits Minister Sheldon Walker, a light-skinned, two-hundred-fifty-pound baby-faced man with a diamond encrusted pinky ring that speaks highly of his congregation's naïve generosity.

"So what's on your mind, Frank?" Rawls wants to know.

"I came down here to ask you to lay off the pressure on the department about this Jackson kid. And to ease up on Officer Richter and the LeClaire Courts shooting."

Rawls takes a sip of his coffee and smiles. "Surely you are not asking us to look the other way when there are injustices going on in our community?"

"No, but I am asking you to look at the facts, especially regarding Officer Richter and the accidental shooting. He's a good cop."

"He may be a good cop, but it doesn't erase the fact that he shot an innocent boy—a *Black* boy—and for no other reason than because he was Black."

"That's bull and you know it. Officer Richter was doing his job and what happened at LeClaire was an accident. It could have happened to any officer whether he was white, Black, Hispanic, or whatever else."

"And yet I still have a mother that cries for her dead son. What am I supposed to tell her? That it was an accident and to get over it?"

There's no real cure for a mother's grief, and I'm not about to pretend I know one. "All I'm asking, Reverend, is that you and the other ministers start practicing what the good word teaches about turning the other cheek and doing unto others..."

"Don't try and tell us about the good word. You're the one who turned your back on God's calling."

"I didn't turn my back on God. I answered His calling by becoming a detective. We always talk about God moving in mysterious ways, so maybe this is His plan for me."

Rawls takes a sip of his coffee. "You know what, Brother Calhoun? Maybe this is God's plan for you—but the Ministers Against Police Brutality must lead God's children to freedom, so that we all may grow to realize His plan." Rawls isn't giving in. If the attacks against the department don't cease, then the streets might go up in flames and the city could have an unstoppable riot on its hands.

"I'm not here to argue about who's right and wrong. All I'm asking is that you look at the current situation from a civic point of view. With citizens and cops being killed, the streets are now hotter than ever. If a riot breaks out, who do you think is going to be affected the most? Now *that's* something to think about."

I rise from my seat and head for the door. Rawls calls after me. "Frank, I respect what you've done—becoming a detective and trying to make a difference in our community... But maybe you should worry about your own house. I hear the foundation is crumbling."

Chapter 52

I'm not sure what Rawls means, but I don't have time to ask him—the DOPS meeting is less than ten minutes away, and I have to hightail it over to HQ.

When I enter the building, I find Lions waiting for me in the lobby. He's wearing a pressed blue suit with a light blue shirt and a black tie. He's even shaved away the few whiskers that were growing on his chin.

"I thought you were going to jump ship," I say.

"And miss DOPS try and nail your ass to the board?"

"They can try, but my story's clean and you know it."

"Do I?" he says.

I pause, trying to read him, but he keeps a stern face. "You're playing, right?"

"I don't know, Frank. Partners usually have each other's backs, but you've been playing lone cowboy, and that's just not how things work."

"I know I was wrong for not filling you in on Jackson and Barnes, and I promise I won't do it again. But you've gotta backup my story in there or things are going to go hard for the both of us."

"I guess we'll have to see how it plays out." He walks away.

When I step off the elevator on the fourth floor, Captain

Haggerty and a short white man in his late fifties are waiting for me. "Frank, this is Officer Charles, from the FOP."

The man extends a hand and I shake it. "The Fraternal Order of Police wants you to know that we'll be backing your story one hundred percent. If this investigation should lead to any type of disciplinary action, we're going to be here to help you fight it." I thank him even though I don't think I'll need the FOP's assistance.

The captain puts a hand around my shoulder. "Watch how you say things in there, Frank. I've seen them beat an officer down with his own words."

"Will do, sir."

I walk on down the hall and enter a room on my left where the questioning will take place. The Department of Professional Standards is an independent review board made up of five members called The Council, comprised of a lawyer, a human rights advocate, an ex-judge, a civilian, and an ex-cop brought in from outside the department. The Council always holds its interviews at a round table, and today is no different.

The off-white room is bright from the fluorescent lights that buzz overhead. Sitting at the round table are two males and a female. All three look up from their stack of papers and eyeball me, their target.

"Please take a seat, Detective," one of the men says. He's wearing a brown corduroy blazer with patched elbows. This man, whom I believe to be the ex-judge, adjusts his thin, wiry glasses and licks his dry, pink lips. The space where his hairline originally started has been replaced with a pasty white wrinkled scalp. I pull out a chair and sit down.

The gentleman next to the judge is a large Black man with rough looking hands. He's wearing blue jeans and a tan

Carhartt jacket, with a T-shirt underneath that reads I LIVE AND BREATHE CEMENT. His eyes are brown, but the sly smile on his face says that he enjoys this part of his job more than anything. I figure him to be the civilian, a working man with a purpose.

"Let's bring this meeting into order, gentlemen," the woman says. She has her auburn hair pulled back and tied into a ponytail. Her gray eyes are unwavering, and she looks at me with a gaze that I can only describe as filled with disgust. *Great. I just had to get the ball-busting advocate.*

The judge picks up his gavel-shaped coffee cup, takes a sip and pauses. "I must inform you that our session will be recorded. You have the right to refuse to answer any of The Council's questions. Now, let us begin. Please state your name and rank."

"Lieutenant Frank Calhoun. Badge number 4416."

"Now if you will, Detective Calhoun... We'd like to hear how yesterday's events unfolded."

This is the part I hate about a DOPS review. Even though they all have the information in front of them, they want to hear it out of your mouth regardless. "At sixteen hundred hours, Lieutenant Fred Lions and I approached a building located in the 800 block of South Pulaski. We had received information that two state's witnesses, Andre Barnes and Yolanda Eddy, were occupying the residence."

"Let me stop you for a second, Detective," the advocate says. "If the two individuals were state's witnesses, why were you looking for them? Were they in danger?"

"No ma'am. We were ordered by State's Attorney Perlenski to track down Barnes and Eddy for re-questioning."

She makes a note in her pad, then sits back to study me. "I see. Thank you."

"Please continue, Detective," the judge gestures with a nod of his head.

"Upon arriving at the residence, Lieutenant Lions and I tried to enter the building but found the outer doors locked. We then separated—"

"Why'd you separate?" the advocate asks.

"Because we had our suspicions that Barnes might run."

"Did you at least ring the building's doorbell, Detective Calhoun?" the worker wants to know.

"At this time, I can't recall... But I'm pretty sure there wasn't a doorbell to ring." We're all silent, and then the judge nods his head. "Once Lieutenant Lions and I separated, I waited in front of the building, hoping that Barnes and Eddy would try to flee."

"How long did you wait out in front of the building?" the worker wants to know.

"Maybe about ten, fifteen minutes and then I heard a shot come from inside the building. When I went to investigate, I found Barnes standing at the top of the stairs with a gun in his hand. He took one look at me and started shooting."

"Then what did you do?" the advocate inquires, jotting down notes.

"I ducked for cover and pulled my sidearm."

"You didn't return fire?" she asks.

"No. By the time I was in a position to return fire, the suspects had already returned to the safety of the apartment."

The judge speaks up. "And what about your partner? Where was he?"

"At the time, I had no knowledge of Lieutenant Lions' status. Fearing that he may have been injured, I pursued the suspects into the residence. Upon entering, I identified myself as Chicago Police, and having not received a response from the suspects,

I proceeded with caution. It was not long before Lieutenant Lions called me to his position in the bedroom of the residence, where I found Barnes holding our other witness, Yolanda Eddy, at gunpoint."

"At that point, did you call for backup?" the advocate questions.

"No, ma'am. As I stated before, my thoughts were with my partner. I didn't have time to call for backup."

"You didn't have time, Detective Calhoun? Or you didn't make time?"

"My partner's life was on the line—so no, I didn't have time. Besides, I was sure that the residents of the neighborhood would call in the shots fired."

The advocate and I lock eyes. I can tell that she's never been in a firefight, or even heard actual gunfire for that matter. If she had, she wouldn't be questioning my reactions.

The judge breaks our silence even though I continue to stare down the advocate. "Whenever you're ready you can continue, Detective Calhoun."

"Upon discovering that our suspect had a hostage, Lieutenant Lions and I attempted to talk the suspect down."

The worker leans forward in his seat. "Excuse me, Detective, but doesn't the department have negotiators for things like that?"

"They do, but we couldn't wait for a negotiator. We had a life on the line—not to mention the public's safety to consider. Eventually, we talked the suspect down and took him into custody."

"Did you take the suspect into custody or was it your partner?" the worker questions.

"I took him into custody while my partner attended to our

victim's possible injuries."

"Did you and your partner ever become separated during the arrest?" the judge asks.

"Yes. After taking the suspect into custody, I exited the residence with the goal of depositing him in the back of our car. But as we were exiting the building, shots rang out from a moving vehicle. Before I had time to react, my suspect was dead and the vehicle was gone."

There is a moment of silence before the advocate leans forward in her seat. "How did you know the shots came from a vehicle, Detective?"

"Because I heard the rev of an engine, and the tires peeling out."

"And you heard all of this over the gunshots?"

"No, it was only after the shots. Plus, how else could the killer have gotten away after shooting my suspect?"

"Do you believe the shots that killed your suspect were meant for you or for him?" the judge wants to know.

"I can't really speculate on that. As the saying goes: bullets don't have names on them."

The advocate jots down a few notes. "Detective Calhoun, let me get this right... You were standing behind the suspect when the shots rang out from the moving vehicle, am I correct?"

"Yes."

"And your partner was still upstairs in the apartment?"

"No, he had just exited the apartment and was standing at the top of the stairs."

"Did you pull your sidearm before or after the shots were fired?"

"Excuse me?"

"I asked if you drew your service weapon while the suspect

was in custody or after he had been shot?"

"I never got a chance to pull my weapon."

"Why not?"

"Because I couldn't reach my sidearm. I was too busy watching a young man's life slip between my fingers. Does that answer your question?"

Chapter 53

Lions is standing outside the council's main office leaning against a wall, cleaning his nails. "Took you long enough," he says.

"You know how it can be with DOPS—they want to know every single detail, right down to the color of the urine when you pissed yourself."

"Sounds like you had the fun crew."

"If you call playing twenty questions fun, then yeah."

Lions pushes himself up off the wall. "You know, Frank, while you were in that room answering questions, I thought about what you said about allowing an innocent man to go to jail."

"Yeah?"

"I kept replaying the moment when you held Barnes in your arms, and you know what I came to realize? That somewhere out there in this city is a murdering asshole laughing at us." He turns and looks at me. "We can't let this case rest. Let's put our differences behind us and catch this fucker."

"Are you done being all emotional?"

"As much as you're done being a cop," he smirks.

"Good. Because I think we might have a fresh new lead."

Lions raises an eyebrow. "How so?"

"You ever heard of G&D Housing? Last night I went through

255

McNabb's real estate records and came across the name. Turns out most of her clients have either rented or bought their homes from this developer."

"So you think we should start with the developer and see where it leads us."

"You read my mind."

We walk down the hall and wait for the elevator. "You know, you would have loved the human rights advocate that questioned me."

"And why is that?"

"Because she had that sexy librarian thing going on that you like."

* * *

The City Clerk's office is located on the first floor of City Hall. The marble floor of the building is immaculately polished, and the ornate marble ceiling and walls give it a palatial feel. An L-shaped hardwood counter separates us from the Puerto Rican receptionist whose curly hair bounces whenever she moves.

"How can I help you gentlemen?"

Lions flashes his badge a bit longer than necessary. "Detectives Lions and Calhoun. We're looking to get some information on a city developer."

The woman, whose eyes are the shape of almonds, sizes up Lions, then stands up from her desk and walks over to where we are at the counter. "Do you have a warrant?"

Lions leans down on the counter. "I didn't think we would need one."

"In order to receive city records, you're going to need a warrant."

"Is that a fact?"

"Yes, it is, Detective."

I take a step back and allow Lions to do his thing. "I was hoping we could come to some type of understanding," he says.

"Understanding?"

"How about we start with dinner?"

The young woman leans back and sizes up Lions again. "Are you trying to bribe a city employee?"

"We're both city employees. But no, I'm not trying to bribe you—I'm asking if you'd like to have dinner with me."

The woman looks offended. "With you? And why would I want to have dinner with you?"

"Because I'm paying, and you'd be in good hands."

The young woman laughs to herself. "I don't need a man to buy me dinner."

"Okay, I get it... You're independent. There's nothing wrong with that, but there's also nothing wrong with a good bite to eat, is there?"

"How about I just give you what you want, and we both go on about our day?"

"Ouch, I'm hurt."

In fact, Lions *is* hurt. A man's pride can only handle so much. "That a deal," I say, before he digs himself into a deeper hole.

"Write the name of the developer down on this piece of paper." She slides it over to me. I jot down the name and slide the paper back across the counter. "Please don't make this a habit," she says from behind her computer. Her fingers go to work, typing out the information that I've given her.

"So, what do you want to know?" she asks.

Lions is pretending to read a text message on his phone. "We just need a name and address."

"Let's see..." She returns to typing. "The company is called Growth & Development Housing. They have an office out in Calumet City."

"Wait, did you say Growth & Development?"

"Yes. Do you still want the address?"

"I think we'll be okay." Lions looks up from his phone. "I'll explain on the way," I say.

"On the way to where?"

258

Chapter 54

The Pocket nightclub is eerily silent when we step through its doors. A fat man with a bald head is tending bar.

"We're looking for Prince Paul."

The bartender picks up a Stella glass and starts cleaning it. "Don't know the man."

"I know Paul owns this place," I say. "I've been in his office in the back... You know, the one with the reinforced steel door?"

"I've never been back there, so I have no idea what you're talking about."

"You don't know what he's talking about?" Lions walks over to the bar. He places his badge down on the smooth wooden surface. "How about I run you in and hold you for seventy-two hours in connection to this double homicide we're investigating? How'd you like that?"

The bartender flares his nostrils and stares Lions down. "You do what you have to do, Detective. Like I said, I'on know nothin' about what goes on in back. All I do is tend bar."

"Then I guess you won't have a problem with us going back there and looking for ourselves." Lions turns to his right and begins walking the length of the bar.

I keep my eyes trained on the bartender in case he employs the old shotgun-behind-the-bar routine, which means I have to be ready to drop him without hesitation. The bartender reaches down behind the bar, and I put my hand on my sidearm, lifting it out of its holster. "Hands! Let me see your hands!"

The bartender slowly puts his hands up. "Damn, chill! I was just grabbing a glass."

"Grabbing a glass almost got your damn head blown off."

"We good?" Lions asks from over his shoulder.

"Yeah, I got him."

At the far end of the bar is a doorway that leads to the club's VIP room. Beyond that and down a flight of stairs is a reinforced steel door that protects Prince Paul's office. I steal a look at Lions as he unholsters his weapon while walking towards the adjacent room.

"I thought you cops were supposed to serve and protect," Prince Paul says from the VIP room's opening, as he steps into the main area of the bar. "Not harass and intimidate."

He's wearing a white tank top that gives us a full view of his Satanic tattoos. I hadn't noticed until now that his chest is much wider than it was a year ago. The muscles in his arms are more defined too, which makes his green tattoos look more like brands burned into his skin. Behind him stands the gorilla known as KP, and the light-skinned teen I nicknamed Smooth.

"Look, we got 'em all in one place," Lions says with a smile, leveling his gun on KP. "This time it isn't going your way. So give me a reason to put one in yo head."

The muscle doesn't say a word. They don't even blink or divert their eyes. Until Lions pulls the trigger of his gun, it isn't real to them—it's just a child's toy, or a figment of their deranged imaginations.

"Yo, Big Tom, back to work," Paul commands. The bartender

does as he's told, even though I still have my gun trained on him. Paul crosses the room and sits down at one of the black circular tables. "Whatcha want, detectives?"

"We came to talk," I say.

"Then let's talk. Ay yo, Detective," he says to Lions. "You mind pointing that gun somewhere else? My people don't look kindly upon rude visitors."

Lions keeps his gun pointed at KP. "As soon as your boys show me they're not packing."

"Come on... Are you here to talk or to make an arrest?"

"Could be both, you know? Get us a two-for-one deal going."

Paul looks to me. "Are we really going to play this game, Frank?"

I holster my weapon. "Let it go, Fred." I pat Lions on the shoulder as I pass. There are about twenty circular highboy tables with four bar stools at each one. Beyond the tables there's a large dance floor. I take a seat at Paul's table.

He looks me dead in the eyes. "You find my brother's killer?"

"Maybe, but I guess that all depends on you."

"On me? How's that?"

I look to Lions and then back at Paul. "Fred, how about you keep your gun on them two? You know, for public safety reasons. Don't want them jumping to any conclusions."

"I got ya."

I stare Paul down. "What's Growth & Development Housing?"

"I have no idea."

"Come on, Paul. It's no coincidence that Growth & Development has the same moniker as the Gangster Disciples."

Paul opens his palms and hunches his shoulders. "How am I supposed to control what people call their companies?"

"Now you're playing with my intelligence, and I don't like

261

when people play with my intelligence."

Paul leans in over the table. "Neither do I."

We hold each other's stares as if looking for a reason to go for a loaded weapon. "Here's something for your intelligence, Paul. Katherine McNabb, the woman that was killed alongside your brother, was a real estate agent, and she kept a record of her clients. One of those clients was Growth & Development Housing."

"So what? How's this have anything to do with me?"

"Because it begs the question: did you have your brother killed?"

Paul narrows his eyes. "What did you say?"

"You heard me. What did Tavares have on you? Money laundering? Fraud? It had to be something big, or why else would he have a cache of weapons stored at his apartment? He must have known you'd come for him. Some brother you are."

Paul leaps over the table and we both go crashing to the floor. His entire 180 pounds are on top of me. His fingers grip my throat. I can feel his nails digging into my skin. "I'll kill you, motherfucker!" he screams. His face is a flash of red madness.

I wrap my hands up under his arms and try to pry loose his grip but he's stronger than I've given him credit. "Come on, Frank! Kick his ass!" Lions yells. I unwrap my right hand and slug Paul dead on the chin. His grip loosens just enough that I'm able to kick him off me. My lungs burn as I inhale a quick whiff of air. "You okay, Frank?" Lions asks.

I look over and see that he still has his gun trained on the muscle. "Yeah, I'm good," I say, standing up.

Paul is up on his feet also. His face is covered with tears. The corner of his lip is busted open. He massages it with his tongue. "Pretty good right," he says. "My brother teach you that?"

It was in fact Tavares that helped me get back into shape. After my last altercation with a murdering ex-chaplain named Keyes, I knew I had to improve my fighting technique. I rub my neck. There are scratch marks from Paul's nails. "I didn't come to fight you, Paul."

"Shit you didn't! Accusing me of killing my brother. My *own* brother! Naw, you ain't come to fight—you came to die." I quickly draw my weapon as Paul draws his.

Lions cocks the hammer on his gun. "Don't you two even think about it."

"You sure you want to do this, Paul?" I ask.

"You sure you wanna accuse me of killing my brother?"

I can see in Paul's eyes that he's ready to die. Sometimes the streets drive you to this point. "Okay, let's say you didn't kill your brother..."

"Nigga," he cocks his gun.

"If you didn't have anything to do with his murder, then maybe you can answer this: why did your brother have an arsenal in his apartment, as if he were gearing up for a war?"

Paul blinks twice. "Naw... Naw, it can't be because of that," he says.

"Because of what?"

Paul lowers his weapon. "Damn, naw... It can't be."

"It can't be what?"

Paul takes a seat and places his gun down on the table. "I thought he was talkin' out his ass." He stares past me to a memory long forgotten. "A few weeks ago, I was talkin' to Tavares. He kept sayin' he was workin' on somethin' big."

"Big like what?"

Paul blinks and I can tell that the memory is gone as fast as it had come. "He wouldn't say. All he kept saying was that when he blew it open, no one would believe a rookie had done it. He said it was going to go down in police history. Now I wish I had pressed him more." He slumps down in his chair. I keep my gun down to my side and approach cautiously. "If I had known it would get him killed, I would've told him to let it go. Aww, man." Paul starts crying into his hands. I quickly step over to the table and snatch hold of the gun. I'm going for my cuffs when he looks up from his tear-drenched hands. "What am I gonna tell my mama?"

The question hits me square in the chest. All this time I thought Paul and Tavares' parents were dead. Now that Paul's feelings are laid bare for all of us to see, I know that he couldn't have killed his brother. I drop my hands away from the cuffs but keep both pistols down near my side. "Let's go, Fred."

Lions nods and starts to slowly back up, while keeping his gun leveled on KP.

We are almost out the door when Paul calls after us. "I want y'all to know this is for my brother, and not for y'all." He pauses and gathers himself. "I knew Katherine McNabb... She was a good lady. And yeah, she worked for Growth & Development. She came over from Carlucci a few months back. But some people weren't happy about that, because she also brought along all her clients. But what the hell did I care as long as Growth & Development was making money? I'm only telling you all this because I never brought my little brother around any of the business I did... So I don't know how he and Katherine knew each other. But I bet if you can figure that out, then you'll probably figure out who killed him."

Chapter 55

We're headed down Madison Street. I'm driving and Lions is sulking. "What the hell's going on, Frank?" he asks me. "Why'd we let Paul go again?"

"Because now he owes us."

"And you expect him to pay up sometime soon?"

"Maybe not today, or even tomorrow. But one day we might have to pull him in for a favor. And a favor from a man in Paul's position is worth his weight in gold."

"You keep telling yourself that, but Paul's just as liable to snatch your life without a thought."

I steal a glance at Lions. He's sitting with his arms crossed over his chest. "Thanks for having my back."

"Don't mention it. For a second I thought I was going to have to shoot Paul to get him off you."

"I didn't expect him to be that strong. You see how fast he pulled that pistol? He'd have the drop on a rookie in no time."

"Who you telling? I barely saw the piece. So where we headed?"

"Downtown."

"At this time of day? Whatta you crazy?"

"We have to go where the case takes us."

"Who said anything about the case taking us downtown? From

what I can see, I think you hit the nail on the head when you accused Paul of having his brother killed."

"That's the problem. I hit the wrong nerve. Paul was upset, he may have even overreacted... But you would too if you lost your brother."

"Listen to yourself, Frank. I think you're reading too much into this."

"I thought so too, but I'm not. What we saw today is Paul's guilt. Not because he killed his brother or had him killed, but because he can never be what his brother was to his mother: a ray of hope in this dark world of ours. I know how Paul feels because I was my father's ray of hope, and my half-brother Blue was the dark stain in his life. I watched Blue try to live up to my father's expectations since we were kids—only to fail every time until his death."

"You still haven't told me why we're going downtown." Lions grumbles as we pass the United Center, home of the Bulls and Blackhawks.

"When I was going through McNabb's records, I came across an address right down the street from where she and Richardson were murdered. I was hoping that it would be a Growth & Development property, but it wasn't—it belonged to Carlucci Development. I thought it was just a coincidence, but after hearing what Paul said about people not being happy with McNabb's departure, I'm thinking it's best to go right to the source and see what we can find."

Chapter 56

"**S**o this is how rich people work?" Lions says as we step off the elevator and into the lobby of Carlucci Development. The space is an exposed brick loft that's been divided into at least twelve cubicles. Fifty feet in, we find a male receptionist wearing a headset sitting behind an oblong desk. He's on automatic, switching lines and answering phones.

"How can I help you?" he asks us in between calls.

"Detectives Calhoun and Lions," I say. "We need to see someone about a previous employee."

"That would be Sheila Hyatt, our VP of HR."

"She here?" Lions asks, breaking away to study pictures on the adjacent wall of Carlucci with Mayor Deal, a few city councilmen, and a couple senators.

"I'll check. You can have a seat."

I join Lions at the wall and we both study the photographs. "Looks like the Carluccis are the development princes of the city."

"It looks that way. All the democratic royalty on one wall. And check this out: there's even a picture of old man Carlucci with the first Mayor Deal. Maybe the title of 'king' is more like it."

The picture shows a short young Carlucci, with a hook nose and dark beady eyes. He's smiling, but his expression tells me he's a ruthless businessman who sees the world and everyone in it as a business opportunity. The first Mayor Deal, Julius, is a tall robust man with an equally dark look in his eyes. I can see how the two men would have come together to do business. Their false cordial smiles look forced and out of character.

"Detectives?" We turn our attention to the receptionist. "I've spoken to Mrs. Hyatt. She'll be right down. In the meantime, can I get you something to drink?"

"We're good," I respond.

We turn back to studying the pictures. "What's the plan?" Lions asks me.

"I'm just winging it. Hopefully we'll learn a little bit more about McNabb's life before she went to work for Growth & Development."

"And then what?"

"I don't know. I guess we'll have to see what fate deals us."

"Detectives," the receptionist says. We turn and follow the nod of his head towards the direction of the elevator. Sheila Hyatt is a tall dark glass of Hennessy, with long black hair and high cheekbones. Her voluptuous body fills out her business suit and accentuates her curves perfectly.

"Detectives Calhoun and Lions," I say, extending a hand.

She shakes it with a firm grip that states she is all business. "Is this about Katherine McNabb?" she asks.

Lions and I exchange glances. "Yes, it is."

"Then, I think it would be better to take this into our conference room. Right this way." We follow her like two dogs in pursuit. The conference room is an elongated, windowless room, with a lengthy wooden table and about twenty black cushioned executive-style chairs around it. As a woman in a position of power, she takes a seat at the head of the table. We both sit to

268

the left of her. She clears her throat. "Let me begin by saying that Katherine was an exceptional employee during her tenure here. We were all sad to hear the details of her untimely death."

"You knew her?" Lions asks.

"Not personally. But from what I've heard around the office she was a wonderful person."

"Funny. We heard that she might have been disliked by a few employees."

Sheila Hyatt straightens up in her chair. "I don't know where you could have heard such a thing, because clearly it is not true."

"Well, in our line of business, you learn to take the truth with a grain of salt," I say.

"That's understandable, Detective Calhoun. But as I've stated, everyone that I've spoken to had nothing but good things to say about her."

"We hear you loud and clear, Ms. Hyatt. How long did McNabb work here?" Lions asks.

She isn't accustomed to being on the receiving side of questions, nor is she used to people interrupting her on her own ground. She looks to Lions. "A few years, I believe. I'd have to pull her records to give you an exact period."

"Nah, you don't have to do all that. I was just trying to get an idea why a successful woman such as McNabb would quit and go work for a smaller company?"

She narrows her eyes at Lions. "I can't speculate as to why Miss McNabb left the company, but I can say that it was on good terms."

"Is there any way we'd be able to speak to a few of your employees?" I ask.

"Yes, I'll arrange a time for you to have a sit down with those she worked with close—"

"And what about records?" Lions interrupts her again. "You know, a client or project list of those that McNabb handled?"

"I'm afraid such documents are confidential," a voice answers from the back of the room.

We turn and find a small man, about five-foot-five, walking towards us. "Mr. Carlucci," Sheila Hyatt says, standing.

Antonio Carlucci, Jr. is the namesake of Carlucci Development. He's wearing a fine-pressed, two-piece black suit with matching leather shoes. His black hair is combed over and he has dark pupils that speak of late-night corporate takeovers in boardrooms such as this. If I had to place him at an age, I'd guess fifty-five.

"This is Detective Calhoun and Detective Lions," Sheila Hyatt tells him. "They're investigating the circumstances behind the death of one of our former employees, Katherine McNabb."

"Good to meet you, gentlemen." Carlucci extends a manicured hand.

Lions takes hold of it. "So, about those records?"

"As I was saying, such records are confidential and can't be released."

"Even with a warrant?" Lions smiles.

"Carlucci Development will gladly comply with any warrant that is issued. But as it stands, I see no warrant."

"We can make that happen," Lions affirms.

Carlucci smiles, never once diverting his eyes from Lions. "Then I will be happy to put you in contact with our lawyers."

"We can hold off on the records for now," I say. "But I'd like to ask you about this rumor I've been hearing about Katherine McNabb being disliked by some in the company, after going to work for the competition."

"Ahhh... You mean Growth & Development. I had heard that

she went to work for a small operation. You know, the big time can be very hard to handle... Especially in this business."

"I get that, but I also heard she took a lot of clients with her."

Carlucci fights back a grin. I can tell by the twitching in his jaw line. "A *few* clients. But we have hundreds of clients, Detective—surely a few can go unnoticed. Katherine McNabb was a good worker, but like many good workers, her time with Carlucci Development came to an end."

"Is that so..." Lions whispers.

"Is there something you want to say, Detective?"

"Yeah," Lions says. "But I don't think you want to hear it."

"You'll have to excuse him," I say, before Carlucci can respond. "He's really passionate about his job."

"Aren't we all?" Carlucci says. "I see now that any further discussion of the late Miss McNabb would possibly create an unwarranted suspicion on my behalf."

"And why would you think that?" I ask.

"Because why else would you be insisting that there was animosity between my employees and Miss McNabb?"

"We're just covering all the bases. Surely a man in your position can appreciate that?"

"That I can, Detective Calhoun. But I didn't get this far by being cautious. That said, I think our business here is done. Any further questions can be directed to my lawyer."

Chapter 57

"How'd I do?" Lions asks once we're back in the car. He's smiling from ear to ear as I pull away from the curb. "You think I gave him my best Denzel?"

"You were all right. But yeah, you did good getting under Carlucci's skin."

"We might have had a better shot at Sheila Hyatt had he not interrupted. She probably would have talked your ear off if it would have saved her from talking to me."

"You do have a knack for annoying women."

Lions takes an imaginary bow. "Thank you, thank you. I try."

We're heading west on the 290 Expressway. The traffic is light, which is good considering we're coming from downtown. "What time is it?" I ask.

"Two o'clock. Why?"

"I need to swing by Jamal's school. He's still being harassed by this uniform. I want to catch the guy in the act. You know... Stick it to him a little."

"Let's roll then. Two angry cops are better than one."

We arrive at Alexandre Dumas Elementary school at a quarter after two. The building is an L-shaped, three-story structure with old, gray-framed windows and chipped tan paint. I park at the corner next to the school and wait for the end of the day bell to ring.

"So after we catch this jerkoff and set 'em straight, what's our next move in the investigation?" Lions asks me.

"I'm not really sure. I thought since you've got a few more years under your belt, you'd have some idea on how to play this."

"A case like this can sit idle until some dumbass needs a get-out-of-jail-free card. Then the stories start to come in about this guy knowing some other guy, who shared a cell with *this* guy, and BOOM, there you go. Two, three years down the road when everyone's moved on and forgotten about the case—except for the loved ones—it's solved. Just like that."

I snap my fingers. "Just like that?"

"Hell yeah. But the hard part will be swallowing the fact that nobody acknowledges that you did your job."

"The next of kin will."

"Hmph. This day and age, you'd be lucky to get a thank you. The word 'police' puts a funny taste in peoples' mouths, even when we solve a homicide."

I sit there thinking about what Katriona McNabb said, about me making my living off of death. I guess it's one of those ugly truths I'll have to live with. My concentration is broken by the noise of children bursting out of the main doors of the school, chasing after one another and throwing things at each other.

"There he goes," I point out Jamal as he walks with three other backpack-clad boys. One of them bounces a basketball as they head up the car-lined street away from the school. They pass a small group of girls that I can only assume are part of the popular clique.

"That's Jamal? Man, that boy has grown since I last saw him."

"Yeah, every inch makes him think he's more of a man, which means he's a new challenge every week."

273

"You know how these young boys are nowadays. They think they're men as soon as they learn to piss standing up. But you had to know that attitude of his was coming. It's like one of those Discovery Channel shows... You know, with you being the new lion and him being the only cub. He feels threatened."

I turn and look at Lions. "When did you become the authority on relationships?"

"I'm just trying to impart some wisdom to you, young buck."

I go back to watching Jamal. He seems happy as he jokes around with one of the young girls. "To think we used to be just like that when we were kids," I say.

"Yeah. Except nowadays these kids are having sex earlier and earlier."

Jamal breaks away from the group and starts walking down the street. He's about twenty-five feet away from his friends when, as if on cue, a blue-and-white patrol car cuts a sharp turn and barrels down on him.

"That's our boy," I say, starting the car and pulling off into traffic. The patrol car jolts to a halt and a lone officer jumps out of the car and points at Jamal. I'm about to hit the gas when I notice the side doors of a parked white cargo van open.

"Who the hell is that?" Lions asks. Before I have a chance to answer a woman with a microphone and a cameraman go rushing towards the stunned officer. As we near the growing commotion, I see Gloria and Reverend Rawls exit a car and start walking towards the officer. "I'll be damned," Lions says. "Look at who the dumbass is."

I slow the car to a casual cruise. The officer caught with his hand in the proverbial cookie jar is none other than Officer Smith. I think about stopping, but the reporter and cameraman are all over him, bombarding him with questions. As we roll by, Gloria looks up and sees me passing. We lock eyes, but then she turns away, focusing her attention back on Smith and the reporter. I step on the gas and head down the street. Reverend Rawls' observation about the crumbling foundation of my relationship with Gloria is suddenly obvious.

Chapter 58

"**L**ions! Calhoun!" Captain Haggerty yells as we come through the division doors. "In my office--now!"

"I wonder if this has anything to do with Smith," Lions whispers.

"I doubt it. Watch Commander is still on duty at the desk. Plus, the media hasn't swarmed the place, so this has to be something else."

The captain is sitting behind his desk when we enter. His bushy brown eyebrows are furrowed as he switches an unlit cigar back and forth from one side of his mouth to the other. After about ten seconds, he finally removes the cigar, sits back in his seat, and cocks his head to the side. "Either of you want to tell me why the Chief of D's just told me that if we harass Antonio Carlucci again, heads are going to roll? I don't know who this Carlucci is—but if the Chief is worried about my detectives talking to him, I want to know why."

"Well, sir," I say clearing my throat. "New information just came to light on our double homicide. Turns out Katherine McNabb was once an employee of Carlucci Development. So we took a trip down to their office to get a better understanding of the work that she did for them."

"And?"

Lions chimes in. "It was nothing that we didn't already know, but we believe that the murders might be connected to the work she was doing for Carlucci before she went to work for another company called Growth & Development Housing. Which turns out to be owned by Prince Paul."

The captain leans forward in his seat. "Are you telling me that both our victims are tied to a murdering drug dealer, and you two haven't thrown him in the box?"

"We don't believe Paul Jeffries had any idea that Officer Richardson and McNabb knew one another. But we do believe that someone at Carlucci may have known. But as far as having a suspect and a motive, we're still stumped."

"Then I would advise you to steer clear of Mr. Carlucci until you have a solid reason to pursue further questioning. Is that understood?"

"Yes, sir."

"You're dismissed."

"I guess we scratched the wrong itch," I whisper as we exit the captain's office. The division room is quiet as the four other detectives are out on the street. "First Smith and then Carlucci. I wonder what else this day has in store for us?"

We both sit down at our desks just as Perlenski walks into the division. Lions flicks a paperclip in my direction. "You had to ask."

"Just the detectives I've been looking for," Perlenski announces, gracing us with that cheap politician's smile of his. "Can either of you explain to me why my only key witness is in the system?"

"You want me to handle this, Frank?" Lions asks.

I throw my legs up on the desk. "By all means."

"Yolanda Eddy is being detained because she lied."

277

"What do you mean she lied?"

"She and Barnes played us, in an attempt to collect on the reward money."

"That... That can't be. They both gave us vital information about Jackson. Information that could've only been obtained from the shooter."

"Well, you're partially right. The information that Barnes and Eddy gave us came from the actual shooter, but here lies the problem: we've come across a video that corroborates Jackson's story. We believe the person that killed Barnes may have also discovered this video and killed him to keep his identity from being known."

"But what about the weapon recovered near Jackson's home?"

"We all know that's circumstantial at best. Without a confession, Jackson is as innocent as any one of us."

Perlenski drops his smile. Lions has thrown a monkey wrench into his plans. He brushes down the front of his suit and narrows his eyes. "Well," Perlenski says, "I guess Jackson's innocence spells your doom."

"Yeah, why's that?" I ask.

"Because if you haven't noticed, this case is as high profile as it's going to come. Which means if it doesn't go down as closed, then you two go down with it. Career and all."

"Wait, you can't pin this to *our* jackets."

"I won't have to. Like I said, this is a high-profile case, being judged by the public. If you want to further your careers, then I advise solving this case and bringing me a suspect I can try in court. Or I guarantee you that the superintendent, and even the mayor, will turn a blind eye to you two and this whole division when it's time for promotions." Perlenski turns and heads out the division doors. If he'd turned around to look back at us, he would've seen Lions standing with his fists balled up, ready to end *his* career.

Chapter 59

"Maybe we're going about this all wrong," Lions says, retaking his seat.

"How so?"

"Maybe we've been approaching this whole case from the wrong direction. We've had our heads so far up Jackson's ass trying to gather evidence and a confession that we haven't done real police work."

"Real police work?" I stand with my arms spread wide open. "And what do you call all those hours of interrogation? Not to mention some asshole taking a shot at me?"

"I call it part of the job, Frank. What I mean is that we haven't looked at all the evidence. We've only been looking in one place. For instance, what's one thing we didn't know about our two vics when we started this investigation?"

"That they're both connected to Prince Paul."

"Exactly." Lions leans in over his desk. "Now working backwards from that knowledge, let's layout what else we know so far." He pulls out a pen and a legal pad from his desk and flips it to a clean page. "We've been working on the assumption that this was a robbery-homicide, committed by one shooter. But I think it's time we revisit the possibility of there being two shooters. We know that McNabb and Richardson were killed with two different guns."

"Right. The .32 caliber pistol recovered near Jackson's residence only accounts for the GSW afflicted to Richardson."

"Which means we've still got a gun on the streets." Lions starts sketching something on the pad, then hands it over to me. It's a crude map of our crime scene, with two X's marking the spots where the victims fell. "We know there were six shell casings found at the scene," he continues.

I draw small circles on the map to indicate the location of the spent rounds. "There were eight," I correct him. "We only recovered seven."

"Oh yeah, the one we pulled out of the kiosk at the conservatory—which leaves us with one bullet unaccounted for."

"Right, our absent witness," I say.

"Speaking of that, did you ever go through the medical reports from the County?"

"No, but they're right here." I put down the pad and pull a file out from under a stack of papers and open it. The list is short, with about twenty names on it. Of the twenty names, four are marked homicides. Two had fallen on our house and the other two to another precinct. With the list down to sixteen, we're able to narrow it down even more by excluding the gunshot victims that don't fall within the designated timeframe of our victim's death.

"I guess it's time we do some cold calling," Lions says, dialing the first number on the list. "Hi, this is Detective Fred Lions of Area Four. I'm trying to reach a Thomas Clay."

There's a pause. I look down at the list and go over the names, cross-referencing them with the time the shooting occurred, along with the type of bullet recovered from the victim. "Fred, hang up the phone."

"What?" Lions says.

"I think I just found our wit."

"Whatta you mean?"

"Look," I hand him the file. "There's only one walk-in out of seven patients that night."

"So what?"

"Look at the time, and at the bullet fragment recovered. It's a nine-millimeter. I bet it's just like the ones found in McNabb. It's gotta be him."

Lions scans the page, running his finger across the information. "I'll be damned. Says here that the wounded patient is a thirteen-year-old."

I swing around to the computer on my desk and tap on the keyboard to awaken it. "What's the name of the patient?"

"Rob Base."

I look up from the screen. "Like the rapper?"

"That's what it says here. Probably gave the nurse a fake name—he might have a warrant."

"What the hell. We've come this far." I open up the ICLEAR system, type in the name and hit enter. Rob Base's photo pops up on the screen with a bracket of information that consists of his height, weight, nickname, and other pertinent personal information. "You've gotta see this," I say from behind the monitor.

Lions rounds the desk and leans in over my shoulder. "What am I looking for?"

I point to a box just below Rob Base's address, that shows he's a ward of the state under the supervision of United Children's Homes.

"Isn't that...?"

"Yep, McNabb's third employer."

282

"We gotta move on this." Lions picks up the phone and dials the number on the screen for United Children's Homes. "Goddammit!" he yells, slamming down the phone.

"What's up?"

"Got their downtown office. They're closed. We're gonna have to go up North to the group home and see if this Rob Base is still around." The division doors part. We both look up to see Ramirez and Gore coming our way. "I'm gonna inform the captain of these new developments," Lions states.

"And what brings you guys by?" I ask Gore and Ramirez.

"Just wanted to check in and see if you were okay... You know, from the other day," Gore says, leaning on the desk.

"Yeah, I'm good. Just trying to keep my mind focused on the case."

"Tell us about it," Ramirez chuckles. "We've got case files backed up all the way to Austin. We bring in one dumb fuck and the courts let three more go."

"How'd our CIs work out for you guys?" Gore asks.

"To tell you the truth, they didn't work out so well. Turns out that Barnes and Eddy were lying, trying to collect on the reward."

"What?" Ramirez says. "I knew something was wrong with those two."

"Okay, you called it," Gore says, smiling. "So how'd you discover they were lying? Let me guess: the girl buckled under the pressure?"

"Actually, we discovered video footage that cleared our suspect. Yolanda Eddy just confirmed what we already knew at that point."

"Which was?" Ramirez asks. "Don't leave us in suspense, bro."

"She didn't really give us anything. Turns out that Barnes was the mastermind behind the scheme. He might have had a partner, but we'll never know."

"You ready?" Lions asks coming out of the captain's office.

"Where you guys headed?" Gore inquires, taking a seat on the edge of the desk.

"Checking out a lead. We might finally have a break--in the form of a witness. Talk to you guys later." We head for the door, leaving Gore and Ramirez at our backs.

Chapter 60

The ride north to the United Children's Home takes about twenty-five minutes. The campus is a few acres wide and consists of three buildings pushed up against a patch of woods that has somehow escaped urban development. We park in the visitor's lot, then head for the administrative building.

A Black woman with a poofy hairstyle meets us at the door. "How can I help you gentlemen?"

We flip out our badges. "Detectives Lions and Calhoun. We'd like to see the director."

"Right this way." The woman leads us down a beige hallway to an administrative office. Once inside, we're introduced to a man by the name of Fernando Cinco.

Lions takes the lead. "Mr. Cinco, we're homicide detectives investigating a murder, and we have reason to believe one of your wards might be a witness."

Cinco sighs. "Which one of my kids is it now?"

"Robert Base," I say.

"I was afraid so."

"And why's that?"

"Robert's a good kid, but when we had to pick him up from the hospital after being shot in the leg, I knew it was only a matter

285

of time before the truth surfaced."

"Did he tell you how he got shot?" Lions inquires.

"He told me he got caught in a drive-by, but I didn't believe him. These kids have trust issues, so it's hard enough just to get some of them to tell you anything."

"We totally understand. Is there any way we can speak to Robert?"

"Yes, of course. I'll have someone bring him down."

We wait inside Cinco's office for about ten minutes before a knock comes at the door. Standing in the entrance is a kid dangling his frail frame between a pair of crutches.

"Robert," Cinco says, gesturing the boy into the office. "These detectives want to ask you some questions."

The kid is about five-foot-five with rough looking hands and an even rougher stare. His nose is small and round, and his complexion is like butterscotch. He glares at Cinco with a nasty, 'you-set-me-up' look, as he hobbles into the office. We stand and allow the kid to take a seat in front of Cinco's desk. This gives us a two-pronged advantage of treating it like a mini-interrogation, while establishing ourselves as the controlling force in the room. It's a gamble because we both know from first sight that the kid isn't afraid of the police.

"I'm Detective Lions and this is my partner Detective Calhoun. We want to ask you some questions about that gunshot wound in your leg."

The kid smirks. "It's just a scratch."

"Well, we want to know how you got that scratch," Lions insists.

"Like I told Mister Cinco, I was just walkin' and all of a sudden somebody started shooting, and I got hit. Simple as that."

"Where were you walking when the shooting occurred?" I

ask.

"You know... Around."

"Around where?"

"I don't really remember." He hunches his shoulders. "It's all a blur."

The kid is playing us. "Okay," Lions says. "If that's the way you want to play it. Let's put all our cards on the table. We believe—no, we *know*—that you were in the East Garfield Park area when your caseworker, and an off-duty police officer, were both gunned down."

Cinco sits back in his seat with his mouth open, stunned by the accusation leveled by Lions. It would have been a picturesque moment had the kid not started to laugh. Lions and I look at one another. *What the hell just happened? What's so damn funny?*

"Oh man, damn—I was wondering when you guys were going to show up. That must mean you're Preacha Calhoun," he says, pointing at me with a giggle. Lions looks to Cinco and then to me. I shrug my shoulders. The fact that the kid knows my street name has me baffled. The only time a cop's name rings out in the streets is when he's crooked. "I tried calling you a few days ago," he says.

"What do you mean you tried calling me?"

"You know," he hooks his thumb and pinky to form a phone. "On that hotline of yours."

"Wait, that was you on the phone?" His voice suddenly becomes clear to me. "You sounded like a little kid."

"Yeah, that was me. Officer Richardson said if I ever needed help and he couldn't be reached, that you'd be the man to talk to."

"Wait," Lions says. "You knew Officer Richardson?"

"Yeah, he taught me boxing up at The Dome."

The Golden Dome is a recreational building in East Garfield Park where residents can take up extracurricular activities, like boxing, and basketball.

"So, were you there when it all went down?" I ask.

Rob stops smiling. "Yeah, I was there. They lit Ms. McNabb and Officer Richardson up."

"Did you see the shooters' faces?" Lions asks.

"Only one of them."

"You think you could identify him if you saw him again?"

"Maybe. I've only seen him once before."

"You've seen this guy before? Where?"

"When Ms. McNabb had me record her at one of her house showings." Cinco gulps and starts wiping his forehead. He's thinking exactly what Lions and I are thinking. *Was McNabb involved in sexual misconduct with one of her clients?*

"You still have the recording?" Lions asks.

"Fa' sho. I thought that was the whole reason y'all had come here in the first place."

Chapter 61

"**S**o, like... Why they call you Preacha?" Rob asks as we head down the gray hallway to his room, which he shares with five other boys.

"Because that's exactly what I used to be back in the day." He hobbles along. "You playin', right?"

"Nope. Went from the calling of God to the call of the Blue Religion."

"How much farther?" Lions asks him.

"Two more doors."

We pass an open door where five boys are lounging on their beds listening to music or reading hip-hop magazines. Rob leads us to his dormitory where two other boys, one white and the other Puerto Rican, sit on bunk beds, trading basketball cards.

"What down?" Rob says to them.

"Chillin'," the white boy says as he slides a card off his deck and passes it up to his cohort.

"Be right back," Rob says, hobbling off on his crutches down the aisle of bunk beds.

The two boys steal glances at us and then return to trading cards. Lions leans over and whispers. "Whatcha think is on the tape?"

"Hell if I know. I just hope it doesn't show McNabb getting

289

down and dirty with him, or with some other kid."

"Yeah, I was thinking the same thing. A tape like that could turn our whole investigation on its head."

"Not to mention it'd be a media firestorm."

"Bitch, you can keep Melo's broke ass!" We both turn to see the Puerto Rican kid drop a card back down to the kid on the bed below.

"Broke? Melo got too much G. He just ain't found the right squad to take off with," the white boy states.

"Whatever, you can keep his bum ass... But if you got a Derrick Rose, I'll give you my LeBron when he was with the Heat." The two boys exchange cards and continue their bargaining without acknowledging that we're in the room.

Rob comes hobbling back down the row of beds with a DVD in his hands. "Officer Richardson said that if anything should happen to him, I should give you this DVD."

"What's on it?" Lions asks.

Rob smiles. "I can show you better than I can tell you."

* * *

The rec room on the floor of Rob's dorm is filled with about ten boys.

"Ay yo," Rob says. "We need to borrow the TV for a sec."

"You betta get yo ass on!" someone yells.

"Change that channel and watch me fuck you up!" a Baby Huey looking kid says as he stands up from his seat. He's nearly six feet tall, with large black hands and absent eyes that possess nothing but murderous intent.

"You're going to do what?" Lions steps up to the kid with his badge in his hand. Baby Huey goes silent. "I thought so. Now everyone clear out and return to your rooms." No one moves. "Now!! Before I have to make an example out of one of you assholes." Baby Huey stares at Lions for a second, then turns to go. "You have any problems with him later, let me know," Lions says to Rob, loud enough for Huey to hear him.

Once everyone has cleared out, I step over to the DVD player and pop in the disc. The TV goes blank, but then Katherine McNabb's voice comes through the speakers. "Over there... Yeah, *there*," she says. The picture materializes, but the image is jumbled for a moment before it's finally straightened. She is standing inside a home, which looks to be under construction because of the exposed wooden beams in the walls, and in the background are pails of paint, a few slabs of drywall, and two wooden sawhorses. "Okay, Robert," she says to the camera. "I'm thinking that will be the perfect spot for you. All you have to do is just stay hidden and everything will go according to plan."

A door squeaking can be heard off camera, along with the sound of footsteps. "Everything ready?" the voice of Officer Richardson asks, before he steps into frame. He's wearing a blue T-shirt and jeans. "Where's Robert?"

"Over there." McNabb points towards the camera.

"Oh wow! He's hidden pretty good. I thought those were just boxes of supplies."

Again we hear a door squeaking off camera. Richardson bends down and looks into the lens. "Okay, Rob... Just keep the camera steady and be quiet."

From behind McNabb and Richardson, we hear footsteps approaching, and then two men appear in the frame with their backs to the camera. "I guess you didn't get the message the first time, Ms. McNabb," one of the men says. His voice sounds oddly familiar, but I can't quite place it.

A paint can soars across the room and lands on the floor. "What do you want?" Richardson asks the men.

"You know what we want, rookie. We know all about your brother's little development plans, and we're here to send a message that this block, and every block like it, is off limits."

"You can't stop what's coming," Richardson says.

"Yeah?" One of the men draws a handgun. "How about I put one in your head right now? See how much of a difference that makes."

"Oh my god! Please don't," McNabb pleads.

Richardson stares down the gunman. "You gotta know that if you pull that trigger, you're going to be asking for a lot of trouble."

"It wouldn't be the first time, rook. You forget, I've got a bigger gang on my side, so you tell your brother to think about *that* before he loses his life."

The gunman gives Richardson a gut-punch that drops him to one knee. "We're not that easy to scare," Richardson manages to mumble.

"You don't have to be scared. But you have to have some type of brains to know that this can only go one way: from bad to worse."

"You have no idea," Richardson states.

"Benny," the other guy says. "Make an example of the woman."

The gunman makes a move towards McNabb. "All right," Richardson relents, still kneeling. "We get the message."

"Good," says the leader. "But if I have to come back, I'm not going to be so lenient." The two men turn, exposing their faces to the camera, and I can't believe it.

"Well, hell—it seems there was a tape after all," that same familiar voice says from behind us. We all turn to find Gore and Ramirez standing there with their guns drawn.

Chapter 62

I stare into Gore's dead blue eyes. He's no longer the man I thought I knew.

"So you know our little secret," he says. His voice carries a hint of death behind it.

"Those are the dudes!" Rob says, not yet realizing that between us are two loaded pistols.

Ramirez trains his gun on Lions. "Let's see those pieces. Slowly."

Lions sneers. "You gonna shoot me, Ramirez?"

"Don't think I won't. I'll put your brains all over that TV set."

"And if you do that, you think you're going to walk out of here scot-free?"

"Probably not," Gore says. "But that'll just mean that there will be a few less kids being adopted this year. Now let's see those guns, and don't forget about the phones." We place the weapons and cells on the floor and kick them over. Gore points his gun at Rob. "You. Get me that disc." Rob turns around and ejects the disc from the player. "Slide it over," Gore demands, but the kid doesn't do as he's told. "I said slide it over. Don't make me have to shoot you."

Rob turns up his lip. "You already did."

Gore chuckles. "I guess I did. Might as well finish the job." He cocks the hammer on his gun. I quickly snatch the disc and toss it over. "See, now that's a good cop. A man who follows orders." Gore stuffs the disc into his inside jacket pocket.

"Okay, you got the disc... Now what?" Rob asks.

"We make you disappear." Gore points to me and Lions. Ramirez grins as he keeps his pistol trained on us. "You two move over to that corner. We're all going to go for a walk," Gore says, stepping over to Rob and taking ahold of him by the arm. "First me and the kid, followed by you two and Ramirez. You try making a run for it and I blow this kid's brains all over that nice gray wall."

We do as Gore says, following him out of the rec room and into the hallway. To my surprise, there isn't a kid in sight. "Ay, yo--where everybody at?" Rob questions.

Gore pushes him. "They got the memo to stay hunkered down. Now shut up and keep moving." We move down the hall as quiet as church mice, save for Rob's crutches squeaking with every step he takes. "To the right," Gore says as he slams Rob into an emergency exit door.

A shrieking alarm pierces the quietness of the hall and fills it with chaos. The door leads out to the back of the facility, near the woods. It's windy and the cold air brushes across our faces. "So you killed Richardson and McNabb over a disc?" I ask no one in particular.

Ramirez shoves me in the back. "Shut the hell up and keep moving." I stumble a bit but I'm able to keep my balance. "The only thing I don't get is why?"

"I said shut the hell up!" Ramirez shoves me again.

"Big man with a gun in his hand," Lions states.

"You shut up, too—before I get tempted to put you out of your misery right here."

We walk on through the low-cut grass. I look up at the baby blue sky and see a few streaks of white from passing planes. We come to the edge of the woods and stop.

"Let's do 'em right here and be done with it," Ramirez says.

"No. We take 'em in deeper, and then we do the job. Your impatience is the reason we're here in the first place."

Ramirez snorts. "You can look at it from that point of view, or you can look at it this way: my actions have kept us out of jail."

"Like I said, we go deeper... If they ever discover their bodies, we'll be long gone."

Ramirez spits. "Fine, we do it your way. You heard the man... Let's move!"

Gore leads the way into the trees.

"Hey! Hey you!!" someone calls out from the direction of the facility. We all turn to see the female security guard coming out of the emergency exit.

"Goddammit." Ramirez curses. "Fucking flashlight cops. I'll talk to her." He puts away his gun and starts walking towards the guard.

We stand at the edge of the woods with our backs to the trees. Gore is about six feet in front of me, holding us all at gunpoint.

"It didn't have to come to this," Gore says, his breath steaming in front of his face. "All you two had to do was take Barnes' statement, arrest Jackson, and this would have been an open-and-shut case."

"We could have done that, but it wouldn't have been the truth," I say.

Gore laughs. "Damn, Calhoun. I thought you knew that in this line of work, the truth is whatever you and your partner say it is."

"I guess I didn't get that memo." I look past Gore and see

Ramirez halfway to the guard.

"Memo? It's one of the first things you learn when hitting the beat. You back your partner no matter what."

"Yeah, and to contradict your partner is a sin—I've heard it all before. But do you really think that justifies you and Ramirez killing innocent people?"

"You know as well as I do that on these streets, it's either kill or be killed."

I look over Gore's shoulder. Ramirez is about five feet away from the security guard. "What hustler did you pick that up from?"

Gore chuckles again. "You learn a lot when you work narcotics. Most developers are just as ruthless as your average drug dealer. The only difference is that they have deeper pockets. If that bitch McNabb hadn't gone to Carlucci, talking about the disc and telling him to ease up on his plans for gentrification in East Garfield Park before she went to the press, we would have never known it existed." I scoot a bit closer to Rob. "No reason to try and shield the kid, you're all going to the same place," Gore says.

I look over Gore's shoulder once again. Ramirez is talking to the guard. The way the security guard is pointing back towards the facility, it looks as if Ramirez isn't quite getting his way.

Ramirez turns as if he's going to walk back towards us with the guard but then he reaches for his sidearm.

BOOM!

BOOM!

The reports from the pistol crack the silence of the outdoors. Gore turns his head around and I quickly grab hold of Rob's crutch and steer it right for Gore's testicles. The narrow shaft of the crutch finds its mark and he falls to his knees, dropping his gun and covering up his balls with his hands. "Ffffuckers..." he moans.

I dive for the pistol while Lions drops to one knee and pulls out the .22 that he keeps strapped to his ankle. *Gotta love the old schoolers.*

BOOM!

BOOM!

BOOM!

Bullets whiz over our heads as Ramirez runs towards us firing. "Let's split up!" I shout to Lions. "I'll take the kid." I throw Rob over my shoulder and run into the woods. Rob screams as bullets tear into the trees, but I can't stop to check on him because we're running for our lives.

Chapter 63

"**T**hey gone kill us!" Rob shouts from over my shoulder. Shallow light falls in between sparse branches as I continue to run deeper into the woods. "They comin'," Rob squeals. I spin with him still on my shoulder, gun extended, but find no one behind us. "They gone shoot us the hell up!"

I can feel the full weight of his body heaving against my shoulder as he starts to hyperventilate. "Listen to me. We're not going to die. Just stay calm."

I start running again. Twigs crack and dead leaves rustle noisily with every stride I take. Once we're deep enough into the woods, I stop and sit Rob down against a large oak tree. The young boy has tears streaming down his face, but he isn't shaking or going into shock like I suspected. He just really doesn't want to die. We remain silent for a few seconds. Listening to the eeriness of a world still untouched by man.

"What we gone do?" Rob wipes his face with the back of his hand.

I stare down into his wide brown eyes and do my best not to show the fear that churns in my stomach. "First, we're going to *whisper...* And secondly, you're going to stay hidden here, behind this tree."

"What? You just gone leave me?" He tries standing on his

injured leg, but the pain quickly forces him to retake his seat.

"You're in no condition to move. Besides, if I don't have to worry about you, I'll be much better at keeping you alive. Now how's that leg?"

"I'll live."

"Good. I'm going to try and double back around to see if I can get help." Rob nods and positions himself against the tree. I cock the hammer of the gun and set out into the woods, determined to make my way back to the facility.

Night is swiftly approaching as the last beams of light from the setting sun turn the woods into a series of shadows. I race through dried, wicked-looking bushes that claw at my skin and clothing, but I keep running.

I'm sure that at the rate I'm moving I'm bound to attract attention to myself, but I can't stop. The sound of gunshots penetrates the tranquility. I stop mid-stride and try to figure out which direction they might have come from but can't determine the location.

There are two more shots. I listen intently for the report of the last one, then sprint in the direction it came from. For all I know Lions is dead and I'm walking right into Gore and Ramirez's hands, but it's a risk I have to take.

Twigs pop as I wade cautiously through the dead leaves, doing my best to minimize the noise I'm making. A bullet grazes a tree just a few feet in front of me. I drop to the ground, searching for the shooter, but all I can see is shadows.

"Those shots were from Ramirez finishing off your partner," Gore shouts. "Just give me the boy, Frank, and I'll let you walk."

The smell of dirt and dead leaves reminds me of a dank basement. My heart is playing pitty-pat with my chest. I bite my bottom lip to keep myself from crying. Tears aren't going to bring Lions back.

"I'm waiting, Frank!" The fact that Gore is yelling tells me that he's had no military training, otherwise he'd know he's giving away his position within a cluster of smaller trees to my right. "This is your last chance, Frank!" he shouts. "I'm offering you the deal of a lifetime!"

"To hell with your deal." I fire two shots in his direction before rising and sprinting the other way. I can barely see in front of me as I race back to where I think I left Rob. My lungs are burning but I know if I stop to take a breather, Gore might catch me off guard. I stumble over a rock and fall face first onto the ground. The gun flies out of my hand and disappears into the sea of dead leaves. I crawl along, searching the ground while trying to keep an ear open for Gore or Ramirez's approach. The leaves disintegrate in my grasp as I rip through them, searching for the gun. *All I need is a little light*, I keep telling myself. The gun's black body makes it impossible to find.

Gore continues to yell out my name. "FRANK!" I frantically search for the gun, pulling up weeds and roots, breaking fingernails, but I have no idea where the gun actually went. "I've got the kid, so come on out!"

Rob lets out a high-pitch squeal that shakes me to my core and makes goosebumps pop up along my arms. "Ahhhhhhh!" Rob screams again. I have to do something, but without a weapon, I'm as helpless as he is.

I stand up and take a deep breath, surrounded by darkness.

"Fraaaaank!!!" Gore calls out once more.

I might not have a weapon, but I made a promise to serve and protect. That alone is enough for me to walk into the darkness and face death.

Chapter 64

Gore has the barrel of his gun pressed against Rob's scalp. "Nice of you to join us," he says.

I keep my shooting arm down near my leg and slightly behind it, hoping that the darkness will give me enough cover to play up the ruse as much as possible. "Well, I couldn't disappoint after all that yelling you did."

"Drop the gun and let's see those hands." I look around, trying to figure out where Ramirez might be, but it's too dark to tell. "Hands, Frank. Or you get a firsthand look at this boy's thoughts."

I slowly raise my hands. "See? No weapon."

"Where's the gun?"

"Buried under a bush somewhere."

"Don't fuck with me, Frank!" He mashes the barrel of the gun into Rob's head.

"I ain't playing you," I say. "I lost it."

Gore chuckles. "If it wasn't for your bad luck, you wouldn't have any luck at all, huh?"

"You know what they say: luck is what you make of it." I move in closer, trying to buy myself some time until I can make a move.

"That's far enough, Frank." Gore squeezes Rob's shoulder,

302

forcing him to cry out.

"All right! I get it. Just stop hurting him." Gore loosens his grip. There's a fallen branch to my right, just barely protruding from a mound of brown leaves. It's my best shot. "How about you let the kid go? I'm sure he won't even remember your face, will you kid?"

Rob shakes his head, trying to be brave.

"If only it was that easy—but you know how this has to play out." I inch over towards the branch while maintaining eye contact with Gore. "Everybody's gotta go," he says. "I've had just about enough slip-ups for any man in my position to have, so I can't leave any witnesses."

"I understand that, but he's just a kid."

"Yeah, maybe so... But one day, he'll be a man." I'm about three feet away from the branch when we hear something moving off to my left. We both turn and look into the darkness, unsure of what's moving within it. "Ramirez, that you?" Gore calls out.

There's no answer. We stare at the dark woods for a few more seconds before I quickly grab the branch and swing it. Gore pushes Rob out of way and raises the pistol and fires once. I drop the branch mid-swing. The bullet feels as if someone has stuck a red-hot knife in my chest, and they're twisting the blade's tip.

I gulp down deep breaths as I fall to my knees. The world starts to whirl around me. I grind my teeth to keep myself from crying out. Tears flood my face, and I can feel my blood soaking into my clothes. I raise my head and stare up into the barrel of Gore's gun. His cold blue eyes seem to have turned blood red. He smirks before leveling the smoking gun to my forehead.

I close my eyes and say a prayer. I'm not ready to die, but I'm not afraid of death either. My father comes to mind, and I think

about all the times we never said, "I love you," or "I'm sorry."
I know that once he learns of my death it will send him on a
collision course with some other inmate's shank.

I take one last gulp of air and an image of Gloria flashes behind
my eyes. She's smiling and I smile back—we're good again and
I'm at peace.

BOOM!

BOOM!

I flinch from the sound of the shots. When I open my eyes
Gore is staggering away, holding his abdomen.

I search the darkness, but I can't tell which direction the shots
were fired from. I fall back into the dead leaves. The stars up in
the sky are bright, and I have to close my eyes to shield them
from the light.

"Frank? Frank..." I feel a slight smack across my face. "Stay
with me." I open my eyes and see Lions' dark face staring down
at me. "Stay with me, partner."

I crack a smile. "You came to meet me in heaven?"

"Far from it. Just need for you to fight a bit longer... I'm going
to get you help." He moves away from me, and I can hear him
off to my right, rifling through Gore's pockets for his cellphone.
I stare up at the night sky, connecting the stars in my mind as if
I'm connecting dots. Lions kneels down next to me. "Help's on
the way."

"Thanks... How's the kid?" I whisper.

"A bit shaken, but he's fine."

"Good to know." My mouth is dry and my lips feel chapped.

"Just stay strong," Lions says. My eyes feel heavy. "Come on,
Frank... Keep 'em open." He slaps me across the face. "I need
you to fight." I open my eyes slightly, but Lions is nothing more
than a blurry apparition. "Come on, partner... Stay with me."

I want to say that I haven't gone anywhere, but my mouth won't move, and I feel so tired... The stars twinkling lights are dimming, and the quiet darkness makes everything feel serene. All I can hear is Lions' faint voice calling my name, but I can't find him in the darkness.

CHAPTER 64

Chapter 65

Be-bop-beep
Be-bop-beep
Be-bop-beep

Jamal is playing one of his video games again. The *be-bop-beep* continues, and though I don't want to wake from this wonderful sleep, I know if I don't say something, he'll keep playing without any consideration for the fact that I'm in the room. He's probably playing the game on loud just to tick me off.

When I finally decide to open my eyes, the room is fuzzy at first, but then everything gradually comes into focus. The *be-bop-beep* is closer than I thought—a bit to my right, near my head. My stomach growls and gurgles for sustenance as I slowly sit up in bed.

"Welcome back to the land of the living," Lions says. He's sitting in a chair next to the bed. His eyes are red and his clothing is wrinkled.

"I don't know if you can call how I feel living." My voice is raspy. I slump back down into the bed. "How long was I out?"

"Three days. It got a little serious when we first brought you in, but you kept fighting."

My throat feels like there are splinters stuck in it. "And the kid?"

"He's good. You want some water?" He pours me a cup before lifting it to my lips.

"So I guess they're going to be giving you the key to the city, huh?" I whisper.

"For what?"

"Like you don't know. You saved that kid's life, and mine... *And* you put down two cop killers. That's gotta be what——two or three commendations alone?"

Lions chuckles. "Yeah, maybe on a good day."

I stare into Lions' eyes and can tell that something is bothering him. "What's wrong, Fred? Did the upper brass just give you a pat on the back?"

He looks down at the floor. "Worse. Perlenski cut a deal with Gore."

"You're telling me that fucker lived?"

"Afraid so. I put two slugs in him, but his vest saved him. At best, he's got a few broken ribs."

I'm silent. The last thing I remember is the sight of Gore standing over me with his gun to my head. "So what type of deal did they give him?"

Lions sighs. "How about we talk about that after you're out of the hospital?"

"That bad?"

Lions drops his head. "Shit's become all political. There's talk of the Feds getting involved."

"The Feds? What do they have to do with this?"

"Look, I've said too much already. Let's pick this up after you're out."

"If you say it's turning federal, that means it's probably all

307

over the headlines. So either *you* tell me, or some anchor on the nine o'clock news is going to."

Lions rubs his hands together like two pieces of charcoal he's trying to rekindle. "Alright, fine... Perlenski is fingering Ramirez as the shooter of McNabb, Richardson, and Barnes, as well as the attempted murder of that security guard. They're making Gore out to be an accomplice who had no choice but to follow Ramirez's orders."

"That's bullshit!"

"That's just the beginning. Gore has turned state's witness and implicated Antonio Carlucci as the ringleader behind the murders."

"If Perlenski pulls in Carlucci, then we're talking millions... Which means the Feds are going to want to stick their thumbs in the pie."

"Perlenski figures that since Ramirez is dead, he eats the three homicides, and turns Gore into a one-trick pony. He can run the case all the way up to federal and get national attention."

"Which gets him one step closer to city hall in the process. That piece-of-shit! He's gonna fuck us out of our own case."

"On the bright side, we still get the clearance."

"And Gore does what? Ten, fifteen years *maybe* before he hits parole. And in the end, he still doesn't have to answer for his part in the murder of a police officer and two civilians."

"I know how you feel, partner. But in the three days you've been out, the game has been in play. Things are moving forward whether we like it or not."

"I hear you. Tell me something... Did the captain and the upper brass fight Perlenski on the plea deal?"

"The captain voiced his opposition, but it's the upper brass who want this to disappear... Especially since Gore and

Ramirez came out of the Special Operations Unit." It's just as I thought—the department doesn't want the bad press, so they're trading favors with Perlenski to keep the case moving without any obstacles. "Almost forgot... The captain told me to tell you that he kept his word: Richardson's getting the full service. The funeral's tomorrow."

"It's good to know that the upper brass is done riding the fence on that one."

"I guess so. I'll see you tomorrow, Frank."

"Yeah, tomorrow." I nod as Lions departs. I sit back in bed and try to get comfortable, but the thought of Gore walking on the murder charges bothers me. I turn on the TV that hangs from the ceiling in the corner. The local stations are playing afternoon movies, but nothing I want to see.

Someone knocks at the door. "I'm decent!" I shout. "You can come in!"

The door swings open and in walks Gloria. She's wearing jeans and a tight T-shirt that says ORIGINAL WOMAN. Her hair is pulled back into a ponytail. When she smiles, I get a slight erection, and I think I might burst open my stitches as I try to sit up and play the part of the strong male. "No need to move on my account," she says. Her gaze sweeps over my body.

"It's always good to see a pretty face when you've been lying up in the hospital."

"Maybe so, but I'm sure there's enough nurses to fill that quota."

"I haven't been looking, but I'm sure none are as beautiful as you." She walks over to the bed and I reach out my hand to take hold of hers. Her skin is soft. I bring her hand up to my rough lips and gently kiss it. She slowly withdraws her hand. *I guess we aren't back to being lovers just yet.* "Sorry, I didn't mean to be

309

so brash. Have a seat. Let's talk."

She hesitates, looking around the room. Her eyes find the heart rate monitor with its *be-bop-beep*. "I was scared," she says, looking more at the monitor than at me.

"I know, but there's nothing to be afraid of. I'm all right."

"No, I was afraid of loving you, Frank. I was afraid you didn't love me."

"But I do, baby. I do."

"You just think you do."

"I know now that I love you, Gloria. And nothing's going to change that."

She turns her attention from the machine and looks me in the eyes. "I wish I had heard it sooner than later. Before we ended up where we are."

"And where are we?"

"We're on two different roads, Frank. You've got your job and I've got my kids. Our priorities are different."

"I hear what you're saying, but that doesn't mean we can't both be heading in the same direction, trying to get to the same destination."

"That's true. But after hearing about your injury and seeing the end result, I just don't think it's something I can live with... Let alone subject my children to."

"I understand."

She leans down and kisses me gently on the cheek. "I'm sorry, Frank," she whispers before leaving.

* * *

I awake a few hours later. This time, there's no one to greet me—only the constant *be-bop-beep* of the heart monitor. My toes are tingling, and suddenly I have an urge to stretch my legs. I sit up and pull the electrode pads off my chest. The monitor beeps, then dies. I throw back the sheets and slide my feet over the side of the bed. They dangle an inch or so from the cool floor. I look down at my chest. The right side is covered with a thick white gauze. I try to lift myself up off the bed, but the pain in my chest shoots straight to my right arm. I fight through the agony and ease out of bed. My legs feel wobbly and I have to balance myself against the chair near my bed to stand up.

I hobble over to the door and step out into the brisk hallway. There's no one at the nurse's station. The clock overhead reads 12:00 a.m. The floor seems eerily silent, save for the *be-bop-beep* that comes from a few other rooms.

I slowly drag myself the length of the hall, unsure of where I'm going. All I know is that I need to walk. Maybe even right out of this city, and this so-called life of mine. I've lost Gloria, and in the process, I've lost a part of myself I didn't even know existed: the ability to love another person.

I turn a corner and head down another hallway. Without Gloria, it seems as if this job is all I have, but my dedication to it is what's driven me to the situation I'm currently in. All I have to show for it is a gunshot wound to the chest.

As I approach the end of the hall, I hear voices. At the nurse's station, there's an Indian woman whose cinnamon-colored skin reminds me of one of Gloria's cosmetic blushes. Leaning against her counter is a uniformed officer with waxy brown hair.

"Just stretching my legs," I say. The officer nods, then returns to his conversation.

"Shouldn't you be back at your post?" the nurse asks.

"Nah, that cop killer isn't going anywhere. He's restrained in his bed." I realize that the uniform has to be talking about Gore.

Lions failed to mention that he's in the same hospital as me, let alone on the same floor.

About forty feet away from the nurse's station, there's a chair positioned just outside a room with a partition of glass in the door. I lean into the doorway and peek inside the room. The lights are low, but I can tell it's Gore lying in the bed. I gently press down on the door latch and slide into the room. It's quiet. Both of Gore's hands are shackled to the side of the bed. He's breathing heavily from his injuries. His entire two-hundred-and-twenty-five pounds explodes with every breath he takes, even as he sleeps.

I stand there for a few seconds, watching him. My mind buzzes with images of him shooting me, then aiming the warm barrel of the gun at my head. I close my eyes and take a deep breath. When I open them, I find my fingers balled into fists, and I'm trembling.

Gore has to die. It's that simple. He's taken too many lives and now he's going to skate on the charges, just so the prosecutor can make a name for himself. I move in closer and stand over him. All it would take to end his life is a hand over his mouth and nose. I open and close my hands, squeezing them as tight as possible to ensure I can do what needs to be done. I'll only have one shot, but that's all I need. I start to lean in when Gore opens his eyes and stares up into mine. I can only imagine what I must look like to him. Death incarnate, most likely.

His cold blue eyes are unwavering as I stare down into them until I can see my own reflection in his irises. "Do it," he whispers. "*Do* it." I take hold of his nose and cover his mouth. His body jerks, instinctively fighting for air, but I hold tight. I'm not seeing red—I'm seeing death. The faces of Richardson and McNabb haunt me.

Then, like a specter, I hear Kat's voice saying to me: "I could never live with a man who makes his living off of death."

I release Gore's nose and mouth and stagger back into a corner as if I'm out of breath. *"Hunhhh..."* Gore gasps, sucking down air. He's breathing hard. After about twenty seconds of silence, he turns his head and looks at me. The light from the moon cuts through the blinds and makes the darkened corner I stand in look like a supernatural cage. "Why didn't...you...finish?" he asks, still gasping.

"Because taking lives isn't what I do. Unlike you, I'm *real* police." I step out of the corner and walk towards the door.

"Finish...it!" he growls. I keep walking, right on out the door. As far as I'm concerned, our business is done. "Finish it!" he barks at my back. Halfway down the hall, I hear him scream yet again. "Calhoun! Get back here and finish it!!!!"

Chapter 66

I'm standing outside the hospital in a tan suit, with a brown long-sleeved shirt and matching shoes. Lions is busy bringing the car around. Since we don't have time to stop by my place to grab my ceremonial uniform, he brought me one of his old suits. I'm not going to mention my encounter with Gore the night before. What happened between us is for our own knowledge, and no one else's.

Lions pulls his Cadillac up to the curb and I get in. He's wearing his department blues. The little gold buttons on his jacket shine like nuggets. His cap sits on the dash, and I can see my reflection in its shield. "You don't look too bad," he says, turning out into the street.

"Yeah, if I was a pimp."

"Hey, that's one of my lucky suits," Lions says.

"*Was* one of your lucky suits. You couldn't fit into this suit even if you started eating nothing but fruits and vegetables."

"That's not what Gloria says."

I chuckle. *If only he knew.*

"I hear the mayor might even show up today," Lions says. "You know, give a speech and all that crap."

"I doubt it. From what you've told me, this case is going to create a huge stink... At least enough to keep the mayor and the higher-ups at arm's length."

"Probably so. The media's still running the whole Prince Paul gangster angle. And now they're trying to say the old Special Operations Unit with Gore and that fucker Ramirez was some type of unfinished street business."

"Anything to boost the ratings."

"You know it."

We head south before making a left on Roosevelt and proceeding east. "So where are they having the service?" I ask.

"Over at the Sanctum. Someone in the department talked his mother into having it there."

"This is going to be interesting."

"Who you telling? With Prince Paul and his crew coming through, who knows how things are going to play."

I nod. The fact that Richardson's funeral is being held in the Sanctum, a Catholic church the department likes to use to send departed officers off in style, suggests that the upper brass is expecting a three-ring media circus.

* * *

Half a block away, we can see a line of patrol cars backed up bumper-to-bumper, their flashers twirling. On the opposite side of the street, the news media crowds the sidewalk, marking off prime real estate for the best view of the nineteenth-century church's stone entrance.

"Might as well park here," I say. "We're not getting any closer." Lions swerves the car into a curbside spot and we exit, stepping quickly up the block, making sure not to acknowledge the press. Inside the church, the pews are filled with a sea of blue. A line has formed to our left for those wanting to view the body and pay their respects before the services. "I'm going to make the rounds," I say. "Save me a seat."

Lions slides into the last row while I stand in the viewing line. The line moves single file around the church. As I near the front, I notice Prince Paul sitting in the first row, staring at his brother's casket with a killer's gaze. His tatted arms are wrapped around a dark-skinned woman whose face is buried in his chest. He nods in my direction, and I return the gesture.

Richardson's casket is silver with a blue velvet lining. There's an eye patch over his left eye. The mortician has done a great job covering up the small scratches and abrasions on his face so that it looks as if he's sleeping. "We got him," I whisper. I turn away from the casket and head down the aisle to my seat. Halfway there I bump into Richter. He's back in his uniform. "I see DOPS did a good turn with you," I say, shaking his hand.

"Decision came down a few days ago. Truthfully, it feels a bit weird, you know. Being back without having Smith as my partner."

"You're better for it. One day you're going to have to show some rookie the ropes. Just remember that being a police officer means more than just wearing a badge and you'll be okay."

"Thanks, Frank." We shake hands again and part.

When I look towards the entrance, I see Captain Haggerty near the doorway. He nods for me to come over. I make eye contact with Lions and nod towards the door. He gets out of his seat and meets me at the entrance.

"Not you, Detective Lions. Just Calhoun. The Chief of D's wants to have a word with you."

"About what?"

"He didn't say, and I didn't ask. But his car is outside waiting on you."

"Hopefully this won't take long." I head out the door and down the steps to the tinted Lincoln Towncar that awaits me. A uniformed officer opens the car door.

Inside sits Gladstone, the Chief of Detectives. I slide into the seat next to him. "First off, Detective, I want to say great job. That was some beautiful police work you and your partner did."

"Thank you, sir. We were just doing our jobs."

"A modest man... I like that in my detectives."

"Not to be disrespectful, Chief, but can we get to why I'm here? Officer Richardson's funeral is going to start soon."

"You're also direct—another quality I like. Detective Calhoun, it has come to my attention that you're the one responsible for Officer Richardson entering the academy."

"I may have encouraged him... Possibly recommended him, if that's what you mean."

"That's exactly what I mean, which is why I'm here to inform you there's going to be an IAD investigation."

"Internal Affairs? For what?"

"The department just wants to make sure you're not involved with the Gangster Disciple nation and the criminal Prince Paul. Or that you played an inadvertent role in Officer Richardson's death."

"Are you serious?"

"Your captain says you're a great cop and that he'll vouch for you on that, but we have to be sure. We don't need any new surprises while—"

"You mean the upper brass and City Hall don't want any new surprises! Especially since the media's been stirring up the idea that Gore's actions could have been attributed to his days when he was part of the Special Operations unit. Which, if I remember correctly, was hand-picked by you at the time. Is that why you're so quick to go along with Perlenski, and to cut a deal with Gore?"

Gladstone fixes his tie. "Listen to me, Detective... You might have brought this case in, but if you don't play nice, you could find yourself buried under a lot of paper."

"Is that all, Chief?"

"I think it's a start. The ball's in your court."

I exit the vehicle and stand on the sidewalk, looking up at the church. Sunlight covers the building in a yellow glow. I did my job and brought a murderer to justice. Now my own brothers-in-arms are telling me that justice isn't enough. At my paygrade, justice is whatever they make it out to be.

I flip open my cell and dial a number. "Arnie, it's Frank. I got a story for you if you're interested. Let's meet at my uncle's restaurant after the service. I'm going on the record about everything. And I do mean *everything*."

By the time I hang up the phone, the sound of a choir singing "Take Me Home Jesus" is coming out of the church. I smile. To hell with the badge and the Blue Religion. After today, justice will be served, and I can live with that.

Epilogue

It's been three weeks since I gave Arnie Ratcliff the story he's been dying for. Within that time, I lost my badge, and Gladstone was demoted, but Perlenski is riding the media wave as far as it will take him—-possibly all the way to State's Attorney.

I'm sitting on the stairs of my front porch, enjoying the last of a surprisingly warm fall day. Behind me, I can hear Jamal and Janai coming out the front door.

"Hi, Frank," Janai greets me.

"What's up, Mister Calhoun?" Jamal says without malice.

"You kids headed to the park?" This is as close as I'm going to get to knowing anything about their lives. Since Gloria and I broke up, I see less of them each day.

"Yeah, gonna shoot some hoops." They bound down the stairs and out the gate. Jamal bounces a basketball while Janai begs for him to pass it to her.

"Y'all be careful," I caution, fully aware that I don't have a say in what they do now.

A loud bump and boom comes from the trunk of a silver '67 Impala as it turns the corner. It makes its way up the block before stopping in front of my home. Prince Paul steps out of the car with a pistol bulging under his white T-shirt. He's the only gangster I know that walks around with a registered gun and an FOID card. "What up, Preacha?" he says.

"Come to gloat, Paul?"

"Come on now—you know I'm better than that. I just wanted to say thank you for finding my brother's killer. That's a debt I'll never forget."

"I didn't do it for you, Paul."

"Oh, I know. But what you did afterwards took guts. I'm just sorry to hear they took your badge in the process."

"Well, you know what they say on the streets: you can be on your knees shoveling shit..."

"Or you can stand tall like a man. I feel you. By the way, they finally got that crooked ass cop Gore on the stand yesterday. He testified about everything."

I shake my head. "So Carlucci goes down, but Gore gets to walk on the murders. Gotta love it."

"Didn't you hear?"

"Hear what?"

"Gore got killed last night. Some dude who had life or something attacked him in the courthouse jail. Stabbed him like sixteen times. That's ironic, huh?"

I rub my chin. "Very ironic."

Paul smiles. "Keep yo head up, Preacha." He jumps back into his car and drives off.

I stand up from the stairs and stretch. Paul is indeed a clever tactician. His lethal move put everything into check. And even though, deep down, the detective in me wants to go after him, I know Gore's death is the result of a never-ending game that I'm done playing—even if it isn't done playing with me.

About the Author

Alverne Ball has a M.F.A in Fiction writing from Columbia College Chicago.

Mr. Ball is the recipient of the 2019 Tin House Graphic Novelist Fellowship. He is the 2018 Chi-Teen Lit Festival graphic novel speaker. He is also the recipient of the 2014 and 2015 *Glyph Rising Star* award for his writing on 133art's *OneNation* and *OneNation: Old Druids.* In 2009 Mr. Ball became the recipient of the first-ever Luminarts Graphic Novel Writing Award. He has also received Three Weisman Scholarships from Columbia College Chicago for his other graphic works. Mr. Ball has also created and written an online comic series, *When we were Kings* and *Zulu,* both published by popular entertainment website, Afropunk.com. He is the author of the crime thriller, *Only The Holy Remain*, published by Vital Narrative Press.

His writing has been published in the literary magazine *Annalemma*, in Columbia College newspaper *The Chronicle*, online at *Brokenfrontier.com,* online for the *Museum of contemporary Photography in Chicago,* online for *Comicbookresources.com*, and an online graphic story for the literary magazine, *Hypertextmag.com.* His short stories of suspense have appeared in the *Sin* anthology by Avendia Press, *Criminal Class Review* as well as the online magazine, the *heatedforest.com.*

Also by Alverne Ball

Only The Holy Remain
http://bit.ly/OnlyTheHolyRemain
302 pp. After discovering the body of Father Pantone, Detective Frank Calhoun embarks on a journey to chase down clues that will reveal the murderer's treacherous intentions. Along the way, he must deal with his own demons such as his father's incarceration as well as his former partner's mysterious death. With the walls closing in around him, Frank must discover the murderous plot before it's too late.